TAPESTRY OF TEARS

MICHELE DRIER

Books by Michele Drier

The Amy Hobbes Mysteries
Edited for Death
Labeled for Death
Delta for Death

The Kandesky Vampire Chronicles
SNAP: The World Unfolds
SNAP: New Talent
Plague: A Love Story
Danube: A Tale of Murder
SNAP: Love for Blood
SNAP: Happily Ever After?
SNAP White Nights
SNAP: All That Jazz
SNAP: I, Vampire
SNAP: Red Bear Rising

Ashes of Memories

Stained Glass Murders
Stain on the Soul
Tapestry of Tears

Copyright 2020 Michele Drier

All rights reserved. Without limiting the rights under copyright reserved above, no part of this publication may be reproduced, stored in or introduced into a retrieval system, or transmitted, in any form, or by any means (electronic, mechanical, photocopying, recording, or otherwise) without the prior written permission of both the copyright owner and the above publisher of this book.

This is a work of fiction. Names, characters, places, brands, media, and incidents are either the product of the author's imagination or are used fictitiously. The author acknowledges the trademarked status and trademark owners of various products referenced in this work of fiction, which have been used without permission. The publication/use of these trademarks is not authorized, associated with, or sponsored by the trademark owners.

Dedication

For Em, because I love you

CHAPTER ONE

She ducked her head and covered her ears. Crushing noise from the waves of horses and men storming up from the beach assaulted her where she hid behind a scrubby dune. She'd counted at least thirty ships pulling up on the shore, dislodging cargos of men in armor loaded with weapons, huge battle horses, even a siege engine. Another fleet of ships was being rowed towards land, probably sailing from the coast of France, less than thirty miles away.

The jangle of harnesses, the shouts of men, the orders from the ships' captains, deafened her. How could anyone know what to do, where to go, in all the confusion? The horses, massive destriers newly shod with war shoes, keened in high squeals and slashed the sand, eager to join battle.

The lead host moved inward from the sand to the low-lying beach grass and began to set up camp, readying it for the rest of the army still in ships in the Channel.

This was going to be the end of her life as she knew it, these hundreds of fighting men. These warriors served a different lord and would take the land as they chose.

Roz opened her eyes and the cacophony of sound died away. Where was she?

CHAPTER TWO

𝒮heep. Faint, slow-moving blobs of lighter gray, occasionally obscured by tilting gravestones, drifted through the mist. Here on the south Kentish coast, the fog came in like fingers, sliding up from the Channel, hiding then revealing objects and movement.

She was used to fog now. When she moved from Los Angeles to the Oregon coast, she'd found the gray mist oppressing, folding over her and trapping her fears. It echoed the fuzziness in her mind, making it not-clear and closing it in.

In LA, on a clear winter afternoon, she saw for miles, awed at the massive snow-capped mountains ringing the flat valleys. She and Winston would drive up into the Angelus National Forest to watch how the flatlands, filled with millions of people, smoothed out to the blue Pacific. Or went to the desert, took the tramway up the San Jacinto Mountains and absorbed miles of sand and stones.

Now, wintering in Oregon's mist and fog cut down the expanse and openness in her mind and built up coziness, a need for smaller vistas and closer ties, introspection.

England was different. Here the fog was a breathing thing, a force that ebbed and flowed and carried centuries of history, shifted battle outcomes, determined victors.

Enough. Roz shook her head to rid it of a thousand years of ghosts. I'm here for my future, she thought.

She picked her way carefully through the damp, tall grass, saying a silent thanks that sheep didn't poop large patties like the cows in the pastures at home. A big patch of fog glided away, and she nearly tripped over a gravestone tipped almost flat. She squatted down and tried to read the mossy inscription, rubbing the lichen-covered stone with a woolen glove.

Almost worn away, but she thought she could read the name Henry Claye and a date of 1546. Birth or death, she couldn't tell.

This is part of what you came for, wanting to be surrounded by hundreds of years of human history, wanting to understand and discover why such beauty of glass and stone sprang up, she told herself.

Roz stretched up and headed for the door of the church that sheltered the graveyard, taking in the shapes and arches added to the building over the centuries.

This began as a Saxon church about 640, remade in the Norman style just after the conquest. As this area of Kent became part of the medieval Cinque Ports, the hugely important center of trade with the Continent, the church upgraded.

A Gothic spire, added around 1350, testified to its long life. She wasn't so interested in the outside as the inside, wanting to see if the stained glass changed as much over the last millennium as the façade.

The heavy wooden door creaked as she pushed it, knowing it warped during its long life in this damp climate. Inside, it was as dank as the graveyard, cold and clammy. How long had it been since there was a congregation or any warmth in here?

Fine hairs on the back of Roz' neck rose as she looked up at the windows. A few small stained glass ones that must have been installed in a Gothic redo because the windows fitted into the pointed arches. Two rectangular ones at the back of the nave remembered local men who died in the two world wars and one window space was filled with frosted glass. A window lost during a World War II bomb and never restored?

Interesting, but unremarkable. Small, out-of-the-way churches dotted this part of Kent, most of them too poor or too plain to be looted during Henry VIII's dissolution of church properties.

She shivered. Her walk through the grass had soaked dew into the bottom of her jeans' legs and the wet denim clung to her, adding to her chill.

I came here to check this church out; I need to make it worth my while; she thought and flicked on her flashlight, moving toward one of what she assumed might be a Gothic window. It looked like a parable of the shepherd with his flock, typical of a window for a population who raised sheep but couldn't read.

This one seemed odd, though. She skirted a row of chairs set out for a non-existent congregation, gazed up and peered closely. There was a smear on the bottom of the window. Looking more closely, Roz saw the smear continued down the gray stone of the wall. She flashed the light lower and saw the smear ended on the floor. At a pool of blood puddled out from a body. A man's body.

Dead? She didn't even want to know, spun around, ran back to the grazing sheep and dialed 999.

******

One part of Roz' mind noted the differences between police procedures here and back home. Here, it took a few minutes for someone to arrive from the police station in Hythe, three miles from this church in Lympne, less time than in many major American cities. The arrival was a young officer, constable she thought to herself, who took his time getting out of his car, adjusting his cap, checking for his notebook and glancing around at the incurious sheep who eyed him then went back to their grazing.

"What's amiss, ma'am?"

Roz, taken aback at the politeness, said, "There's a body in the church."

"A body? A body of what?"

"A body, a man's body."

"I see. Is he dead, then?"

"I have no idea. I didn't touch him, or touch anything." She hoped not all the law enforcement in Britain sounded like they stepped out of Wonderland. "Shouldn't you take a look?"

"Yes, ma'am, I'll do that now." The constable took off his cap as he went into the dank interior, with Roz trailing after him.

"Over there, under that window." She pointed out what could have been a pile of clothes but was a man's body.

The constable went over to the wall, Roz keeping behind him, stepping carefully. The officer squatted down about four feet away and shone his flashlight over the body.

"Do you know him?"

"Uh, no!" What a dumb question. Then Roz wrinkled her nose. On reflection, it could have been a companion of hers.

The young man stood. "I'll just go call this in," he said, and went outside to report and wait for the teams to respond.

"Ma'am?" His voice took on a more decisive note. "Ma'am, you'll have to come outside and wait with me. Are you cold? This vile weather just soaks into your bones unless you're like them." He waved a hand at the sheep, calmly mowing the graveyard grass, paying no attention to the soft drizzle.

CHAPTER THREE

*F*irst to arrive was a patrol car with two officers. They conferred with the young constable, opened the trunk—she translated from "boot"—and pulled out rolls of blue and white crime scene tape. Her first friend, she'd finally asked his name and he said, "Fisher, ma'am. Constable Peter Fisher," stood guard at the church door while the other two wound the tape across a few gravestones and the porch.

"Why so much tape, Officer Fisher?" Roz wasn't sure about the correct address for a constable, but "constable" just sounded too much.

"We don't know where he came from. How he got into the church. This way, if there are any shoeprints, besides the bloody," pink washed over his cheeks, "pardon me, the sheep prints, we can mark them."

While they waited, one officer went back to his car, rummaged around in the trunk and came over, offering her a blanket.

"You must be chilled, standing around in the damp. Until the detectives and SOCO get here, this should help."

"SOCO?"

"Yes, ma'am. Scene of Crime Officers. The ones who search the scene, pick up clues, look for tire tracks, fingerprints, all that evidence." He looked around the churchyard, seemingly gathering a picture of what may have happened. "At least this time we'll be inside, I hate the ones we find out in the open. Have to drag in tents, lights, cables for all the equipment. A right pain in the rain."

Roz wondered if he'd ever wanted to be a SOCO, what at home they called a CSI.

The sound of cars bumping down the graveled road, which served both the parking lot for church and Lympne castle, interrupted her thoughts. Unlike at home, a car with two detectives, an ambulance and a SOCO van arrived with no lights or sirens.

She guessed two detectives—a man and a woman dressed in business clothes—came over and held a quick conversation with Officer Fisher, who pointed her out to them, before putting on the white coverall and shoe covers the SOCO people handed them. When the SOCO people were covered in zip-up jumpsuits, the group moved into the church, hauling portable lights, cameras and evidence collection equipment. She heard their muted voices talking about camera angles and blood spatter, then a lone man carrying what looked like an old-fashioned doctor's bag came up, took a jumpsuit from the van, put on gloves and went in.

"Who's that?" She turned to Officer Fisher.

"That's the medical examiner, ma'am," he said. "No one can touch the body until he's declared the victim dead and done his preliminary exam."

Other than watching episodes of CSI, Roz' total experience with the role of law enforcement at the scene of a murder comprised watching as the local police in Oregon took the body of her neighbor away. The local chief wasn't impressed with the way it was handled, and he now required all the cops in the small town to attend classes on evidence gathering.

What she was watching now was a well-orchestrated ballet, everyone taking much-rehearsed parts.

One detective, the man, came out, shook off the top of the jumpsuit, put on a heavy jacket and walked over to where Roz stood.

Tapestry of Tears

"I'm DI Harold Fitzroy. You found the body?"

"Yes." Roz suppressed a shudder. Stumbling across a body unnerved her, pulled her from the past she'd reveled in. This, though, had nothing to do with her; she was simply in the wrong place at the wrong time. Besides, she hadn't seen anything. If it hadn't been for the blood, she might have thought the man asleep, just come into the church to get out of the drizzle.

"Did you know him?"

"No, no. I didn't even look at him, couldn't see his face."

"Well, can you look at a picture?" Fitzroy motioned for the one of SOCO's who came over and hit a button on his digital camera, pulling up a close-up of a man's face. Odd, thought Roz, he didn't look dead, merely asleep. The face of a man verging on middle age, maybe in his mid-forties, regular features, brown hair that covered one closed eye. A trickle of blood ran from his left ear down to the corner of his mouth.

Roz was silent, searching her memory, but, "No, it's no one I know."

"You're from the States?" Not a tremendous feat of intuition, her accent pegged Roz.

"Yes, from Los A…from Oregon."

The DI gave her a frown. "Is there a Los something in Oregon?"

"I'm sorry, I lived in Los Angeles for years and moved to Oregon recently. It still doesn't come naturally."

"And now you're here. Ms…?"

"Ms. Duke. Roz. Rosalind Duke."

"Are you on holiday? We don't get a lot of Americans here."

"Not a vacation. I'm here sort of on business."

At this, the DI raised his eyebrows. "Business? What kind of business? This part of Kent is off the usual tourist track and there's not a lot of business to be had beyond a few farms," he paused, "and you don't look like the farmer type. No Wellies?"

Roz's mouth dropped open. I guess they do all talk like Wonderland, she thought, until "Wellies" translated into Wellingtons, those ubiquitous high rubber boots beloved by everyone who had to wade through rain, mud and pastures. She glanced down at her own sneakers, perfect for walking the trails and sandy beaches at home.

"Oh. Maybe it's not exactly business…"

"What is it, then?" Fitzroy's tone suddenly wasn't so chatty.

Roz swallowed. This wasn't so hard, even though the officer might think her strange, but the English were used to strange.

"I make stained glass windows. I'm here doing research."

"Hmmm…I should think there are many other places in England where you could study better, more glamorous stained glass than here. We don't have any soaring cathedrals or fancy castles in this part of the world. What hotel are you staying in?"

The shift startled Roz. "I'm not in a hotel, I rented a small apartment on the grounds of a church in Hythe. I come down here for a week or so at a time, just looking at the history, how the earliest glass was made."

"You come all the way from Oregon for a week or so?"

Roz was telling this badly. "No, no…I took a, I suppose, a sabbatical, for a few months to come to England. I have an apartment, a flat, outside London. This part of Kent intrigues me because so much of modern England began here with the Conquest."

"Yes. The Conquest." Fitzroy ran a hand over his face, whether wiping away the moisture or in frustration, then Roz mentally smacked herself. Fitzroy. A surname that came in with the Normans. "Fitz" meaning "son of" was adapted by the bastard sons of Norman royalty.

Tapestry of Tears

Was she talking to someone whose family lived here for almost a thousand years?

CHAPTER FOUR

"*I* have a few more questions." Fitzroy took out a notebook and Roz sighed. It looked as though she was in for the long haul.

He saw her involuntary shiver and said, "Let's go to the car and get out of this," gesturing at the billowing grey around them. "If you're used to L.A. this isn't familiar. You'll be warmer."

"Thank you." Roz slid into the car, still warm from the drive. "I'm getting used to fog and mist, but I probably didn't dress for it." She looked down at her T-shirt, jeans, light jacket, tennis shoes. The bottoms of her legs were cold from the wet denim, her top warm from the blanket the constable gave her.

"You're on a sabbatical? Do you work for the church or a university?"

"No, no. I used that word, but it's not really a leave. I'm self-employed. I have a business selling stained glass kits that people can make at home and I do commissions, some large, for churches, public buildings, homes, anyone who wants stained glass and can pay my fee."

"Are you working on a commission?"

"Yes…no, well, sort of. I have a project I'm designing for a university art gallery, more of a history museum."

He stopped taking notes. "Does it have anything to do with why you're here?"

"Yes, it does. I'm looking at the stained glass, the colors, the patterns, the way the caming is soldered. Early glass was made of many small pieces, like rose windows…" Her voice trailed off, she was losing him with the details. "Today, we can work with much larger pieces." Stop now, she told herself.

"You're here just looking at small pieces of glass? That hardly seems worthwhile."

Roz was warming up now and shook the blanket off. "Well, that's not all. The commission we've agreed on is some of the Bayeux Tapestry. It's easy to get across the Channel from here, and I spend time in the Museum, deciding what I want to include." She and the university chose the embroidered tapestry, sewn by nuns in the eleventh century, to document the Norman conquest of England, as an appropriate theme for a history museum.

Fitzroy looked at her. "That's pretty ambitious. Are you taking Harold's side or William's side?"

She smiled. Was he showing a sense of humor? The smile faded as she wondered if he felt some rancor about the Conquest, even a thousand years later.

"Neither. I'm planning to do about a dozen panels, showing both sides. Not so much the battle scenes as the historical events leading up to the battle. The comet over Westminster, the Normans building the ships. I'll have to include a few battle scenes, I love the horses and it clearly shows medieval armor."

"Do you have a contact phone?"

Oops, she probably bored him to tears with her drivel. "I do." She rattled off the number, gave him her email address for good measure and scrolled through her contacts to read off the name and phone of her contact at the Hythe church who was the renting agent.

"We'll expect you at the Inquest. By then we'll have an identity and autopsy results. How long are you planning to stay in Hythe?"

"I was thinking I'd go back to London next week, but I'm flexible."

He jotted something down, then, "By the way, please stay in the country until we've cleared you."

"Of course." She nodded, then the impact hit her. "Wait, you mean I can't go to Bayeux? I was planning to next week."

Fitzroy grinned. "We may have tight ties with France, the Chunnel and all, but it's still another country. I'm afraid any trips are a no-go until we get a few things straightened out." His tone changed. "Do you need a ride back to Hythe?"

"No, I have a car, a long-term rental. I knew I'd be driving a lot this trip."

"You're welcome to leave if you'd like. We'll be in touch." Fitzroy got out of the car to speak to his partner and a SOCO officer who walked toward him.

Roz sat there, brain churning. Had she said too much? Not enough? She didn't know the victim and he couldn't have any bearing on her travels or work, but she still felt a niggle of concern. She had no involvement in her husband Winston's shooting; no connection with her neighbor in Oregon who had been stabbed some fifty times with one of her knives, but men seemed to fall dead around her.

She shook herself to stave off a headache that wanted to form behind her eyes, got out of the car—after folding the blanket and leaving it on the seat—and headed across the parking lot. While she was here, she'd spend some time in the Norman castle, built within a few years of the Conquest.

There was history here, centuries. Battles, an invasion, probably treachery. The discovery of the man's body shook her. She wasn't exactly frightened, but unsettled. Why her? Why now? Did this man have anything to do with her and her expedition here? She needed to immerse herself in the long history of this building that had been on this site for better than 800 years. The horror of this morning didn't even register as a blip on this span of time.

The castle was gray stone as well, small as castles went. It sat close to the bluff and had a view across the Channel. She imagined on a clear day she could see the coast of France. Below the cliffs were some remains of both the ancient Roman port and the pilgrim landing place at an Anglo-Saxon fort. This was once the terminus for the road to Canterbury, but all that was on private land now and off limits.

Inside, it was clammy again. These medieval buildings were always cold, probably why people wore layers of clothes and didn't remove them often. Plus, rooms would have fires. It was a wonder any forests were still standing with the volume of trees that had to be felled to keep a vast castle warm. Roz let her mind idle as she walked from empty room to empty room, visualizing tapestries, fires, trestle tables and benches set up for a meal, servants lighting torches, dogs nosing for bones in the rushes on the floor and people dressed in vibrant colors, gathered in groups around the central room.

Climbing a stone staircase, she thanked the health and safety people for installing a wrought-iron railing along the wall of the stairwell. Pictured herself in a floor-length skirt with kirtle and apron, moving up and down these treacherous stairs with her arms full. Surely servants carrying wood or water for a bath or clothing or laundry up and down these stairs all day long could have fallen. If they did, there probably wouldn't have even been a record of their injuries or death.

As the stairs opened out into the second floor large solar, tomb brasses from surrounding churches lined the walls. Roz had a frisson of recognition when she spotted one from the 15th century. Winston, an art historian who'd taught in L.A., had done a rubbing from it, framed it and given it to her as a birthday gift. She tamped down a sudden rush of nostalgia and longing for a life that was never to be again.

There was more light and slight warmth here on the second story, as they had installed glass in window openings. Not much to see, though, beyond stone walls, empty fireplaces and a few tomb brasses. Roz heard a rumble, realized it was her stomach, looked at her watch and knew she'd better leave, or she'd miss lunch. Her rental of the apartment in Hythe included three meals, prepared by the Altar Guild, if she wanted them. The apartment had an electric kettle for coffee or tea and a microwave to heat things up, but no real cooking facilities. She alternated between eating the provided meals (nutritious, not gourmet) and choosing local restaurants and pubs in the surrounding area.

Walking out to the parking lot, she saw that the detectives and the medical examiner had left with the body, but SOCO people were still bent over like white birds of prey, shooing sheep away and stooping through the grass.

CHAPTER FIVE

*"H*ello?" Liam's voice held a trace of sleepiness.

"I hope I didn't wake you. I probably should have waited to call tonight." Roz tried to keep a schedule for the eight-hour time difference between England and Oregon in her head, always surprised that talking to someone more than 8,000 miles away could make her feel homesick. A former newspaper reporter, Liam was now a novelist and had become a trusted friend. Or maybe something more.

"You didn't, just haven't had my second cup of coffee yet. What's up?"

"Things hit a little wrinkle this morning, or really early this afternoon."

Now Liam was awake. "Hit a wrinkle?" He knew Roz was initially nervous about driving on the wrong side of the road, but she'd been in England for three months now, so should have adapted.

"Not hit while driving, hit because I can't leave the country."

Liam was wide awake. "What happened? Have you been arrested? Are you hurt?"

Roz gave a weak laugh that morphed into a sad sigh. "No, not arrested or injured." He heard her take a deep breath. "I found a body this morning."

"What!" Liam dropped back into his newsgathering mode. "Who? Where? When…"

"Slow down, I don't know most of the answers. I'd driven over to the castle at Lympne. It was the usual misty, overcast morning and I walked over to the church to look at its stained glass. A few of the windows are very early…"

"Cut to the chase." He knew if Roz started down the road of explaining glass, they could be on the phone for hours.

Now the sigh sounded like it held an edge of tears. "When I went in the church it was cold, damp, and I saw what looked like a pile of clothing. I thought someone had come in to get out of the fog and mist, so I tiptoed over to the window above him, her, whatever, and that's when I saw the blood. There was a smear down the stone wall that led to the guy's head."

"The guy? Do you know who it was?"

"I didn't bother to look, just ran outside, called 999 and waited."

"And….?"

"Oh, you know, the usual. English cops ask pretty much the same questions and make the same assumptions as cops at home." She went over the conversations with both the constable and DI Fitzroy, ending with the warning not the leave the country.

"Which is a pain in the butt. I was planning to catch a ferry to France tomorrow for another visit to the Tapestry. I bought one of the tourist DVDs and a book showing scenes, but there's still nothing like seeing the actual work, looking at the stitches, putting myself into the workroom with the nuns, trying to figure out how they laid the story out."

She could almost feel Liam nodding impatiently, so she dragged herself back from the eleventh century. "I need to check in with the local constabulary, I talked to DI Fitzroy—interesting, you can't swing a cat here without hitting some remnant of the Conquest—and I have to attend the inquest."

"Why do you have to attend? What do they think you know?"

"I'm so tired of this." Liam detected frustration mixed with anger.

"Why are you angry? They're just doing their job."

He heard Roz take a deep breath, let it out slowly. "I know. And I know I was the one who almost stumbled over the body, but I'm so tired of looking like a 'Person of Interest.' First Winston, then our neighbor, now this."

She was silent long enough that Liam said, "Are you there? Should I come over?"

Roz laughed. There were times in her life she could have used a white knight, but this was just irritation. She had nothing to worry about. Really, right?

"No, I'm fine. I didn't think coming this far, my dead-body curse could have found me."

"Dead-body curse?" It was Liam's turn to laugh. "What makes you think you have a curse?"

"You know the saying, nothing's coincidental, it all fits together in a pattern. We can't always see the pattern, though." She closed her eyes and saw the man's body again. "I'm gobsmacked if I can see any pattern here. A random man, here on a random morning, in a place I've been to once in my life?"

"It does seem coincidental. Too many events, people, to fit together. I think you're going to have to wait and see what plays out at the inquest. Maybe if you learn who he is, or why he was in the church, or maybe even how he was killed, it'll give you more of the puzzle."

"Yep, but now that I've been told I can't leave England, I'm itching to get on a ferry." She laughed again. "That old song, *Me and Bobby McGee.*" She could almost hear Liam nod. Then the segue. "How's Tut?"

She'd left her dog, a rescue greyhound named Tut, in Liam's care. The quarantine period to bring pets into England changed in 2011, but was there was still paperwork and requirements she hadn't wanted to deal with for only a few months. Besides, she'd be going back and forth to France, plus she didn't want to be responsible for anything but herself. This was a test of her resilience.

"He's fine. We walk on the beach, he loves my truck—not a good omen for when you're home—and I take him to Portland." Liam kept a studio apartment in Portland for those times when he needed to be more accessible and involved. The small beach city of Hamilton, Oregon, was a balm for the frazzled soul of urbanites but lacked the pace of a city.

"Don't spoil him too much." Roz' warning was empty air. She knew both Liam and Tut would do what they wanted, whether or not she was there.

"I'm not. I take him to your house every couple of days so he knows you haven't left him, he still has his own bed and toys."

"Where's he sleep at your house?"

There was dead air. Liam cleared his throat.

"Oh, no, you don't…"

"Well, he sleeps on my bed with me." Liam's mumble was faint.

"Great! I had to break him of that when he came to live with me, and now you've ruined all my hard work!"

Liam started to apologize, then heard the undertone of hilarity in her voice. "You had me worried for a minute, but I know how much you spoil him. This is small potatoes. Wait until he wants to take a shower with you."

"You don't…do you?"

"Got'cha." Liam laughed and Roz cracked a smile. In the two months she'd been gone, she missed the easy banter with him. Hearing his voice with its American drawl gave her another twinge of homesickness. She shook her head, closed her eyes. She was here to do a job. And to exorcise the demons of Winston's death and the death of her Oregon neighbor.

CHAPTER SIX

"*Ms*. Duke?" The man's voice was English.

"This is she." Beyond its Englishness, Roz had no clue who was calling.

"This is DI Fitzroy. We met yesterday at the church in Lympne?"

"Yes, Inspector. I remember." How could she forget? This was the man who mucked up her plans to go to France this week.

"I wondered if you'd be free to come to the station this morning. We have a few more questions you could help us with."

Roz thought for a moment. Help them? She knew nothing yesterday, and certainly not any more today.

"We can send a car for you if you'd like." Fitzroy's voice was business-like, not at all threatening.

"No, as I told you, I have a rental. You're not far from here, right?"

"If you're in Hythe, at the church, we're less than a mile away."

"It sounds as though I could walk. Will this take long?"

Fitzroy's voice softened a bit. "I shouldn't think so. Most of your information checks out."

What! Roz was miffed. They'd checked her out? What did that mean? Email inquiries to Hamilton? Oh, lord, one to the LAPD? She mentally cringed, remember all the hectoring phone calls to the detective about finding Winston's killer. It didn't put her in the best light.

"I hope I came through the check in one piece," she said, trying to make light of what she felt was an intrusion on her privacy.

"We didn't delve too deeply." Fitzroy sounded almost jovial. "Just asked if this person known as Rosalind Duke was a resident of Hamilton, Oregon, late of Los Angeles and did stained glass. And once we were satisfied, we went to Google. I had no idea we had such an illustrious artist looking at our small windows."

A flush rose on Roz' cheeks, making her glad she was on the phone, not in person. It gratified her that Fitzroy took the time to look her up, discomforted her with his use of "illustrious". There must be some place between "Person of Interest" and "Illustrious" she could hide.

"I can expect you shortly?" Fitzroy was back in his cop role, polite but terse.

"I'm almost ready." Roz looked at her sneakers, still damp from yesterday's slog through the wet grass, put "Wellies" on a shopping list. "I'll walk."

"See you soon.," and Fitzroy clicked off.

At home, Roz would have run this by Tut, asking for input. Now, she went to her window that looked out on the church's rose garden.

"Which way is this wind blowing? They surely haven't put me in the Person of Interest category? He didn't record me yesterday, probably wants a witness statement for the inquest." She racked her brain, scraping to remember any British police or murder series that included inquests, seeking help on what it entailed.

The roses had no more answers than Tut would have had. She sighed, put on her sneakers, grabbed a light sweater and headed off to the station. It was a 15-minute walk, even with lingering to look at a shop displaying gardening tools and a selection of Wellingtons.

Hythe's police, a branch of the Kent Constabulary, occupied a nondescript building, probably put together in a fit of modernization in the mid-1960s. She thought it too much to hope a late medieval or even early Victorian building had been renovated. England had suffered from the same craze that towns and cities at home succumbed to—raze the old, slam up the new.

She asked the woman at the reception desk for DI Fitzroy, the women said, "Just a mo," and announced to everyone that DI Fitzroy had a visitor in the lobby.

Great, Roz thought. If she'd had any intentions of keeping a low profile with the local cops, this blew it to pieces. As she stood, trying to seem interested in the "If you see something, say something" posters, Fitzroy materialized.

"Ah, Ms. Duke. Thank you for coming. This way, please," and he ushered her through a set of double doors to a largish room lined with cubicle offices. "Over here." He gestured to a small office with a window and a door, mercifully. At least she wouldn't have to tell her story in a large, open room with several sets of ears.

"Would you like some tea…or maybe coffee?"

Roz hesitated. The designer coffee craze had spread to England and coffee wasn't the pale liquid of years ago, but this, in an industrial setting, may be a throwback. She tossed a mental coin, said, "Coffee, black, would be wonderful." and sat back to see what appeared.

What appeared was DI Fitzroy carrying two cups of a steaming liquid that smelled deliciously of a dark roasted coffee. He set the cups on his desk and took one of two chairs in front of it.

"I'll have to record this, but it is a conversation and I think it might be easier if we chatted instead of being formally behind a desk." He could give some lessons to the cops at home, Roz thought. They weren't rude, exactly, but always seemed to have a secret suspicion that "just a conversation" meant "push for the confession."

"Fine, what do you want to know?" Roz picked up her cup and sipped. Wow, this was not days-old, overheated from a huge pot. Could he have just brewed it? Maybe a new technique to disarm a suspect into giving up secrets?

"As I told you on the phone, we checked out who you are and why you're here—partially, of course. I'd like to hear more about why you're on the coast of Kent, in backwater small towns, instead of looking at glass in some of our cathedrals. Or even those in France. Chartres, Notre-Dame, Blois."

"This trip I'm not so much looking at the windows as at the glass. Some of the colors used by makers in the twelfth through the fifteenth centuries we have a hard time replicating. And some names of their coloring agents. Rose madder, for instance, had been known since the Egyptians. Today, we know it has two active ingredients, which give different hues and depths…" She trailed off, watching his eyes begin to glaze over. Once she started down the teaching and research path, she kept on when she should have stopped. "I'm particularly interested in glass made in the twelfth and thirteenth centuries," she wound up, bringing this dump of information to an end.

"And that's because…" Fitzroy probably knew, but he wanted her to say it.

"It's because I'm trying to replicate some of the Tapestry. The dyes used on the woolen thread still vibrate with color, but it's subtle, and I want to recreate this."

"You said that's why you chose this area. I'm unclear on your commission, though."

Roz grimaced. "I'm a bit unclear, too. I pitched this to a private university in Wisconsin, as part of a new history building. It's designed with a small museum of artifacts—and a few reproductions. Obviously, they can't get the

Tapestry, but I may be able to design a good alternative in glass."

"Hmmm…" Fitzroy set his half-drunk coffee down. "If you don't have the commission, then what are you doing?"

"I'm planning to give myself another two or three months of research into twelfth century glass-making, draw up one scene from the Tapestry, make it in glass. That will tell me I have the ability and technique to do a larger commission and be a strong visual for the university's purchasing panel."

Fitzroy nodded. "Makes more sense, now that I've heard this story and checked you and your credentials out." He was quiet for a few seconds as he stared out the window, and Roz worried she'd lost him with too much detail.

Then he gave a shiver, turned to her. "You've heard about the 30,000 pieces of medieval stained glass they discovered in one of the attics of Westminster?"

"Yes. It was a stunning find and one catalyst for me to try such an old design. I know experts are still working out what to do with all that glass."

"I tell you this as an expert in the field, but it's not for public consumption. Almost half of the find has disappeared."

CHAPTER SEVEN

Roz sat, unable to grasp what Fitzroy said. "What do you mean, disappeared? Lost?"

"We don't think lost. We think stolen."

"But that's crazy…" Roz began, then stopped, considering. "For ransom? There's a big black market in stolen and 'recovered' art. Holding a piece of art until its owners fork over the ransom is hushed up, but most of my colleagues think there's a huge underground trade and market for this."

The DI nodded. "I'm not directly involved; the Met has a small art forgery, theft division, who work with the international teams. Interpol has one as does your FBI. I read an estimate that art theft was a $6 billion business in 2018, valued after arms, drugs and human trafficking."

Roz shook her head. "Stealing pieces of old stained glass can't be more than a tiny drop in that bucket."

"True. A big part of those billions are from pieces looted in Iraq, with Afghanistan and Syria running close behind. None of that has been recovered. It's anybody's guess if it ever will."

He looked at her. "I wondered for an instant at the coincidence of you showing up with a dead body at a remote church in Lympne. An expert on medieval stained glass and windows."

Parts of the puzzle slid into place for Roz. It was no wonder Fitzroy had her checked out. As she knew, there were no coincidences. Until there were.

She was silent, the information about the loss of the glass echoing in her head.

"Are you hungry? There's a pub close that does everything from a ploughman's lunch to a decent curry." Fitzroy smiled and his eyes lost some of the sorrow evidenced when he talked about the theft of art.

"Yes, that sounds good." Roz skipped breakfast, wanting to get to the police department, get the dreaded interview over. What she'd found was a decent man doing his job, with a strong streak of compassion.

*****

Three blocks away, the sign of The Baron's Arms pub creaked in the breeze off the water, but the fog had lifted and sun shone on the old building. It rewarded Roz with a Tudor, half-timbered structure with mullioned windows and glass that distorted the view. A massive fireplace covered one wall of the taproom, and several centuries of spilled ale scented the place with a yeasty-malty-fusty smell.

New owners remodeled a dining space at the back and Fitzroy headed for a table by clear, new windows that overlooked a garden, beginning to die off in autumn colors.

"In the spring and summer they put tables out." Fitzroy glanced over at the chalked menu. "Lamb curry today. Sounds good."

"I'll have the same." Roz usually reserved curry for a good South Asian restaurant, then again, the Raj cross-pollinated, so Indian food loomed large in England.

The DI sat back in his chair, squirmed a bit, leaned forward, crossed his arms on the table. "I wanted to talk more about the theft and explain why you initially set off bells with us." He cleared his throat, took a sip of water. "The art theft guys have no leads, not even ideas, about how the Westminster glass went wrong. Or why. Or where. It's a big 'who knows' and far down the list of things to look for, but important. It's heritage, it's valuable, it may even be salable. We just don't know."

Roz worked her face into a look of concern mixed with interest. In fact, her to-do list included tracking down the found glass during her visit. This still didn't explain why Fitzroy was interested in her.

"When you called in the body in the church yesterday, we assumed it was either a vagrant or someone you knew. Then, when I interviewed you and found you were a stained glass expert, and from the States, and planning to go to France...the bells got louder. So I checked on you."

He had the grace to turn his hands up. "You were, are, who you say, and your appearance in Lympne was a coincidence. Then, it occurred to us, maybe you could help. Maybe give us some tips on who might buy old stained glass, maybe even pose as a buyer."

"Me?" Roz's turn to sit back in her chair, "Why would you think anyone would take me for a buyer of stolen art?"

"You have a reputation in the stained glass world as someone who knows her stuff. You've written articles on replicating medieval and Gothic windows. You're known to be interested in finding old recipes for glass. Who better to be involved in what happened?"

Roz couldn't contain a laugh. "Wow, you're making an assumption that leaps over the Grand Canyon, DI Fitzroy. I'm such a nerd that even my friends and colleagues make fun of me."

"Please, call me Hal. If we're working together, DI Fitzroy is a stumbling block. And, yes, we sort of found that out about you. Particularly since we have a possible identification on the dead man."

"Were you planning to tell me?"

"Yes. One reason I asked you to lunch. Like the theft, his identity isn't public knowledge yet."

"And?"

He grinned at her impatience. "We think he's a Serb, traveling on an EU passport, in the UK as a student. His name is Dragan Ilic, a fairly common name. His prints came back as that."

"Why would a student from Serbia wind up dead in a church no one ever heard about?"

"Go ahead, say it, 'in a tiny village in England'."

She nodded. "It doesn't make any sense."

"If you read his background, it might. He's been questioned about trafficking in stolen artifacts. Icons, church relics looted during the latest Balkan War. Never arrested, nothing ever stuck, but he's been watched."

"And you think…"

"We don't know what to think. We're just sticking things in the file." He smiled over at her. "This, at least, takes you out of the game."

They finished their lunch and as he laid money on the table casually asked, "During our check I spoke to a detective in the LAPD who said your husband was killed."

Here it comes, she thought. All her past sorrow and anger and neediness. This man might think her a fool. "Yes. He was shot in a drive-by. They found the shooter, but I still don't know why he was at that mall."

"Does that concern you?"

She drew patterns with a spoon in the condensation on the tabletop. "Yes, a little. He was miles away from home, at a place we didn't usually go. Why was he there? What was he buying he couldn't find close to home? Was he meeting someone? All the questions when events don't fall in their usual places. I know who shot him, but all the other unknowns…it left me with a nagging feeling that the man I knew, the man I loved and who I thought loved me, was a stranger."

Fitzroy was silent and Roz cringed. What was she doing, telling this stranger secrets, feelings she hadn't shared with Liam…or even Tut.

Then he said, "I think I know that feeling. That incompleteness. Questions you'll never have the answers to. My wife and son were killed in a motorway accident. She was driving on an A road twenty miles from here, going in a direction we never went. I'll never know where she was headed. It could have been as simple as finding farm fresh strawberries for dessert."

CHAPTER EIGHT

*T*hey stared at each other, surprised at the unanticipated revelations. How little we know what's in another's heart, Roz thought, but felt less alone, less prickly after Fitzroy's, Hal's, spill.

"Thank you for telling me. Yes, it's the incompleteness, the never knowing, that's so hard to take. When I'm at a low ebb, my mind goes to it, worrying it. It must have been to meet someone. Another woman. One of his students? What would happen if a young woman showed up at my door with a child, telling me it's Winston's?"

"That's an awfully low ebb. Do you have any reason to think it might happen?" Fitzroy held the door for Roz and once on the street she answered.

"No, no. There were a couple of girls, young women, who were his students—he was a popular and well-respected art historian. Well-traveled, good-looking, great sense of humor. His annual lecture on sex in painting was always standing room only.

"He never saw any of his students outside of the university. Occasionally, one of the young women would develop a crush, send him notes, follow him on Facebook, but he didn't respond."

In front of the police department's front door, Fitzroy stopped. "Grief is hard. We are angry, in denial, live in magical thinking. No matter what, in sudden death there's always an unknown that survivors continue with forever. Thank you for coming out to eat with me. If anything develops in the art theft area, I'll be in touch. Please let me know when you go to France, or even back to London. If I suspected you may be involved, others may think the same and you could be in danger."

"Danger? I hardly think so. I told you, even my friends think I'm boring and nerdy. Thank you for lunch and I hope we can talk again. Now I'm off to find some Wellies!" She laughed and left him smiling as she swung down the street.

Who knew? Once in the store, she was taken aback at the selection of Wellingtons. If she'd thought of them at all, she'd pictured tall black rubber boots, dirty with muck and mire from fields. What the store had were fifteen different colors, plaids, polka dots, flowers, stripes, the combinations seemed endless. She ended up with a siren red pair, unable to bring herself to get pink polka dots or the cute yellow ones with green frogs. Wellies aren't a fashion statement, she told herself as she handed the clerk a credit card, hoping to deduct them as a business expense.

Free now to travel to France, she spent the afternoon writing up notes about the glass in the small church, wondering if she'd ever be able to use the research without picturing the dead man, Dragan Ilic. She Googled him, coming up with so many hits on that common name, that she gave up and instead booked a Roll-On-Roll-Off ferry ticket. She promised herself she'd take the Eurostar before she went home, but this was a sensible option to get both her and her car across.

Her car. This was one of those stupid minor issues. She'd finally gotten comfortable driving on the left, well, still the wrong side of the road, she thought. Going to France was a toss-up whether to take the English left-hand drive or rent another car in France. Since she was doing much more driving on the English side of the Channel, she always toughed it out for the short drive from the ferry landing to the Tapestry Museum in Bayeux, white-knuckled all the way.

Tapestry of Tears

Roz let her mind drift, going through the steps for the trip. She'd be gone for a couple of days so didn't need to pack much, a change of underwear and tops, maybe two t-shirts. Her sketch book, laptop, camera. She'd spend at least one full day at the Museum, walking back and forth around the Tapestry, choosing, photographing the panels that might do and would reproduce best in glass.

The battle scenes? Maybe one or two. She planned on using more of the scenes that led up to the battle, although she loved the border of dead soldiers, some missing their heads and all in chain mail.

Bodies? Her mind jolted back to Ilic's body, which bubbled memories of home up, her new home on the Oregon coast. There were physical similarities. The cool gray, the expanse of water, the small-town atmosphere, sudden, violent death.

She didn't often write or email Liam, uncertain at putting words together because he was a writer. Starting out as a reporter, he'd semi-retired and now wrote freelance articles as well as less-than-best-selling fantasy books.

Talking with him that morning had been comforting. Maybe writing him would help her synthesize her emotions—give her a chance to describe where she was and showing him another step to understanding the glory and mystery of glass. No, her inchoate feelings of awe couldn't translate to anyone else, any more than faith could, it was internal and personal.

She pulled a chair up to the small table overlooking the roses and some beehives and opened her laptop.

"It's so timeless and peaceful here. It was a good choice to rent this studio apartment. The church isn't medieval, but there's a feeling of an ambulatory in an older abbey or cloister."

She stopped typing and let her eyes unfocus as she stared at the garden. Now she saw cowled and robed figures talking with workmen. There was a quiet cracking sound as workers chipped and fitted pieces of glass into a wooden form. Where was this? Not in this little backwater, somewhere larger, a place where a cathedral was being built.

A figure in white appeared and dragged Roz' mind back to the now. One of the scene of crime officers? Why were they here? She shook her head, wiping away the images of medieval workmen, and watched the figure who carried a small, smoking can in one hand.

Wait, what was the sound? What had been a background hum became a louder, more angry buzzing as the beekeeper sedated the swarm and reached in to pull out a frame of golden honey.

This quiet church hadn't been an abbey with monks and nuns producing all they needed to be self-sufficient, but beekeeping was still necessary. In fact, had come back into favor with the die-off of bees world-wide. Beyond pollination, the church's hives provided honey, probably for sale at the local markets and certainly filling the pots Roz dipped into at breakfast.

Fitting that this timeless occupation was still around and thriving after probably two millennia.

"This area is playing with my mind—I find it hard to stay in one century. Just now in the garden, I saw and heard men who looked like monks talking to workmen who were putting together a window. I was a silent observer, but could see, hear and feel the carefulness of the workman and the urging of the monks to hurry the process."

Was she saying what she meant, what she wanted to tell him? When it came to the glass, she knew her windows spoke in simple messages, sharing joy, beauty, peace. In words, not so much.

She and Liam both had deep feelings, emotions that need an outlet. They'd chosen, or been given, different ways of expression, and maybe she shouldn't try to use his. She saved the unfinished note and began an internet search for stolen or missing art.

Google pulled up 59 million results for stolen art.

Oops, she thought, better refine that a bit.

Typed in stolen religious art.

Well, that was better. Only 22 million results.

This wasn't the best winnowing process, so she entered stolen stained glass.

A mere several thousand were available, including a story from early 2019 that 13 windows in a former church, possibly donated by Andrew Carnegie, had been stolen. The Braddock, Pennsylvania police were asking antique dealers, online sale sites and pawn shops to be aware and report anyone trying to sell them.

Roz started to bookmark some of the sites, then did a head smack. Chances were good that Hal, DI Fitzroy, already saw them, read them, bookmarked them. What she had that the cops didn't was knowledge of and access to people who dealt in glass. Most of her suppliers were people she'd dealt with for years. They knew her and her orders. Some had even filled special orders for her, usually for colors they didn't normally stock.

She called the Hythe police, asked for DI Fitzroy, was told he was out and left a message. "This is Roz Duke. I wanted to tell you I'm headed for France tomorrow on the ferry and expect to be gone three days. I've begun some internet searching on thefts of stained glass and you were right, there's a big market for it. When I get back, I'll start looking on places like Facebook, Etsy, eBay."

With not much more she could do, she walked to the church's community room for dinner, taking a book on glassmaking with her. An early night, then the ferry and a different country, different language, different food. She always looked forward to time in France.

CHAPTER NINE

*P*ortsmouth was teeming. Driving through the clogged streets, Roz was glad she'd avoided the summer tourist influx. Now in late September the weather was still good, getting a bit of a chill in the mornings but warm days. She pulled her car into line to load, sat back with a book, and in less than an hour was walking the ferry deck for the six-hour ride across the Channel to Caen.

Out on the water, she appreciated what an amazing barrier the Channel was to possible invaders. It wasn't so wide, but it was almost always windy and rough. She remembered watching documentaries about the Allies' invasion of France on D-Day, not far from where she was crossing. Eisenhower had watched the weather for days, then finally gave the invasion order and hoped the weather would hold.

Her area of interest was 900 years earlier, the only time England was invaded by an army set out to conquer. On one of her trips she drove the coast road from Caen to Bayeux and stopped at the spot overlooking Omaha Beach, where German rip-rap still sat partially immersed and concrete bunkers watched the water. Said a silent thanks to the men who'd died there, saving Europe from further ruin and ending the worst theft of art in history, the rape of Europa.

******

In Bayeux by dinnertime, she checked into a favorite small hotel converted from a chateau with a reasonable room price and a bar that served Calvados, the apple brandy of the region. She sent a text to Liam, having promised him he'd be able to find her as she moved around, had a wonderful dinner of cassoulet, went to bed and read. Her book this evening, a history of the Cinque Ports of medieval England—those towns that were given royal privileges in exchange for providing the first line of defense from a hostile France—didn't keep her interest.

Bach's Toccata and Fugue in D Minor blasted her out of bed. She seldom set her alarm and forgot what she'd chosen. This morning, it jerked her away from shouts of men, impatient horses, sounds of a departure. Maybe it was time to change the alarm to something quieter, more lyrical.

Awake, she showered, dressed, headed downstairs for coffee, croissants and drove to the Museum at the door when they opened. As a regular visitor over the past couple of months, the attendant nodded a hello to Roz and the docents waved her in. She began in the side room with the video that told the invasion story, with actors in medieval clothing. It was in French and English and gave visitors an overview of the political issues during the conquest.

Back out in the main hall where the Tapestry lived, she began her slow walk along the U-shaped glass case that held it. The tapestry wasn't actually a tapestry so much as an embroidery, a 230-foot long strip of woven linen 20 inches high with the scenes stitched in wool thread.

It was commissioned by William the Conqueror's half-brother, Odo, Bishop of Bayeux, to be installed around the nave of his cathedral and its colors were still bright and fresh. As she walked, she stopped and took close-up photos of portions, panels that showed the history of Harold and William, initially friends and allies.

Roz knew one of the challenges she faced was the background linen. It would take a lot of glass, and she wasn't sure if any of her regular suppliers could blow glass that imitated the weave of the linen. She put that question aside, took out her sketchbook, began drawing the scene where a comet appears over Westminster while an astrologer tells Harold that it's a bad omen.

Drawing, she looked at the faces of Harold and a group of his subjects who watched the comet in fear. The nuns embroidered the tiny features, but Roz planned to take the medieval tactic of painting small things—faces, details of flowers—onto the glass. As it was, she'd have to use the most narrow caming she could find for most of the piece, and she worried about the structural integrity of the finished window. She worked quietly, seeing the glass she'd have to find, planning the cartoon, placing the glass just right so she'd waste little.

She moved on, to a scene of the Norman ships ferrying William's army, along with battle horses, to the English beachhead, then added a detailed sketch of the Normans readying a camp and preparing a meal. Not sure what she'd end up doing for the panel she'd present to the acquisitions committee, she wanted to have as many drawings to choose from. These were the foundation for the ultimate window. She'd enlarge them to the correct size, project them onto a heavy paper, and carefully trace a complete cartoon, the pattern she'd use to cut the glass.

Her usual creations were constructed as a whole regardless of the size, but here she had to pull selected panels from the entire tapestry to give the viewer an idea of the sweep of the events pictured. This prep work was tedious. The sketches and cartoons had to be exact replicas of the original, with little ability to change or shift the focus of the piece because of the medium.

The lights in the big room dimmed, and she jerked her head up. Were her eyes going? She spun around and realized the attendants were starting to usher visitors out and looked at her watch. Gave a jolt when it said 5:15 p.m. She'd worked right through lunch.

She began to put her sketches in order, pack up her things and, as she worked, felt her neck stiffen and arms feel heavy. No wonder, she'd been holding a sketch pad and carefully drawing for close to eight hours and her muscles reminded her of it.

Today's work gave her enough to begin laying out and creating the detailed cartoon which she'd take home to Oregon to translate into the glass. Then she stopped. That had been her original plan. Now, surrounded by the history the piece represented, the emotion of being at the place where so much happened, maybe she'd work on the window here.

But first, a soaking bath to loosen her muscles and a wonderful dinner followed by a comfortable bed. Maybe a call to Liam to tell him of her progress. Should she mention a shift in plans? If she were to make the window here and ship it to the university, she'd be gone for possibly several more weeks. Would Liam think she was taking advantage of his dog-sitting?

And would DI Harold Fitzroy pull her further into the investigation of missing glass?

CHAPTER TEN

"*W*here are you?"

Liam's voice sounded echo-y and drifted off.

"I'm headed to Portland. On the freeway. Why?"

Roz blew out a phhut, said, "You sound funny, kind of fading in and out."

"It's this cheap hands-free." Liam let out a groan. "Next time, I'm buying a truck equipped with Bluetooth."

Roz had ridden in his old pickup. Not any kind of luxury. "Why are you taking your truck?"

"It's your fault," Liam laughed. "I'm taking Tut. I even installed a doggy harness to keep him in the seat, but he keeps whining he wants to stick his head out the window. Told him his mom may let him do that, but I won't."

"It's true, I do let him, but only around town. That's nice of you to take him."

"I'm liable to be there a few days. Doing some research and I want to visit the *Oregonian* office, talk to some friends. I couldn't leave Tut home alone."

"Thanks for that." Roz paused. Should she tell Liam about Fitzroy pulling her into his investigation of the missing stained glass? Sure. She blurted, "Did you hear about the theft of stained glass from Westminster?"

"What? Some windows are missing?" Liam's voice rose a notch. "How could anybody steal a window from Westminster?"

"Not windows." Roz went over the story of the find and then told him nearly half the glass was missing. "Apparently

Interpol, the FBI's Art Theft section and Scotland Yard are looking."

"That seems a lot of activity for some pieces of glass."

"It's considered a national treasure. They're assigning it to the major art theft division. Fitzroy said the thieves will probably hold it for ransom." Roz broke off, then, "I did a cursory search for stained glass art theft. You wouldn't believe how much there is!"

She heard "Oops," and "Sit!"

"What's going on?"

"Some idiot changed lanes without a signal, I swerved, Tut slid off the seat. All fine now. So, you were telling me about some glass gone missing. And…?"

Roz sucked in a breath. She didn't have to give Liam a reason for her getting involved, why would she keep it from him? Or maybe it was none of his business. The pedophile ring in Oregon was his business, the murdered priest had been their neighbor, but this? Still, she needed to share it.

"And, Fitzroy asked me to work with them, to find the thieves. He said because I'm well-enough known in the glass world that I'd probably hear about some being either sold or ransomed sooner than they would."

"This English cop wants you to put yourself out there as a, what, decoy?"

"Overstating, Liam. He wants me to start trolling some of the sites where hobby stuff, glass, is sold, alert him if anything looks wonky or suspicious."

Silence. She didn't hear screeching brakes, metal or glass crashing, horns. Just empty air.

"Liam?"

"I'm here. I'm thinking. Is this safe?"

"Of course it's safe! I'm only scanning some sales places where interesting glass may show up, in fact…" Could Liam hear her thinking? "In fact, if you're going to do research, maybe you could help."

"I'm sure I can find the original story of the discovery, but you already know that. I could look for any stories on the theft."

"Hal, DCI Fitzroy, said the theft hasn't been mentioned yet. They've all agreed to keep it quiet, not give the thieves any publicity. His theory is the silence will force them to rely on back channel markets and shady dealers and keep down the number of false claims."

"Hal?"

Fudge, Liam picked up on that fast. "He asked me to call him that since we're going to be working together. I don't know much about him." A white lie may calm any ruffles until she could figure out who was who in this muddle. She and Liam were close, but not intimate and hadn't discussed anything that might be related to a relationship. They were friends, respected each other and, she admitted, had an attraction, but it was far from a commitment.

"What do you want me to look for?"

Did she detect a note of coolness in his voice? "I thought you could do a Lexis-Nexus search for anything fraud-related to art theft, stained glass theft. Is that too wide to search?" She made her voice smile.

"That's doable. It's pretty broad, but I'll narrow when I see what comes up. It may be a day or so, though."

"Thank you, whatever you can find would help."

"Are you in England?" Liam was back to his easy banter, just friendly conversation.

"No, I'm still in France. I'll go back to Hythe tomorrow." She paused. Was this a good time to talk to him about her possible change in plans? "Are you and Tut doing OK together?

"Yeesss, I sense a deeper question there."

"Well, I've changed my mind about something."

"Hey, Tut and I are fine, but I don't think I'm his forever home. What's going on?"

Roz managed to tangle herself up in so much chat she'd aroused suspicion.

"It's just that my original plan was to do a cartoon of some panels of the Tapestry then construct them at home. After examining it, I think I want to make a panel here, while I have the original to look at, work through, then ship it home. And it will probably be easier to get the glass here."

"That makes sense. So where do Tut and I come into this equation?"

She sighed. "It means that I'll probably be gone a few more weeks that I thought. Maybe as much as six weeks. And that will give me time to help Fitzroy find Ilic's murderer."

CHAPTER ELEVEN

"Ilic? Who the hell is Ilic?" No question, now Liam was upset. Pissed? Hurt? Surprised? Probably all three.

Backtrack, Roz, she told herself. Tell it in a straightforward way.

"Ilic is the body I found in the church. A Serb national who traveled on an EU passport and had been suspected in art thefts of religious works like icons, and in fencing stolen art."

"And you discovered this when? Were you planning to tell me?" Liam's tone was so stern, so icy, she heard Tut whine. Great, he was pissed and her dog was frightened, nice work.

"Sure, I was going to tell you, although I don't think it's a very important fact."

"Not important? A guy, an art thief, is murdered, you find the body, your English boyfriend gets you involved in looking for stolen stained glass. Possibly the stuff that got the guy killed, and you don't think it's important? Have foreign countries rattled you so much you're not thinking straight?"

"Low blow, Liam. It has nothing to do with being away from home, I'm just not sure if all this is tied together." She huffed, then: "My English boyfriend? Where do you get off?" He'd succeeded in pushing her to the same angry place where he was. Calm down, she told herself. This was a stupid argument to have at any time, let alone when they were 8,000 miles apart and he was barreling down an Oregon freeway, probably at more than 80.

"'English boyfriend' might be rude, but here's a guy who wants to involve you in helping find a thief, possibly one who's already killed one person. I'm cranky and worried."

"Cranky, yes. Worried? Why?" Eep, why should he be worried? "I managed to get through Winston's murder with no problem and even though the archbishop tried to kill me, I'm still around."

"True, but you were attacked in your own home in a town where you're well known, with friends surrounding you. Now you're in a foreign country where no one knows you, you found a body and have already been tagged by the local cops."

"Wait. Just wait. You're not making sense. I'm working *with* the cops."

"My point. This can make you more visible. Before, you were just an oddball woman with a pathological interest in stained glass. Now, you may have a bull's eye on your back."

Roz couldn't help herself, she laughed. From Liam's silence, she may have made him even more upset until she heard a slight sound. He was stifling his own laugh.

"I don't know which I'm more tickled at, the pathological or the bull's eye, but you sling a good mixed metaphor." She walked across her room to grab a bottle of water, took a sip and coughed.

"Are you alright?"

"Fine, water went down the wrong pipe."

The moment of laughter stopped the bickering and brought them back to civility. She heard traffic sounds mounting and said, "You must be coming into Portland."

"Yep, and traffic is close to a standstill. I can't figure out where all these people came from."

Roz nodded, realized he couldn't see her, agreed. "I know, we're probably becoming small-town people, not comfortable in the big city."

She heard the screech of brakes, then; "I better get off the phone now. This car sludge needs my attention. Call again, soon, and watch your boyfriend."

"Right. Take care and give Tut a treat and hug from me." She clicked off.

Boyfriend? Where did he get off jumping to that conclusion? There was no boyfriend, even including Liam—was there? She'd enjoyed the brief times she'd spent with DCI Fitzroy, Hal, but it was just business.

Enough, this was edging close to confusion and complexity. She'd left L.A. after Winston's murder to find a quiet place, where no one knew her or her past, where she could build a safe life with her dog. And found herself smack in the middle of a murder investigation, even being a "Person of Interest"—she always thought of that term in quotes—setting her aside from normal people.

Do what you came for, she told herself. This is a challenge, a thing that has never been done before. Even in her usual world, her creations pushed the boundaries. The recent commission for a cathedral in Colorado comprised a design from the Hubble telescope's photos, a star nursery at the beginning of the universe. To her, the work spoke more to the universality of creation than to the concept of one religious sect.

If she could pull this off, transferring a masterpiece from one medium to a completely different one, her place in the world of stained glass would be cemented. She didn't do these creations that pushed her skill to the edge solely for money; she had enough of that. And she didn't do it for the recognition, she was already a star. She did it to prove to herself that she was worthy, that she mattered, that she was deserving of Winston. She did it to still that questioning voice of why he was at that place where death came from nowhere.

The call to Liam interrupted her evening's plan, she'd called him as she got out of the bath. Now, she dressed in a casual skirt and loose-knit sweater and headed down for a glass of Calvados and dinner, tonight a classic coq a vin.

After, she went up to her room, gathered up clothing, sketches, materials, laid out clothes, tickets, passport for tomorrow. As much as she loved France, she didn't feel fluent in the language and looked forward to being where people spoke English—well, English and not American.

Should she call Hal? No, there wasn't anything important, just that she'd catch the early ferry and be back in Hythe mid-afternoon, texted him that.

Tonight, she read about Martello Towers, those small forts built along the southern coast of England. Constructed between 1804 and 1812, they were to defend against another invasion, that of Napoleon. The French Emperor never managed an invasion, but the possibility lived on when mothers told their children to behave or the Bogeyman will come and get them.

She fell asleep, dreamed of Frenchmen storming across the beaches, woke to a weak sun breaking through the mist. She grabbed a fast shower, dressed, packed up the last few things, had a quick café au lait with the inn's owners and was at the ferry landing with half an hour to spare.

The crossing was smoother this time, less wind and fewer whitecaps and they landed a few minutes ahead of schedule. Waiting in her car to drive off, Roz heard her cell ping with a text from Hal. *Good, call when you get to Hythe.*

She didn't have time to worry about the text, the loaders were moving cars off at a steady pace and once on land, she was shuttled into a lane that took her directly to the coastal A road.

Tapestry of Tears

Okay, he'd said when she reached Hythe so it would have to wait. Rationally, she thought that; the "why" though made her stomach feel nibbled by rats.

CHAPTER TWELVE

She was on the roundabout toward Hythe when her cell pinged with another text from Hal. *Come to the station.*

Terse, to the point, no please, no thanks, hardly a boyfriend.

Well, it was an order, and she'd follow it. Didn't mean she had to respond. She pulled into a municipal lot, got out and stretched. The weather had warmed since France this morning, so she left her jacket crumpled up in the seat, went in the front door.

The uniformed constable smiled, said, "Can I help…" and the door to the squad room slammed open.

"There you are!" DCI Fitzroy held the door and motioned her in.

"Actually, I'm almost fifteen minutes early…" Fitzroy took her arm, and all but pulled her into a side office where he closed the door.

"Wait a minute, what's the big idea?" Maybe Roz had been lulled with a false sense of politeness in her prior dealing with the British cops, this was reminiscent of the L.A. force.

"I didn't want to say this on the phone or text, but we may have a break." Fitzroy's grin reached his eyes.

"That's great, but why the manhandling?"

"Sorry, I've been wanting to tell someone this. None of the regular staff here are assigned to this case, it's all very hush-hush, so I have good news and no one to share it with."

Roz sat in an uncomfortable chair in front of a desk, sliding it around to watch Fitzroy, now pacing. "And what is it?"

"We have a possible break. An antiques dealer, one who's always on our watch list, got an email from someone asking if he dealt in stained glass. He said occasionally, what did the seller have in mind? Our guy never heard back again. By the time the dealer got around to telling us about it, the email account was taken down."

"Can't you trace it?"

Fitzroy ran a hand through his hair, making him look like a little boy who'd been tousled. "We're trying, no luck so far. I do think this underlines our, my, supposition that there'll be a ransom demand. I think the email was just the beginning move to find out what the market will bear for the glass."

"Well, where do I come in? I'm no good at computers."

"If we can trace this email path, maybe even through the dark web, we can have our IT guys set you up with an account. You can start a query about where to buy old stained glass for a project."

Roz started to protest, then thought about her conversation with Liam. She'd asked about help thinking Lexis-Nexus, but possibly the dark web? Liam's friend knew about that, he'd done some research on an archbishop and a defrocked priest that led to a murder and cracking a pedophile ring in the diocese.

"I have a friend who may be willing to help." She recounted an edited version of her conversation with Liam last night, leaving out the "boyfriend" cracks.

"And he'd help us, why? Can he be trusted?"

"Yes, and yes. He's a journalist, semi-retired now and writes sci-fi, fantasy novels. He's real, has an agent and a publisher, just not a best-seller, yet. I, we, could talk to him, maybe offer him a book deal after it's all said and done."

"Why would he write a book about stealing medieval stained glass? Sounds like a narrow interest niche." Fitzroy stopped running his hands through his hair, was sitting and listening, focused. She had his attention.

"It's not just this theft, it's all the art that's been stolen and never found. Look at the theft from the Isabella Gardner Museum in Boston. A priceless Rembrandt. Look at all that's missing from Iraq and Iran, Afghanistan or stolen by the Nazis. And there's probably a lot that never gets reported. Big business, as I found out from Google."

"Hmmm, we seem to have gone from an obscure theft to global grand larceny. I'm not a publisher, but that seems too big for one book." He smiled and his entire face warmed. Why had she thought the English austere?

Roz smiled back. "I'm not a publisher, either, but this is just supposition on my part. I think if we throw the possibilities out, Liam may grab them. He knows his business."

"Liam. Irish, then?"

"No, or at least I don't think so. Names in the States don't carry as much weight as they do here. Parents latch on to a name they've heard, or like, and use it."

Fitzroy was silent for a few seconds, then: "Let me run this idea by some other team members. We've all been as quiet as the depths, one step away from using code. I don't want to think what our futures would be like if we can't find and rescue this glass. Not quite the crown jewels, but still…" His eyes shifted to a picture of the Queen and Roz shuddered. Was he anticipating a future of walking a beat somewhere in the wilds bordering Scotland?

She moved to pick up her purse and Fitzroy came back from wherever. "Have you eaten? Of course you haven't, I practically demanded you come directly here. Would you like to have dinner?"

Not a boyfriend, but an invitation to dinner. Where did this fit? If she was going to work with Fitzroy and ask Liam to help, it would be good to get on friendly terms with both of them.

"Sure, if that's not an imposition. My car is here. I'd like to go to the church, drop my bags, get changed. Can I meet you somewhere?"

"You don't have to meet me, I'll come pick you up. There's a pub I know that's going upscale, Waterford Grange. Food's good, it's quiet, out of the way." He grinned. "Which here means hard to find. Shall we say 7:00?"

"Fine." Roz shook his hand. Did he hold on to it a beat too long? Knock it off, she thought. This is a nice man, a dedicated cop who's proud of his job and his country, and she'd do what she could to help him find this treasure and the scum who took it.

Her rental still didn't feel like home as she unloaded her overnighter and computer bag and brought them into the flat, but it held traces of her; a vase of roses she'd cut and left on the table, now drying, her scent in the bathroom, the duvet carelessly pulled up on the bed. Travel, seeing new places, finding new adventures always charged her up. The conversation with Liam, though, where she pictured him, Tut, the old pickup, the heavy traffic around Portland, gave her a moment of loneliness, a longing in the pit of her stomach.

She sorted out dirty laundry, pulled a pair of linen slacks and a silk shirt out of the closet to wear, redid her make-up and was slipping on a pair of sling-backs when there was a knock at the door. Opened it and saw…no one.

How odd, she thought, Fitzroy knew which flat was hers. She glanced at her watch, saw it was still a few minutes before 7, turned to go back inside when she noticed a white envelope on the mat. I don't remember that before, what is it? I'll never know if I don't open it.

Inside a folded piece of paper with "Stay out of this. Go back to the States" printed on it.

Roz took a deep breath. Don't panic, she told herself. She walked as calmly as she could down to the corner of the building and looked out at the street. The only car besides hers was Fitzroy pulling up.

She stood like a stone as he walked up, said, "Are you ready?" He looked at her, took her hand that was holding the paper and said, "What's wrong?"

CHAPTER THIRTEEN

"*I* don't know what's wrong." Roz dragged her look from the paper in her hand to Fitzroy's face, gave it to him, her hand trembling. "There was a knock at the door, no one there, but this was on the mat."

"Was there anything else?" Fitzroy glanced at the sheet. "Did it have an envelope?"

She shook her head. "Of course, but there nothing written on it," she said, handing the blank envelope over. "I don't know what you can figure out from this."

He was silent. "Do you have some tweezers? Drop both the note and the envelope on the table. I'll get my things." He whirled out the door, she heard a car door open and close and he was back with a clear plastic bag.

"Tweezers?" He looked at her. She went into the bathroom, got hers from the counter and handed them to him. He picked up both pieces of paper, put them in the bag and sealed it.

"Probably a case of futility, but the forensic people may be able to trace something." Now he looked at her, and she thought he shifted from a cop to a man on a date.

"I focused on the evidence, not on you. How are you? I imagine this shook you a little." His eyes, more hazel with tints of gray than Liam's soft brown ones, held a question and compassion.

"I'm fine, I think. This did startle me. I didn't think anyone knew I was here, well except you and the whole constabulary in Hythe." She stopped for a pause. "And the church ladies here, and my landlady in London and the rental car place and all the staff of the museums I've visited and the glass factories I order from…" Her voice trailed off like rain in the desert. "Come to think of it, a lot of people." She gave a wry grin. "It never occurred to me to be stealthy about my movements."

"I know." Now Fitzroy was wry. "When we checked your cell phone and banking records, it didn't look as though you were covering anything up."

Roz straightened up and glared. "You looked at my phone? And my bank account? What gave you the right?" She stormed to the door to open it and throw him out, discovered it was open, stood there with the knob in her hand then slammed it shut. She was so angry her hands shook. "That's a gross invasion of my privacy. I don't know what your laws are here, but at home you'd have to have a warrant or suspicion or something."

He stayed outwardly calm, but two hectic spots of color on his cheeks reflected his inner turmoil. "It's much the same here. You were the reporting party for a murder and the only one there. You were an alien, no fixed residence in England, your movements included travel to the Continent. You were an initial person of interest and we got permission to look deeper into you. I told you we'd Googled you."

"Google me! That's all public knowledge. My phone, my bank, are private! You had no right!" She was so angry she felt tears forming…frustration, not fear.

This felt like he'd used her, gone behind her back, spied on her and broke the beginning of confidence. She seethed, sure her anger and disappointment showed, which was fine, He needed to know how angry she was.

Fitzroy's face crumbled around the edges. "It looks so bad in hindsight. All we were trying to do was clear you of any involvement. And we did. You are exactly what you said you were, a famous stained glass artist, getting an international reputation. An expert on medieval stained glass. Widow of a noted art historian." He paused, ran a hand down his face. "And an intelligent, attractive woman. One I'd like to know better."

"What? Didn't my phone records give you enough information about me?" Why did cops on both sides of the Atlantic feel they had the right to pry into her life? If there was a next time that she found a body, she'd let someone else be the goat and tell. She was tired of trying to be a good citizen.

"I'm sorry, Roz, Ms. Duke. I understand why you're angry. We have no information on what the conversations of the phone calls were, only the numbers. We found that most of them were to hotels, ferries, a few to a number in Oregon. Nothing suspicious, and we never looked at your computer and search history. It was never meant to hurt you, only to clear you. We needed to make sure you were legitimate before we asked you to help."

Her eyes narrowed. "You mean you did all that before…"

"Before I asked you to work with us. Before we went to lunch to talk about it. Yes."

Her anger abated slightly. "At least you weren't asking me out for meals and trying to pump me for information."

"No, not at all. Once we knew you were more than above board, they asked me to get you involved in the hunt. Your background is sterling, we couldn't have found anyone with better credentials." His eyes were tinged with sorrow. "I felt I needed to tell you about it before we went any further."

"On a business or personal level?"

"Either. Both. If we're going to work together, we need to have no secrets." He tucked the plastic bag into an inside pocket in his jacket. "I'll get this to forensics tonight." Paused, then, "Are you still willing to have a meal with me?"

Roz looked at the floor. Did she want to spend time with this man? He'd gone behind her back and pried into her life. At least he'd come clean, and she knew from her involvement with the cops in L.A. and Oregon that what he'd done was just procedure to rule out possible suspects. And she'd been nervous but flattered when he'd asked for her help.

She raised her eyes, found him watching her with a wary expression. If she were going to continue working with the team, plus figure out the threat she just got, she'd be better off closer to him.

"Both of us need to eat, so I suppose so. If I do this, I don't want any other surprises, no digging around. My personal life is off-limits. Right?"

A small smile tugged the corner of his mouth. "Right! You'll know what we're planning when we do it."

Hmmm, she thought. That statement had enough ambiguity to allow ferrets to dig holes, but she could live with it for now. She picked up her purse, opened the door, checking to make sure nothing broke when she slammed it, locked it after him and followed him to his car.

*****

Waterford Grange was as Fitzroy had described. She never would have found it driving herself, it was a few miles outside the village of Limpley Stoke, tucked up against a small meadow and at the apex of four rural paths. This was off-the-beaten-path England. It wasn't medieval but it was a thatched building, Tudor half-timbered and white-washed. Large picture windows had been cut into the largest room, so that dining tables overlooked the front garden and meadow.

A nice selection of traditional English and Continental entrees made Roz' mouth water, she decided to treat herself to a glass of good wine, a Beaujolais.

Tapestry of Tears

Conversation was awkward as they waited for food.

"How was the crossing?" Fitzroy took a sip of his own drink.

"Uneventful." Roz swirled her wine around, watching the red sheen the glass. "I forget there are still some English teens who go over to France, try to drink it dry, then come back obnoxious and vomiting. The ferry bathrooms are iffy."

Fitzroy smiled. "Are teens different in the States?"

"Not really, but the circumstances are. They just find someone to buy them alcohol and go off in the woods. They're not drunk and rowdy in public, they know they'll get picked up."

Dark had fallen by the time they finished. A silent ride home, but when he pulled up in front of her apartment he said, "Thank you for tonight and for giving me another chance to get to know you. Please call me if you get any more letters, threats, anything that doesn't seem right to you. I'll be in touch with any results on the note."

Roz reached for the latch, but he'd already come around and was opening her door. "I'll walk you up and make sure there's nothing else," he said. "I doubt it, he probably thinks he's warned you enough,"

"'He.' Do you think it's a man?"

"Not officially, but women tend not to give warnings, they make decisions then act."

She let that remark go by, said, "Thank you for dinner and showing me the Grange. It's a lovely spot, even though I probably couldn't find it again. I'll hear from you tomorrow?"

"I hope so." Fitzroy walked to his car, Roz got ready for bed and reflected on a day of revelations and surprises. Tonight, she made sure she checked all the windows and the door. The note jarred her more than she initially thought.

She opened her laptop, began making notes and wondered if she'd walked into a hornets' nest.

CHAPTER FOURTEEN

Roz pulled an old library table under the window overlooking the rose garden and beehives. It differed from her vast view of the Pacific at home, but more compact, maybe more fitting to replicate a piece of the Tapestry. She hung a white sheet on another wall, projected some pictures she'd uploaded from yesterday. Flipped through them, assessing, rejecting, finally settled on two, a section with the comet over Westminster Abbey and one of horses being loaded on the Norman ships. They both showed a lot of detail; she hoped she'd be able to capture it.

She was taping a large piece of rough sketching paper on the sheet when her phone rumbaed to the edge of the table, letting out a factory-default ringtone. Unknown caller. She sighed, had the robocallers chased her around half the world? She stared at it, then it clicked…Fitzroy. She hadn't added him to her contact list.

"This is Roz Duke." A neutral answer.

"Ms. Duke." His English accent was discernable even in two words. Something about the way they formed the vowels she guessed.

"Yes, DI Fitzroy. How are you? Do you have some news?"

"I'm fine. And yes, some news but not perhaps what you were hoping. Forensics found nothing on the note or the envelope. Plain printer paper, envelopes you can buy by the gross, self-sealing. The person wore gloves, no prints. A complete dead end."

"I guess I'm not surprised. It was such an anonymous thing."

"He, whoever, is good at this. Not a phone call, text, email that could be traced. We're holding on to it, but I guess to just begin building a file. You haven't had any other contact?"

Why would he ask that? Did he think she was holding back, hiding something?

"No, I've been quietly working. This location is good for that. I find myself drifting in time. The other day I watched some beekeepers, you know, in their white coveralls, and at first glance, thought they were cowled monks. Strolling in the gardens." Should she have told him that? He'd probably think her on the edge. Oh, well.

She took a deep breath, shut her eyes as though she didn't want to face this next truth. "It makes me angry that the quiet I found here has been invaded."

"Invaded?" Fitzroy's voice tensed. "You mean something else has happened?"

"No, at least nothing I'm aware of. It's just that someone's been watching me, knows where I live, maybe followed me to France. I feel exposed, creepy."

"Have you talked to your landlady?"

"No. Why?"

"Maybe she's the one who told the person where you lived."

The phone began to shake in Roz' hand. Were the ladies in the church guild involved?

"I'll tell you what," Fitzroy said. "I'll come over there and we can talk to her together."

"It's not a 'her', the church guild is responsible for the rentals and food. I'm not sure where any of them are, but we'll find someone."

Roz didn't want Fitzroy to think she'd taken extra care for him, but she went into the bathroom, rinsed off her face, did a quick swipe of blush and lipstick and ran a brush through her hair. As she put the brush down, Fitzroy rapped at the door.

When she opened it, he smiled at her. "Are you ready to go? Where is the manager or landlady located?"

"In the rectory." Roz stepped out the door, pulled it shut. "Follow me."

She skirted around the line of apartments, took a path through the rose garden into the colonnade of the next building, and entered the offices where two women sat. One was embroidering a piece for the altar, the other was at a computer. Both looked up as she and Fitzroy came in.

"Ms. Duke." The woman at the computer stopped typing. "We don't see you here often. Is everything alright?"

"Yes, Mrs. Lewes. I've had a curious incident, and this is DI Fitzroy from the Hythe police who'd like to talk to you."

Mrs. Lewes gasped and stood, her hand at her throat. "A policeman? We don't usually see police here. What's happened?" The other woman stopped, her needle in the air, a look of astonishment on her face. She didn't speak, but leaned forward to catch every word.

"It's not serious, but Ms. Duke received a note last night with an implied threat. We'd like to know if anyone saw someone, we assume a man, coming up to Ms. Duke's door between 6:00 and 7:00 yesterday evening?"

Two sets of eyes widened, two voices gasped. The women paled, looked at one another, shook their heads.

"No, no, we haven't seen anyone. And at that time, we're busy with dinner for those of our guests who eat their meals here." Mrs. Lewes took the lead, and the other woman nodded in agreement. "Besides, as you might know, Ms. Duke's front door faces the street away from the church grounds proper. The chance of any of us seeing a visitor is slim unless we happen to be walking to the shops."

"I did notice that." Fitzroy's tone was calm, probably not wanting to frighten the women. "And her presence is casual. She travels and can be gone for a night or two, but I wonder if we could make her arrangement with you a bit more formal."

Wait a minute, Roz thought. Was he going to ask these ladies to keep track of her? Babysit her? She cleared her throat, then saw a quick eye movement from him and stopped.

"What I'd propose, if both you and Ms. Duke agree, is that she lets you know any time she's going to be away overnight and that she checks in with you when she returns. If she's gone for more than a day longer than she planned, I'd appreciate a quick call."

The two Alter Guild women exchanged a glance, then agreed. "We usually don't keep too close an eye on our guests, but then I don't think we've ever had a guest threatened." Color returned to Mrs. Lewes' face. "Would you be agreeable to this, Ms. Duke? We don't want you to feel that we're imposing on your privacy at all."

What could she say? Roz' usual reaction was to answer to no one, but now someone knew where she was and wanted her gone. At home, there were neighbors, people who knew her and her routine. And if she needed to leave for a few days, people who'd take care of Tut.

Here, even though she'd interacted with a lot of people, it was all casual and no one would notice or think anything if she disappeared. Well, maybe if she didn't pay a bill, but that could take weeks, months possibly.

"Yes, that's acceptable and I'm sorry if my presence has disrupted your peace. That's one thing I cherish about it."

"Please don't be concerned. The church has always been a sanctuary in troubled times or for troubled people." Mrs. Lewes took one of Roz' hands.

As they left the office Fitzroy said, "I have one other request."

"What now, that I clock in and out with you? That I tell you every time I get in my car?"

"Not exactly. I'd appreciate it if you'd give up your other flat outside of London and move your base here."

"Why here? I still do a lot of research in and around London, and the glass was stolen from Westminster. If it were going to get fenced, it would more likely be in London, or a major city. It'd be too easy to trace in a tiny town like Hythe."

"All good points, but here's where the murder took place, here's where you were warned and here's where I, we, can watch out for you. And you don't have to tell me when you get in your car, you know we have CCTV."

CHAPTER FIFTEEN

CCTV? Roz thought of what that meant at home. Cameras stuck in convenience store corners and big box retailers, designed to deter theft. Now, used by the cops for forensics, tracing the movements of crime victims or possible suspects.

In Britain, they were ubiquitous, recording pedestrian-filled streets, highways, ferry crossings, village round-abouts. She realized Fitzroy could track her to London and beyond. England was a hard country to be anonymous in.

"Would you really follow me?"

"Don't think of it as following you, look at it as keeping threats away from you. If anyone were to drop off another note, we'd have a picture of him." He thought for a moment. "Or her."

Roz grinned at his attempt to be politically correct. Even the mother tongue was undergoing evolution and change just as it had for more than a millennium. With more than a million words, English had been changed by the Angles, Saxons, Vikings, French, Hindi, all layered on Celtic and Latin bases.

"It could be a her. I don't imagine there's any sex-linked characteristic to leaving an envelope on someone's doormat." She smiled, her light teasing language reminding her of Liam.

Liam. She'd have to tell him she was moving from her north London flat to Hythe and he'd ask why, and she'd tell him…what? Well, she'd think of something. Right now, she had to figure what she'd left in her other flat. Would it all fit in her rental car? Some clothes, several boxes of glass and cames, a roll of drawing paper, books. A lot of books. Mostly history and studies of stained glass.

"I can help, you know." Fitzroy's voice broke through her inventory-taking.

"Help?"

"I'm going to follow you up to keep an eye on you. I'll have my car and can help move things." He was bouncing his keys in his hand and glanced at her with such innocence she had to snicker.

"That's a sneaky offer to watch me." Roz felt a tiny flame of resistance, belligerence but tamped it down. If she said no, would he do it anyway?

"Are you ready to leave?"

"You want to go today?" Roz wrinkled her nose, calculating how long it would take to throw things together.

Fitzroy raised his brows. "It's only about two hours, depending on where you are in north London. Up and back in four hours or so. I'd think a displaced Angeleno wouldn't think much of it."

"I still have to pack stuff up, load the car, let my landlord know and turn over the keys. How about we plan to spend the night somewhere up there after I get everything packed?"

"That will work, we can time ourselves to miss the worst of the commute crunch. I usually take the train, it's just over an hour to Liverpool Station and no traffic to deal with." He hesitated. "Unless there's a rail strike or something."

Roz smiled to herself. People made a big deal about traffic in California and forgot how bad it could be in other places. She remembered the Arc de Triomphe traffic circle as a nine-lane parking lot and a trip to Amsterdam where they watched a driver next to them finish reading a book in the 45 minutes they sat on the highway.

"Good. I'll pack a few things for overnight. Are you ready?"

"I am, I usually have things with me. Never know when I'm going to get called out. Let me run down to the station and let the team know I'll be back tomorrow."

She nodded. "I shouldn't be more than fifteen minutes. Should I meet you somewhere?"

"Why don't you come to the station? If the note-leaver is still around, we might want him," he paused, "or her, to think they've scared you off when they see you driving off with a case."

"A case?" She gave a mental slap. A backpack or overnight bag. "Right."

In less than half-an-hour they were on the M20, headed northwest, Roz in the lead, Fitzroy following alert for anything odd.

By 7:00 that evening they'd packed up all of Roz' things, loaded both their cars and set off to find an inn for some food and rooms so they could get an early start the next morning. This time Fitzroy took the lead and suggested Waltham Abbey.

"It's a bit quieter but close to the highway," he said. "We can have a leisurely breakfast and still be in Hythe by noon."

They found a converted coaching inn, booked two rooms, had dinner, then Roz started reading a tourist brochure. "Good cover for us. Let's us look like tourists," she pointed out, adding, "I'm sorry, I can't start out early."

She showed Fitzroy the page on Waltham Abbey Church. "It's been a place of worship since the seventh century. I haven't been here, don't know how I missed it, but I want to see the glass."

She looked reproachfully at him. "If you hadn't forced me to move, I probably would have found this on my own and spent some time here. As it is, I guess I'll have to be satisfied with a rushed trip."

Fitzroy wouldn't be bullied. "Forced you? This is for your own well-being. I need to keep you safe if you're going to be the lure for the thieves, not to mention the murderer. Have you forgotten?"

"Lure? I'm not sure I like that. I agreed to help you track down the stolen glass, I didn't volunteer to be a target." After a moment, she added, "If I'm going to be a lure, it makes sense for me to visit as many churches and see as much stained glass as possible. Our trip back will have to wait a bit. I'm going to bed." She gathered up her purse and sweater and strode out of the restaurant.

How had she gotten off course? This sabbatical time was supposed to be research and design, stretching her abilities to work with glass. Damn that body, what was his name, Ilic? Being in the wrong place at the wrong time had detoured her down this rabbit hole where the police were watching her, where she got threatening notes, where she was forced—well, to be fair, urged—to give up her London flat and its access to museums and churches.

The exercise of walking up two flights of stairs to her room took the edge off her snit. She had to admit that being slightly more than an hour by train, or less than two hours by car, to London wasn't exactly out in the sticks. She could still spend time in the city when she wanted to, and truthfully, she was at a point when working on the design and the window was most important.

And to do that, her apartment at the Hythe church was ideal, quiet, out of the way with the added fillip of transporting her reveries back centuries. She crawled into bed, closed her eyes and conjured up white-cowled monks strolling in the gardens, discussing designs for the new stained glass windows.

CHAPTER SIXTEEN

$\mathcal{A}$ bell. Ting, ting, ting. Calling the monks to Matins?

No, her phone, chiming. She groaned, picked it up. Two a.m.? Then saw the caller's name, Liam.

"Liam. What's up? Do you know it's 2 a.m.?"

"You're the one who moved eight time-zones away. It's 6:00 in the evening here and I called to find out what you're doing."

"I'm sleeping, or at least I was. What did you expect at this hour?"

"I expect you to tell me." She heard a tenseness in his voice.

"That's a bit cryptic. What on earth are you talking about?" She was fully awake now. If they were going to have a tiff while 8,000 miles apart, she needed her brain cells in fighting shape.

"I got a call from the landlord of your London flat. You'd left me as an emergency contact, and he called to say you left a box behind." A 30-second pause. "Behind?"

Roz flipped the nightstand lamp on, looked around the room, looked at her phone. Great, a missed text she'd slept through. The landlord's number. And now Liam knew she'd packed up and fled.

"I was planning to call you today and fill you in. I'm fine."

"Fine? More bodies? Is that why you're moving and not telling anyone?"

"No, no more bodies, it's just that…" How much. What to tell. "I found a note on my doormat at the church in Hythe. It said to butt out, basically."

"Butt out?" Liam's voice took on volume. "Butt out of what?"

"That's just it, Hal, DI Fitzroy, didn't know exactly what. I've been searching the web for any trace or discussion about the missing glass. He's pulled in Scotland yard and Interpol on the murdered man. So far, nothing. I'm going to contact some of the shady glass dealers who are always trying to sell me stuff, but no one knows about that. In fact, I was going to ask if you'd turned up anything."

"Nice segue. When were you going to tell me? And why did you leave London? And where are you going?"

Roz sighed, loud enough that Liam said, "Don't roll your eyes at me. Those are all legitimate questions."

"They are. Hal was concerned that someone involved with the theft or murder knew who I was and where I was staying. He all but ordered me to give up the London flat and move everything to Hythe so he could watch me."

"You don't sound all-in on that plan."

"I'm not. He convinced me I'd be safer there because there are fewer people, fewer strangers coming and going. I complained that I'd be too far away from museums and research facilities and he pointed out it was just over an hour by train to London. And made a snide remark about how former Angelenos thought nothing of that commute."

Liam laughed. "That's hitting below the belt, there isn't much comeback to that."

"I know. There's almost nowhere on earth you can get to easily anymore. Have you found anything?"

Liam was silent for long enough that Roz said, "Are you still there?"

"I am. I'm trying to synthesize what I've learned—or not learned—so far."

Tapestry of Tears

"Not learned doesn't sound too good."

She'd leaned on Liam's contacts in the world of the dark web, hoping that there'd be some trace of the stolen stained glass for sale—or for ransom. If there were no traces, it'd be up to her to troll the shady dealers.

"Sam, you remember Sam, has been searching, slowly and quietly. So far, he hasn't found any discussions about stained glass. It's a pretty esoteric item. I'd think anyone wanting to either buy or sell would already have contacts."

"Hmmm…" Roz' mind churned. He was right, but a piece was missing. "Let's not think about selling it, let's think about ransoming it. Hal said this hoard of glass was considered a national treasure because it was found at Westminster and there's so much of it. That could mean not only the church, but the government as well, might pay to get it back. And both those are seen as having deep pockets."

"Well, if I were looking to get a ransom from some national treasure I'd stolen, I wouldn't be talking about it on the internet, dark or not."

"Wait." Roz' thoughts were outrunning her brain's comprehension. "What if…what if someone hacked into, say, the British government's sites and put their ransom demand there?"

Now Liam was quiet. Then, "That's something possible. If the government was hacked, they wouldn't go public with it, it would make them look like none of their information was secure. And the same would go for the church. Speaking of which, I assume the glass by default belongs to the Church of England, not the Catholic church."

"I don't know. I'll have to ask Hal." Roz didn't write it down, sure she could remember until morning.

"I'm not so sure about the Hal guy." Liam's voice took on what sounded like a note of petulance. "You two seem to be getting pretty chummy."

"And that would bother you, why? Do we have some kind of relationship I don't know about? Some exclusivity?"

"No, no…" Now Liam sounded as though he were stammering, searching for the right words. "We're friends, sure, but I kind of thought we…"

"We may come to that," Roz said. "For now, we're friends who help each other out. I appreciate all you've done, are doing for me. The research, taking care of Tut—speaking of Tut, how is he?"

"He's fine." Now on solid neutral ground, Liam was his usual bantering self. "Here, say hello, I have you on speaker."

Roz heard a rustling then a slight whimper, probably not Liam she thought. "Hi, my sweet boy, I miss you." She felt somewhat awkward, talking doggy to a dog over a satellite bounce. "Is he still sleeping with you?"

"Most of the time, but I leave it up to him. When we go to your house, he scours the place for you but comes to me when I call him."

"He's not in your way, is he?" Roz knew well that without Liam and his willingness to watch Tut her sabbatical would never have happened. She hadn't come up with anything she could use to pay him back. "Are you able to write with him there? What are you working on?" Another safe topic.

"My agent is working to sell a fantasy trilogy. I'm about 45,000 words into the first book."

"That's terrific, Liam! Working mostly in Hamilton?"

"Yep, I'm trying to stay here and stick to a schedule. For this book, I don't have any reason to go to Portland. Tut and I are being homebodies."

Both seemed to talk more easily about everyday concerns than when the conversation veered to relationship areas. Roz figured they'd have to address that at some point, but not while they were so far away.

In the meantime, she'd continue to call DI Fitzroy, Hal, and would gloss over any snitty comments from Liam.

"That's good, Liam, and I'm sure Tut likes to have a regular routine. And back to Sam, would he be able to find out if any part of the British government had been hacked? Or had gotten any communication about the missing glass?"

"Not sure. I'll ask him. I'm heading to the beach for an evening run and later I'll look for the green streak for you. Keep in touch, I don't like the threat and I guess I'm glad that the English copper is watching you. I hope you can go back to sleep."

"I think so and I'll be better at calling if anything else happens. Give my love to Tut and the beach and say I'll see them soon."

Without Liam's voice, Roz lay back in the bed. A sudden surge of homesickness and the mention of the green streak, a flash of green on the horizon just as the sun slipped into the Pacific, washed over her and a tear slipped out. What was she doing here?

CHAPTER SEVENTEEN

Roz struggled to get out of bed. She'd had a hard time getting back to sleep after Liam's call, and her alarm at 6 a.m. forced a groan. Get up, she told herself. Hal would probably want to get on the road early. She could stall him for a bit and give herself an hour or so in the church.

The small town was quiet as she walked the few blocks to the Abbey, hoping an early service meant the doors were unlocked. They were, and she pushed through the door and entered. This was a full-scale Gothic building with much of the interior redone in the nineteenth century. Disappointing.

She picked up a guidebook, saw that an original wooden church on this site dated to 610 AD. The stained glass was a bust, although the rose window and two lancet windows were good, if not medieval. What was early medieval was that this church held the tomb of King Harold, buried at the high altar after his death in 1066 at Hastings.

She took a few pictures, made a note to follow up on research about this church and was back at the inn by 8:00 a.m., drinking coffee in the small breakfast room as Hal walked in, ready to start his day.

"Let's have breakfast before we begin," he said. "The traffic will calm down. And," he smiled at her, "don't you want to visit the church?"

"I already did. The glass was a disappointment, but it turns out that Harold was buried here after the Battle of Hastings." Roz raised her eyebrows. "Did you know that?"

It was Fitzroy's turn for raised eyebrows. "No. I know a bit of the history around the invasion. This part of the coast still has traces."

"I wondered about your name." Roz thought this was as good an opening as any to find out his roots. "Were you named for King Harold?"

Fitzroy's stare bored through his coffee cup. It looked as though his mind was reeling through a century of family history. "I don't know. It's a name in my family over the years, probably eight or nine Harolds. I never put it together with the king." Now he looked directly at her. "My last name, though, means that someone way back was the bastard son of a Norman lord, or even one of William's relatives. There's always been talk that someone maybe 600 or 700 years ago held a manor house in fief from a Norman earl."

Roz stared. She couldn't fathom a family history that went back that far. "Has anyone traced it?"

"One of my great-grand-uncles, a cousin of my great-grandfather, was searching church records, but he was killed in World War I and nobody took it up after that. That war ripped apart English society and culture, and people didn't have time to recover before the Second World War hit. Since then, no one in the family has had the interest."

He smiled. "My parents gave up the rural life. My dad is a solicitor and my mum's a teacher. The live in Canterbury, where I grew up. My grandmother still lives on the small farm she inherited from her grandparents outside of Folkestone."

He laid down money for the check, grinned at her and said, "So you see, we haven't stirred much. Are you ready to go?"

In reply, Roz pushed back her chair, grabbed her backpack and purse and stood. "Yes. I'm anxious to get back to Hythe, get these things moved in." She hadn't mentioned her conversation with Liam last night. Should she? How much should she share?

They hit the tail end of the commute traffic on the M20 and it took more than two hours to get to the Hythe exit. At Roz' apartment, Fitzroy made her wait while he checked inside to make sure nothing had been disturbed. It miffed her until she remembered that they, whoever the "they" were, watched her. Maybe even followed her to London and back?

She and Hal unloaded their cars, stacked the boxes and bags in her bedroom. She'd have to ask the guild ladies, maybe Mrs. Lewes, if there were any available wardrobes or chests of drawers or bookshelves she could use for storage. Everything would have to fit into her bedroom, she needed the living space to use as her studio and have enough room to lay out the patterns.

"I need to check in at the station," Hal said. "Maybe we could have dinner and go over anything that's come up."

Ahhhh, a few hours' respite before she had to give Hal a version of her Liam conversation. "Good, that'll give me some time to work on transferring a slide to the paper pattern I started. Would 7:00, work? Meet you somewhere?"

"I'll pick you up. After the note, I don't like to think of you out on your own. We don't know who's watching you."

Roz still was uncomfortable being coddled, then remembered she was the bait that Hal was using to trap a thief and murderer. Well, now, bait put a different slant on it. Maybe she wasn't being confined but kept safe.

She worked steadily through the afternoon, eating some cheese and bread—ha, a ploughman's lunch, she thought—while making minor adjustments that would allow glass to be cut and shaped more easily. The bottom border of this scene included five empty boats resting on waves, not colorful but an omen of the invasion, and she needed this to tell the story.

A knock at the door pulled her away from her work, and she looked at the clock. Not Hal, it was only 4:30. Who? Someone leaving another note?

"Who is it?" Normally she wouldn't ask, just open the door, but was relieved when she heard Mrs. Lewes' voice. "I just wanted to make sure you'd gotten home safely."

Roz pulled the door open and the Guild woman stood on the mat holding a vase of flowers.

"We don't want to be intrusive, but the Guild thought we should check up every so often. Particularly since you were away overnight."

"Thank you. I'm learning people can be caring and watchful without being pushy. Lovely flowers."

Mrs. Lewes handed over the bouquet. "Did you get everything moved from London?"

"We did. And now I have to ask you if there are any empty pieces of furniture around that I can use." Roz waved her hand at some of the boxes that could be seen in the bedroom. "I hadn't planned on having all this here," she said ruefully.

"We may find a bookcase or two, but how about letting you store things in one of our empty apartments? The one two doors down from you is empty and we don't have any reservations for it."

"If that's not any trouble." Her concern touched Roz. "I want to pay you for it, though. I know the Guild runs on a small budget."

"Small, yes, but we have sufficient to keep the church up. We wouldn't charge you the full rent because you won't be living in it. But maybe 15 pounds a month?" She backtracked at Roz' look. "It that too much?"

"No, no, Mrs. Lewes, it's probably too little. Thank you so much. I liked the flat I was renting in London, but now this is beginning to feel much more like home."

Tapestry of Tears

"We're so glad." The Guild woman shook Roz' hand. "I'll just go and get the keys. You can move things over whenever you want."

With the interruption, Roz decided to put her work away for the evening. She'd have time to move the boxes, get things settled before Hal came for her. She scanned the cozy room, letting a sense of home seep into her.

CHAPTER EIGHTEEN

By the time Hal knocked, Roz had sorted the boxes, rearranged books, tools, glass and was ready for a quiet dinner. And a full description of Liam's involvement, both in her life and in the search for the glass.

"I thought we'd done enough driving for today," Hal said. "We can just walk to a pub in town if that's alright with you."

"Fine," Roz said, glad she'd opted for a pair of flats. Walking on cobblestones, so abundant in Europe, was a tricky proposition that she hadn't completely mastered. Once in Germany she'd been looking at some carvings in Worms and stepped wrong, twisting her ankle and causing her and Winston three days of bed rest in their small hotel while she healed.

It was a calm evening with cloud banks forming over the Channel, a light breeze carrying the smell of the sea. Roz felt settled, the next few weeks of work and research clear in her mind and she took Hal's arm.

He jolted slightly then patted her hand. "Were you able to work this afternoon?"

"I was. And Mrs. Lewes had another apartment available, so I stored those things I didn't need. I could have managed with all the stuff I brought down from London, but this way it gives me room to work. At home, I have a complete house and a converted garage is my studio." She described the sight and sound of the Pacific outside her studio, painting Hal a mental picture of her life away from here. She didn't notice a sadness that settled on his face.

"Here we are." Hal took her hand off his arm, opened the door and the smell of an English pub enveloped her. Beer, cooking fat, onions, even a trace of cigarettes, though smoking wasn't allowed inside anymore. A few centuries of smoke permeated the walls and ceiling, mixing with a slight underlay of gin.

They chose a table by a tall window away from the bar to be able to talk. Hal had a steak and kidney pie, Roz a fish stew. She was adapting to English cooking, but couldn't manage organ meats, didn't do liver or sweetbreads or kidneys. When she thought about it, she occasionally considered becoming a vegetarian.

Dinner finished, Roz cleared her throat. "I didn't tell you everything that happened last night," she began.

"Did you get another note?" Hal's jaw clenched and he all but slammed his coffee cup into the saucer.

"No, nothing like that. But I talked to Liam Karshner."

"Liam? Oh, your friend in Oregon. And?"

"He'd gotten a call from my landlord in London saying I'd left a box behind."

"Ahhh, we'll have to have it shipped." Hal watched her, a puzzled look in his eyes. "I don't think it's a big deal."

Roz agreed it wasn't, then, "What Liam was upset about was that I hadn't told him about moving everything down here, to Hythe."

"Are you supposed to check in with him when you travel around?"

"No, no, it's just that I'd left him as a contact person with the landlord. And well, a few other places. Plus, he's keeping my dog so I want to make sure he knows where he can find me."

"Doesn't he have your mobile number?"

Tapestry of Tears

"Of course he does, that's how he called me. But when I told him about the note and that you wanted me to move everything to Hythe to monitor me, he got kind of upset."

Hal was silent. Then, "Upset because of the move or because of me?"

"Possibly a bit of both. I told him about you and your search for the glass—and Ilic's murderer—and he's willing to help, then I make a move without telling him. He just felt left out of the loop."

"How's he planning to help?"

"He has a friend," and Roz told him about Sam and his abilities to trace things on the dark web.

"And this Sam is able to find things we, The Yard, Interpol, can't?"

Great, Roz thought. Now I've insulted all the English police abilities and probably dissed Hal in the process. She tried to backpedal. "No, it's not that you can't, it just that Sam's looking for any discussion about stolen glass. I asked him to do that. I don't want to have to get in touch with some slimier merchants I occasionally use."

Hal pursed his lips. "You buy stolen glass to use in your own creations?"

Oh god, now he would think she was part and parcel of rings of thieves. "No, I think these guys make the glass under less than wonderful circumstances. Some of it is made in Southeast Asia, and I suspect there's a lot of child labor involved. All my glass is from qualified makers in the States and Europe, but every so often I get a notice of some off-beat color available from a different source." She put her napkin on the table and pinned Hal with a stare. "As you said, I'm an internationally known stained glass artist. Anybody who's making glass knows about me. These makers most often do business with the large-scale retailers of kits or the sweatshops that churn out small pieces you buy as souvenirs."

She hadn't worked through this conversation well. Said too much about suppliers, not enough about Sam's search and why she'd asked Liam to take it on. Took a deep breath and began again. "One thing Liam said was that Sam hadn't found any mention of either glass for sale or for ransom and when I told him they considered this glass a national treasure he said, what if the thieves hacked into government sites and demanded the ransom there? The government wouldn't advertise that they'd been hacked."

It was now Hal's turn to stare. "I don't know that we've taken that angle." He put his head in his hands. "Lord, there's so much there, it would be like peeling onions, layers after layers."

"But you could look, right? Liam's friend is good with the dark web, but I don't think hacking into a foreign government is what he's best at."

"Foreign government?"

Roz opened her mouth, then it hit her. She wasn't talking about anything foreign, this was Hal's government and he was a representative, charged with keeping things safe and legal.

"I misspoke. Hacking into the files of a government other than ours."

He smiled. "I knew what you meant. I'm not sure where to start, though. Can't just google 'British government' and have an email pop up saying, 'Give us a billion pounds if you want to see the Westminster glass again'."

Roz almost giggled. She hadn't expected a wry piece of humor like this. "No, I don't think so. Where would this demand even go?"

"Hmmm, don't know. The Exchequer?"

"Who would look into it? MI 6?"

Hal let out a snort. "You've been watching too many Bond movies. It's the Security Service, MI5, that's responsible for internal security. Like your FBI. That and

Scotland Yard. I'll bring this up at our next liaison meeting tomorrow." He pushed his chair back. "Are you ready to leave? I have some work to do tonight."

She reached down to get her purse, pushed away from the table and stood. "Yes. What with Liam calling me in the middle of the night, I underslept last night. I could use an early bedtime."

CHAPTER NINETEEN

"*B*ond. James Bond."

The words were right, but the voice was different. And this Bond looked like Hal Fitzroy.

Roz shook her head, reached out to touch the man, hit her ebook reader and groaned. She always had such vivid dreams that crossing from them to reality was difficult. This time she tried to trace where the impetus for the famous spy came from, going back over her conversations yesterday. There it was, Hal talking about MI 5 and MI 6.

She lay in bed sifting through the brief discussion of some department of the British government being involved in the missing glass. She appreciated Liam's and Sam's search through all the permutations, but this was just too far-fetched.

What was on her agenda for the day? Today was work. She had no firm deadline for presenting the window sample to the university; she doubted there was even another bidder for the contract. In her rarified world, there were only a few people who'd be offered a chance at a commission, and unless it had to go out to bid, the buyers usually got in touch with her directly.

This project was a challenge to her, though. There were few enough things she copied. She had permission to use a section of "Starry Night" for her front door, but usually her commissions were her own designs. Until this one came along, and she couldn't pass it up. Not only the test of her abilities, but the chance to use glass made to medieval specifications.

With a prospect of the entire day lost in the Tapestry, Roz swung out of bed, went to the kitchen and measured grounds into the French press. She drank the first cup of coffee at her desk, watching the bees begin their dance through the garden. This was such a slower paced life. Her little slice of Oregon didn't bustle, but there was a newness, a rawness to life in the States. Here most things moved at the pace of a person walking and followed patterns laid down centuries ago.

She took a shower, put a bagel in the toaster oven, pulled on a comfortable pair of jeans and a soft cotton sweater, powered up her computer and watched the Tapestry's comet over Westminster come to life on the sheet she used as a screen. The sheet of paper she'd pinned to it had little more than half the scene traced. Now she had to decide about how much glass and caming she'd cut each day.

The completed sample window would have to be shipped to Wisconsin in a special-made crate, but there were people Roz knew who shipped art around the world. It could be done, but she planned to keep the sample somewhat small. The Tapestry itself was only 20 inches tall, so the proportions had to remain consistent. For now, she'd trace the panel in its original size. When it came to the finished piece, it would have to be blown up perhaps three times its size to be seen in the clerestory windows planned for the museum.

With some Telemann and Vivaldi on low, she traced Harold enthroned, conferring with his astrologer telling him the comet is a bad omen. She hummed to herself, idly imagining how the women who worked the linen would feel, learning the omen, now known as Halley's Comet, would incubate a new nation, destined to be a world power and breed a new language, English.

Tapestry of Tears

She jerked and tore a hole in the tracing paper at the knock on the door. What time was it? Who would visit her?

"Who is it?" Roz' voice was scratchy from lack of use.

"It's Mrs. Lewes. You didn't answer your phone, and we began to worry."

Roz tugged the door open. "Mrs. Lewes, I'm so sorry! I switched the ringer off thinking I'd feel the vibrations, then went off and left it on my bedside table. Is everything alright?"

"Yes, yes, I mainly wanted to tell you we're about to close up lunch. We didn't see you for breakfast and wondered if you were hungry. Also, that nice policeman asked if we'd just take a quick peek to see if you needed anything."

What? Roz, sucked in a breath, counted to five. Hal was checking up on her? This was going to be more difficult than she thought. If she couldn't be unplugged for a morning to work, she was going to feel stifled, boxed in.

"It's all fine, Mrs. Lewes. When I'm working, I tend to lose all idea of time. My former husband, Winston, used to come in and bring me food. He'd tell me that was enough, I had to stop and eat with him."

"I didn't realize you'd been married." The Guild woman's face looked curious, avaricious, at learning gossip about their famous tenant.

Roz sighed. She didn't tell many people, every telling brought up the hurt and anger. "I was. He was an academic, taught Art History. He was killed in a drive-by shooting in Los Angeles."

"Oh my, I'm so sorry!" Mrs. Lewes looked stricken, but it seemed there was just a tinge of titillation at the thought of a murder.

"It was almost two years ago, and they caught the murderer. Winston was in the wrong place at the wrong time." Roz wouldn't go into the why's of either the place or time. Maybe someday, but not now. "I am getting hungry, though. Can I come over for a bite of lunch?"

"Yes, please do. We have a bit of Shepard's pie and a jam roly-poly. Plain, but comforting. Will you join us for dinner tonight?"

Would she? Maybe a short hiatus from Hal would be a good thing. Give both of them time to assess what, if anything, was between them beside murder.

CHAPTER TWENTY

Roz appreciated Mrs. Lewes and the Guild ladies, and she decided both lunch and dinner was a onetime occasion for home-style English cooking. After hours of work, she didn't have the energy to go out to a pub.

Following the Shepherd's pie at lunch, dinner was fish, chips and mushy peas with Spotted Dick for a dessert. Several years before when she'd discovered the name of the dish, she couldn't wait to try it. Then she found out it was a steamed pudding with dried fruits served with custard, closer in theme and taste to plum pudding or a moist fruitcake. It never made it to her favorites list, so she passed, feeling righteous at declining dessert.

She hadn't spent much time with the other tenants, beyond nodding a hello when they met. Now she forced herself out of her shell and sat with two middle-aged women. They turned out to be teachers on leave, researching the history of the Norman invasion with the idea of writing a children's book.

The women spent a two-week holiday every year in Hythe, staying at the church apartments, but this year had set aside two months to dig into the local history. Jocelyn Burns, the younger of the two, carried a book with her on the history of the Cinque Ports and kept referring to it when something of interest popped up.

"Have you noticed the Martello Tower remains?" She scooped up a spoonful of Spotted Dick. "There used to be about thirty of them along this stretch of coast, most built to repel an invasion from Bonaparte. That never happened, so a lot were left to ruin. There's a redoubt in Dymchurch from the period."

"I have." Roz stirred a cup of decaf, wondering how anyone could enjoy a mishmash of raisins, currents and a thick, heavy cake made with suet. "Those are beyond my interest, too recent though."

Jocelyn Burns sat back, looked at her friend. "Too recent? What's the time period you're interested in?"

"I'm interested in the medieval period, specifically the years around the Norman invasion here. I'm trying to recreate a stained glass version of a scene in the Bayeux Tapestry."

"The Tapestry?" Now the other woman, Phoebe Shedd, took notice. "We've been thinking of centering our book on the Tapestry. There's so much history in that, not just the actual invasion, but all the shenanigans, possible double-dealing, medieval politics and philosophy. It's a microcosm of medieval thought and actions."

Roz hit a nerve. These women were as passionate about their quest as she was about hers.

"Do you teach history?"

The women looked at one another and burst out laughing. "Goodness, no." Phoebe took a sip of water. "We're games mistresses at a girls' school outside of York. I suppose what you'd call a P.E. teacher. We'd like to advance into administration, that's where the money is, but we need more rounded credentials for that."

"We think that a book, one on the history of how England became England, would give us gravitas with the directors." Jocelyn pushed away her not-quite-finished dessert. "Besides, this is a part of England our students don't know well, so we spend time walking and taking pictures to share. Hope to get some of the girls interested in lifelong physical fitness."

Tapestry of Tears

They both pinned Roz with a stare. "Is your interest in the history? Where are you from in the States? Do you teach?" Jocelyn took the lead.

Roz laughed. "Wow, what are my bona fides? I'm originally from Los Angeles. I design and make stained glass windows, usually big commissions for churches, businesses. Anyone who can afford me. I don't teach but my late husband did, Art History at a Los Angeles university. We used to travel every summer, so I've seen a lot of glass, but much of it is either reproduction or later than medieval. When a commission came up for a history department museum at a small, private university, I had the idea of translating the Tapestry into glass."

"Interesting." Phoebe slid her chair back. "Would you like to join us for a nightcap?"

"A nightcap? Here?" Roz looked around.

"Not in the church, in the Guild office. They set out some sherry and port for the tenants. It's all very civilized and lasts less than an hour, as a getting-to-know-you gesture."

The three women headed outside toward the office, now hosting a low murmur of voices.

"Welcome," Mrs. Lewes waved. "I'm so glad you've met some of our other guests, Ms. Duke. Can I get you a drink?"

"Yes, please. I know I haven't spent much time getting to know people, but between traveling and working, I'm usually busy. Now that my headquarters in England is here in Hythe, it's nice to meet others." She took a small cordial glass of ruby-red port. "Jocelyn and Phoebe were telling me about their plan to write a children's book."

At this, both the other women paled. What? What had she said?

"It's still in the talking stage." Jocelyn cleared her throat. "We don't talk about it much. You said your headquarters are here now? Where were you before?"

Nice gentle segue, Roz thought. "I had a flat just north of London. I was focusing on the medieval stained glass techniques but coming down here to find earlier glass." She took a sip. "And to make travel to the Tapestry easier. The ferry from Portsmouth is cheaper than the Chunnel and not as crowded."

Both Jocelyn and Phoebe agreed and slid into a discussion of how terrible travel was these days, how inundated all the decent spots in England and the coast of France were, everywhere was overrun with tourists, how the influx of Americans had made everything so much more expensive.

"I'm glad to have met you," Roz said, standing and moving to the door, "but I'm at a spot where I need to continue tomorrow, so it'll be an early day for me. I hope I'll see you both again."

She took the path from the office through the garden, scented with the last of the roses' aroma released in the evening air. It had been a productive day, she'd met new people, felt settled into her new home. A fleeting moment of question about why the two women paled at the mention of their book, but it might just be teasing karma to talk about it.

Roz didn't keep a journal per se, but tonight she sat at her laptop, recapping thoughts. She'd gone a full 24 hours since seeing Hal, hadn't spoken to Liam for two days, was claiming her own time and space. Was this good?

Roz jotted a few notes about things to do tomorrow, including to having dinner somewhere other than the church. Maybe with Hal? Was she interested in something beyond business with him?

She was borrowing thoughts. Take a step at a time. He wanted her to help him trace down the missing glass. How best to do that?

She added "talk to Liam: re dark web" and "troll Asian markets" to her to do list, shut the laptop down. Turned off the sitting room light, brushed her teeth, pulled off her clothes and went to bed.

The explosion woke her.

CHAPTER TWENTY-ONE

A dream? No, this was here and now.

The initial blast jerked her from sleep. She heard the tinkling of broken glass hitting the pavement and smelled something burning. The building?

Her hands shook as she pulled a hoodie on, grabbed her phone and inched to the door. Good, it wasn't her apartment that exploded; hers was intact. Should she open the door? Some lessons learned from the fire department when she was a kid came drifting back and she gingerly touched the door. Never open a door hot to the touch, she remembered.

This one wasn't, so she gently eased it open. The cool night air brought a hint of fog which didn't cover the burning smell. But was smoke mixed with the fog? She left her door ajar and carefully took a couple steps onto the sidewalk. The acrid smell was stronger here and seemed to be coming from her right.

Voices drifted through the fog and smoke and she found herself the center of a group of women, yelling over one another.

"A bomb?"

"No, a gas explosion."

"It was an attack."

"An attack? Against who? What?"

The voices sorted themselves out. Mrs. Lewes, Phoebe and Jocelyn huddled in nightclothes and bathrobes, eyes as wide as lemurs, while they tried to work out what happened.

"Wait! Did anyone call 999?" Roz looked at Mrs. Lewes, hoping she'd take charge.

"I did." Mrs. Lewes pulled her bathrobe tight against her lanky body. "I didn't know whether to ask for fire or police so I think they're sending both."

Now the group heard the rising-falling of emergency vehicles and blue lights bounced off the layer of mist. First up was a fire vehicle. Three people poured out, one yelled, "Where's the fire?" Spotted smoke from an apartment two doors to the right of Roz'. They grabbed their axes and ran.

"Wait, wait!" Mrs. Lewes headed after them. "That unit is empty, no one is inside. Please don't hack the door down, I'll get a key."

As the Guild woman headed toward the office, Roz realized the apartment belching smoke was the one she'd just moved her overflow into. She had a key, whirled around, picked it up from her hall table, ran to the firefighters and handed it to the one in the lead. "I think the Guild is worried about damage," she said.

The firefighter slowly pushed the door open. No flames billowed out, and the smoke seemed to be easing so the crew moved into the apartment.

"Doesn't look like much damage besides the broken window," the leader said. "You said no one lived here, but there're things, boxes, in here. Is it just storage?"

Roz and Mrs. Lewes exchanged a look, then Roz said, "Those are my belongings. I don't have room for all of them in my apartment so I'm temporarily renting this unit. I hope there's no damage."

Pushing the shield on his helmet back, he said, "Let us go through to make sure, but it looks as though someone threw a smoke bomb through the window."

Roz gasped. Maybe this wasn't a random act. Maybe she was the target.

Tapestry of Tears

"I think you were the target." Roz jumped, spun around and saw Fitzroy behind her.

"Why, why would anyone throw a bomb? And at a place I don't even live in?"

Fitzroy held up a hand. "Let me talk to the fire brigade and see what they've found." He put paper booties over his shoes, walked into the damaged room, pulled on a pair of gloves. Spoke to the lead firefighter.

Roz watched the two men confer, saw Fitzroy reach down and pick up some shattered window glass, watched the firefighter pick up what looked like an empty can.

Holy crow, Fitzroy was acting as though this was a crime scene.

"What? What did you find?" Roz couldn't help herself, she had to know.

Fitzroy came over to her. "We believe someone threw a smoke bomb through the front window. Most of the shattered window is inside the room, indicating that the object came from outside. And Lt. Vincent has seen that same kind of smoke bomb, canister, before." Fitzroy sounded glum. "It's the kind police and special forces use."

"You mean the person who did this has some connection with the police? That doesn't make sense." Roz ran her fingers through her hair, trying to make it behave, stop falling into her eyes. It would probably take more than one washing to get the smoke smell out.

"I doubt it's somebody associated with the police. You can buy these kinds of canisters online."

Adding to the traffic jam in front of her apartment, a SOCO van slid to a halt, disgorging two techs dressed in the ever-present white coveralls. They nodded at Fitzroy and the firefighters, said, "What do we have here?"

"It looks like an attempt to scare rather than injure." Fitzroy wiped a hand down his face. Roz thought he'd probably been sound asleep when the call came in about a possible fire and recognized the address. "Ms. Duke received an earlier threat."

Roz watched him. Unsaid was any personal concern about her. Would he have moved as fast if it were anyone else? She didn't know him well enough to suss out his reactions, but he seemed to take charge.

"Any fire? Do we need the arson squad?" Fitzroy looked around at the growing crowd.

"No sign of fire." Lt. Vincent stored his equipment back on the truck, took off his helmet and gear. "We found the canister. Nothing damaged beyond the window, but everything in here will smell like smoke for a while."

Roz was quiet. The things she had in here; books, rolls of paper, stained glass, leading, wouldn't be damaged by smoke, but the furniture that belonged to the Guild might be. There was an upholstered love seat, two chairs, bedding. Extra linens stored in a closet may have been spared, but they'd certainly need washing.

"Mrs. Lewes, I'm so sorry. This wouldn't have happened if I weren't here. Please let me pay for any damage or clean-up that's needed." Roz walked over and put a hand on the older woman's shoulder, looked at her, saw pain and shock in her eyes.

"No, no, I'm just grateful that you weren't in there when the bomb went off. We've had no violence here in the past 30 years I've been with the Guild. This isn't your fault, it's the fault of whoever has tried to harm you." She turned to Fitzroy. "I assume you're working hard to find out who this person is?"

Roz stifled an internal smile. For Mrs. Lewes, that wasn't a request, more like an order. Her well-brought-up persona had been rocked by the bomb, the appearance of both police and fire in the middle of night, the aberrant turn of events. This wasn't part of the well-ordered daily life in either the church or Hythe.

Roz turned to Jocelyn and Phoebe and shrugged. "I expect this is beyond what you were expecting in your stay, as well. I probably should have warned you, lately I seem to be a lightning rod for bizarre events."

"Do bombs follow you?" Jocelyn's tone was light, but there was an underlying fear.

What to say? Oh well. "No, not bombs. Mostly bodies." Roz did a quick recap of the Archbishop in Oregon and the body in the Lympne church. She didn't bring up Winston, there was too much personal in that story.

Both Jocelyn and Phoebe made sounds, little murmurs of excitement. Maybe wanting to hear more? Not tonight, there was plenty of electricity still sparking between Fitzroy and Roz for her to tackle any explanations.

She wondered if she'd be able to go back to sleep. There would be plenty to talk about at dinner tonight with Fitzroy. And it better be something other than mushy peas.

CHAPTER TWENTY-TWO

It took another half-hour to get things sorted out, people off to where they'd come from, darkness and quiet to be restored.

Fitzroy stationed a constable in the smoky, smelly unit until daylight and the Guild could get a glazier to come and replace the window. Then, they'd pay to have a crew come and sweep up the glass, clean the furniture and scrub everything else.

"I'm so sorry you were woken up. I've managed to disrupt everyone's sleep tonight." Roz started back to her own apartment. "Would you like to come in for some tea or something? Maybe something stronger?"

"Perhaps tea. I'm not sure I'll be able to go home—there are reports to fill out and I want to see if the SOCOs found any evidence."

Roz busied herself getting tea, cups, sugar out and filled the electric kettle. This simple ritual kept her hands occupied, but her mind raced down dead-end alleys. What if she hadn't found that body? What if she didn't know about the theft of the stained glass? What if she'd never come to England?

The last "what if" was ridiculous. No more sensible than wondering why Winston was in that particular mall at the particular time. It was all just weird coincidence, right? Well, until it wasn't.

"I'll be off after this cup. You must be exhausted." Fitzroy took a cup on a saucer from Roz.

"I don't think any more than you." She yawned.

"Well, yes, but I'm more used to getting woken up with middle-of-the-night calls."

"Mrs. Lewes says this is a quiet place, and even you've said there aren't any murders to speak of. Why else would you be called out at midnight or whenever?"

He smiled at her. "Murder isn't the only thing that can interrupt sleep. There are vehicle accidents, domestic incidents, fires. Anything that takes looking into, filing reports." He dipped his head and rolled his neck. "I suspect that the law enforcement departments in the States are as awash in reports and paperwork as we are."

She watched him closely. He exuded what could be the English low-key, stiff-upper-lip syndrome, but his body was giving off other vibes. Maybe he was used to being blasted out of bed in the night for an emergency, but it looked as if it was wearing on him.

"Do you think tonight has anything to do with Ilic or the theft? Am I being targeted? Will this fit in with your idea of me as bait?"

He stared at the wall behind her, finally caught her eye. "Well, I should certainly think so. They, whoever 'they' are, know about you. Know you found Ilic's body. Know where you live. Watched you move things into the other apartment. The only misstep was they assumed you were living there."

"Do you think they'll try something again?"

"Oh, I should think so."

Roz jerked back. He was so matter of fact about it. Was she in danger? Or was this just a maneuver to frighten her, to cause her to go back to Oregon? Whatever it was, tonight, though it was nervy, only strengthened her resolve to figure this out, to find the treasure of medieval glass.

Fitzroy put his cup in the sink, came over and touched her shoulder. He was close enough that she could see the tiredness in his eyes, his unshaven cheeks and a wave of tenderness welled in her chest. He might seem insouciant, but this affected him. On top of a murder and a theft to figure out, he now had her to worry about, even though she felt she played an equal part in the hunt.

"Thank you for the tea, it helps. What time do you want to go to dinner this evening?"

"Are you still planning on it? I thought you'd be too tired." Roz intended to go back to bed and she could sleep as late as she liked, but he'd likely power through.

Fitzroy wrinkled his nose. "I'm not going to let some two-bit hood ruin a nice meal with an attractive dame," he said, in a parody of Bogart.

Roz burst out laughing. "You've seen too many old American gangster movies," she giggled. "And if that's supposed to be Bogart, you sound more like Jimmy Cagney. 'Youse dirty rats'." This, the teasing, the banter that covered up interest, was what she'd missed being away from Liam.

At the door, Fitzroy paused. "You may be right. These days, though, you don't get those old black and white, clear cut bad guys. Would 7:00 tonight be good?"

"Fine. Are we walking or driving?"

"I don't know yet. Does it make a difference?"

"Not a lot." Roz glanced down at her feet, still in the flip-flops that served as slippers. "Just wondering what shoes to wear."

From his expression, Roz could tell he was trying to assimilate this comment, digging in the file drawers of his mind for the correct slot. He must have given up because now he waved as he stepped out to the street, then stopped.

"Hmmm, I think, maybe, we'll see…" His verbal musing pricked Roz' ears.

"What? We'll see what?"

"Oh, just talking about the new CCTV cameras we installed. I don't know if they were switched on when the vandal showed up."

"Are you going to check?"

"That's one task for this morning. By tonight, I should have some answers. We can talk over dinner. Good night, I hope you get some rest."

With that, he crossed the street to his car, parked at a probably illegal angle where he'd pulled up and left it.

Roz turned to go inside and caught sight of one of the CCTV cameras. Could this unblinking eye have captured whoever was after her?

CHAPTER TWENTY-THREE

"Well, hi there." Liam's American drawl echoed in her ear from across the miles.

"Hi your own self. Are you busy?" Roz felt a wave of homesickness.

"No, just beginning to think about dinner. Hey, it's what, 3:00 a.m. for you? Why are you up at this hour?"

Roz was buoyed at Liam's quickness, his ability to sense things without long explanations.

"I've been up since just before 2:00 a.m. The explosion woke me."

"What?" Liam practically squawked. "OK, quit dancing around, cut to the chase."

"Well, someone threw a smoke grenade into a unit two doors down from me. Woke me up, woke up some other tenants, the landlady. The cops and fire brigade showed up. Lots of action in the middle of the night."

"It wasn't your unit, though?"

"No, not the one I'm living in."

Liam must have detected a note of omission in her voice. "That's a weaselly answer, what are you not telling me?"

"You know I've moved out of the London place and have all my stuff down here..." Roz went on to tell him about the move, renting the empty apartment for storage, the damage the smoke grenade did to the place.

"Did you lose anything?" His voice was tense.

"No, at least I haven't seen any damage. The forensic guys were there, arson squad, DI Fitzroy, Hal."

"Any leads, suspects?"

"No, not yet. Hal thinks it was just meant to scare me, warn me. I'm going back to bed, he went to the office to check out forensics and see if the CCTV caught anything."

"Some warning!"

"Nothing's harmed beyond fixing. There's a constable in the apartment for tonight because whoever threw the grenade broke out the front window. And here's a little wrinkle, the smoke bomb was a canister, the kind of canister the police use to smoke out suspects."

Roz heard Liam blow out a breath then, "That's not necessarily a link to any law enforcement. Those things can be bought on the internet. Let alone the black market and dark web." A pause. "You'd be surprised at what you can pick up on the dark web."

"I appreciate your shopping tip. That's what I wanted to talk to you about."

"You called me in the middle of the night, your time, to talk about shopping on the dark web? Do you have smoke inhalation?"

Roz smiled to herself at Liam's mild sarcasm. He had a way of making her look at things in a different light, one that wasn't so dire. "No, I'm not shopping and I'm not oxygen deprived. Hal hasn't asked, but have you found anything out? Has Sam run across any references to stained glass for sale?"

"The last I told you still stands. He hasn't uncovered any discussions, not even hints. Anything on your end?"

"Beyond getting a lesson on the difference between MI 5 and MI 6, no. Hal did seem surprised, well maybe more pensive, when I mentioned the government being held for ransom."

"What's he doing about it?"

"Nothing that I know of. We're going to dinner tonight. I'll grill him then."

"Dinner?" She felt Liam's eyebrows rise.

"Yes, dinner. I'm lying low today and he's swamped at work, so we need some uninterrupted time to talk about things. We certainly can't talk about conspiracy theories involving the British government at the police department in Hythe. And I'm not comfortable having him over here for hours."

Her reasoning made Liam say, "Hmmm…you may be right. There is one thing, but I don't want you telling that Hal guy. Sam has found a hacker who claims he could get into any—and he repeated, ANY—government office, either here, there or anywhere."

"Liam!" Roz was aghast. "Anywhere in the world? Are you sure he doesn't work for, like, the NSA or something? I'd think he'd be the most valuable asset any government can have."

"I asked Sam that. He says the guy is only interested in the coding and hacking, not the politics. Remember when 45 poo-pooed the Russian hacking charge? He said something like 'it could be a 400-pound guy sitting on a bed in the basement' or a comment like that. No one knows who these guys are and for many of them, it's a game to see if they can outsmart the establishment."

Roz was silent long enough for Liam to say, "You still there?"

"Yes, just thinking. I won't say anything to Hal, but are you going to talk to Sam's friend?"

"I don't know yet. If I do, I'll let you know first. Do you think you can casually pump Hal for some info on how the government works over there? What would be the place that a hacker should get into to see if there was a ransom demand?"

"I'll dig a bit, although he did mention the Exchequer."

Roz heard a whine, then "OK, ok, dinner's on the way."

She raised her voice so Tut could hear her, aware he had better hearing than his human beings and knew she was talking, he just didn't know where she was. "Hi sweet boy. I miss you. Are you being a good boy for Liam?"

For an answer she got a loud snuffle and Liam laughing. "Yep, that's her, Tut. She's talking to us but not coming home right away." Then to Roz, "I'll keep poking around on this end and let you know what I find. Watch out for that Hal guy, I don't trust those foreigners. And please watch out for whoever's targeting you. I don't like knowing someone has you in their sights."

"Right." Roz laughed back at Tut's immediacy. He lived in the now of walks, dinner, pets. "I'm perfectly safe. Tonight was kind of shocking, but nothing harmed, no injuries and the Hythe constabulary is on the job. The one who's probably most stunned is Mrs. Lewes, the Guild lady who rents the apartments out. She's not prepared for violence."

"It may be the last time she rents to a crazy American. Hope you can sleep, and I'll talk to you later."

Hanging up with Liam, Roz felt some of the night's adrenaline seep out. He was such a good friend, solid and dependable, with his own life and demons but willing to help out when she needed it.

She took two acetaminophen to relieve the dregs of tension and was out when someone pounded on her door.

CHAPTER TWENTY-FOUR

Roz struggled out of bed. Why was someone banging on her door so early? Then she realized the sun was streaming in her window, looked at her phone. It was 10:15 a.m.

A remnant of last night? Someone come to see if she was still here, still alive? She slipped a long t-shirt on and padded to the door, calling, "Who is it?" When she'd rented the apartment, she didn't notice there was no peephole in the door—nor would she have thought she'd need one.

"It's Jocelyn and Phoebe, Rosalind. We're just checking to see if you're alright after last night."

Roz pulled the door slightly open and peeked around it. The two teachers were dressed for a day of walking it looked like, in jeans, light sweaters and hiking boots.

"We're sorry if we woke you." Phoebe stretched out an arm and rested her hand against the doorframe. "We're going to the church and castle at Lympne and wanted to know if you'd like to go with us."

Quick, what was the answer? "Thanks, but I do have some work I have to get done. DI Fitzroy and I talked until almost 3:00 this morning, and I also want to check with him to see what information they have on the smoke bomb. Why are you heading to Lympne?"

She wouldn't mention her last trip to the church and Ilic's dead body, nor the subsequent meetings with Fitzroy. Nor, for that matter, the theft of the stained glass.

"It was one of the earliest Norman castles on the coast." Jocelyn sounded in her teaching mode. "If we manage to write our book about the Invasion, we want to include the impact the Normans had on the land, as well as the structure of government."

"And let's not forget the language," Phoebe smiled. "I've even taken some classes in Norman or medieval French because so much of the historical records and legal documents are in that."

Last night, the two had exchanged a glance when Roz mentioned the Tapestry, today, they were willingly talking. Had Roz imagined their shared look?

"Do you have a proposal for the book? I only ask because a friend of mine at home is an author. He writes fantasy books and he's publishing a non-fiction one on a pedophile ring and cover-up in the Church."

"Oh. My, that's way ahead of where we are." Jocelyn was pink. Embarrassed? Reticent? Surprised?

"He's a retired newspaper reporter, so writing seems to be in his blood." Roz took a step across the doorsill and Phoebe moved back.

"We should be off," Phoebe said. "It's going to be a fine day and the mist will have burnt away by now. We want to take pictures of the Channel from the castle and we'd like to go down and look back at the cliff and the castle, but it's all private land now."

"As much as we can, we want to be immersed in the eleventh century, see what the Normans saw, how they brought their culture with them." Jocelyn seemed to be looking at a distant past. "Even though there wasn't too much difference between the cultures at the time."

"Perhaps some other time, then. We can compare notes. Will you be here for dinner?" Phoebe's question seemed innocent enough.

"No, I'm having dinner out." Why didn't she say with Fitzroy? A feeling of squeamishness came over her, as though the teachers were prying. Stop it, she told herself. They were just being friendly after a bizarre night.

They waved and walked to their car. Roz waited until they got in before she closed her door, leaning against it. The vandalism, late night, conversations with both Hal and Liam, had spooked her. All she was piling up were uncomfortable feelings and no solid leads or information.

Showered and caffeinated, she took the key and went to the bombed unit. Mrs. Lewes had been busy. A glazer was just finishing up with putty and Roz heard a heavy-duty upholstery cleaner. She'd check on all the things she'd stored later, not wanting to interfere. The young constable who'd spent the night was on his way out, and she asked him if there'd been any other disturbances.

"No, ma'am." He nodded and pink tinged his cheeks. Did he know that she and Fitzroy had been working together? Or had even had dinner together? Could it look like they were dating?

Putting an apartment inspection near the bottom of the to-do list, she walked back to her unit, tacked up the sheet and drawing paper and continued tracing a scene from the tapestry. As she worked, she jotted notes about colors she'd use, following the original as closely as possible.

She broke off early afternoon, sliced some Cheddar and ate a container of yogurt while thumbing through a picture book of the Tapestry. There was so much there. She loved the horses, thought the pieces where the Normans were building and preparing the ships to cross the Channel were important, telling as they did about the daily lives of the people. Jocelyn's comments earlier about the similarities in the cultures were so true. For people at this level of medieval society, both sides lived alike, building fiefs, swearing allegiance to an over-lord.

Although the structure of Norman and Anglo-Saxon laws was different, the quarrel that led to the invasion was akin to a fight between brothers or cousins over the estate left by an older relative. A disturbingly common event in European history where so many ruling families were intertwined through kinship and marriage.

By early evening she'd completed tracing one panel, carefully rolled the paper and took the sheet down. Tomorrow she'd begin looking through stained glass dealers. Order what she needed. While at it, she thought she'd try some sketchier sites, scoping out any medieval glass for sale.

She changed into a slouchy Cashmere sweater and fine-spun wool slacks, was standing in front of the closet with a heel in one hand and a flat in the other when Fitzroy knocked, exactly at 7:00 p.m.

"I just have to put shoes on," she said as she opened the door. He'd taken some time to clean up, shave, but still looked tired. "Are we walking or driving?"

"Driving. I thought we'd go to Dymchurch. We could take the train, but it's only a few miles."

Roz stared at him. "The train?"

"It's the Romney, Hythe & Dymchurch line, the smallest public railway in the world." He looked at her. "You don't have children, do you?"

Startled by the change of subject, she said, "No. Not married, no children." Was this leading up to something?

"I just wondered if you've ever heard of the children's book and TV show, *Thomas the Tank Engine*. The whole rail line reminds me of that. Shall we go?"

Roz slipped on one heel, limped to the closet to get the other one. Was the evening going to be as cryptic? She wasn't sure what his agenda was but needed to talk about her conversation with Liam and mention Phoebe and Jocelyn. Not reporting them, just talking over the small qualms she had. Were they being less than forthcoming or was she imagining things?

Tapestry of Tears

The drive was only about ten minutes along the road, skirting a long, flat beach. Fitzroy spent the time talking about how this section of Kent attracted vacationers and now the area subsisted primarily on tourism.

Watching the flat sands roll by, a sudden homesickness struck Roz. This could be Oregon.

CHAPTER TWENTY-FIVE

Dymchurch was tiny, smaller even than Hythe. Fitzroy chose a restaurant just a few yards off the beach, and they got a table by windows that overlooked the Channel.

Roz couldn't help herself. "This is so much like Hamilton. Our most popular restaurant is called Jules and is just back from the beach. And the beach itself is so similar. Long, flat sand. Instead of the Channel, we have the Pacific. The storms sweep in from Asia."

Fitzroy smiled. "Sure, the Pacific is huge, but we have our own little storms here. One was the storm that swept the Spanish Armada to Ireland. You might remember?"

Wait a minute, was he playing one-ups-man-ship with her? She narrowed her eyes. "I wasn't comparing storms I was saying this reminds me of home. And in a good way."

"I think I put my foot in it. I didn't mean to compare or lecture, I mentioned the Armada because there's so much history that the south coast has witnessed." A wash of color climbed up his cheeks. "I'm sorry if I came off as nitpicking."

"This tidbit of discussion hits on some things I wanted to talk about tonight." Roz picked up a menu, glanced at it, and set it down. "Jocelyn and Phoebe dropped by this morning and asked if I wanted to go to Lympne with them. They were visiting the church and the castle. I said I had too much to do, and they seemed taken aback. There wasn't anything I could put a finger on, but I sensed a flash of ..."

"Fear?" Fitzroy leaned across the table. "Did they say anything or behave in a way that you found threatening?"

"Not as strong as 'threatened', but there seemed to be a nervousness. Maybe like they wanted to get me away from my apartment for the day. In the end, they went off together."

"Didn't you tell me they were writing a book about the Invasion?"

They ordered and were quiet while the server brought their food, cautious about being overheard. Roz picked up her fork and scooped up a bite of sole. "They said that. I assumed a children's book, although I'm not sure they told me. One of them said they wanted to look at the Channel from the top of the cliff where the castle is, to get an idea what the Normans would have looked at."

She glanced out the window. "It's so flat here you wouldn't get much of a view, though."

"Are you feeling like they aren't what they say they are?"

"No, I don't think it's that strong. But you could check on them, right?"

Fitzroy pushed his plate to the side and took a sip of wine. "I could, I suppose. Where are they from?"

"They teach at a girl's school outside of York. I don't know the name. Did you get their names last night?"

"One constable did. What do you think they're up to?"

"Not so much 'up to' as not being honest. Like they were hiding something." She folded her napkin, placed it by the plate. Then, "There's something else. I spoke with Liam after you left early this morning."

"Liam? Ah, your friend in Oregon. What did he have to say?"

She nodded her thanks as the server picked up her plate. "To begin with, he was concerned when I told him about the smoke grenade. Then he said, just like you, that those could be bought online." Paused. "That led into a discussion about the dark web and the shopping available."

"Are you planning to shop on the dark web? That could be dangerous."

"Yes and no. If I can figure out how to get on it, I thought I'd look for anyone who was selling medieval stained glass. Beyond that, no, I have no intention of spending time there. What Liam did say was that his friend who knows about all that stuff—hacking, tracing people—said he knew someone who could hack into anything. And Liam repeated *anything*, regardless of any government firewalls."

"So, what do you expect his next move to be?"

"I told Liam that we were having dinner tonight and we'd talk about it," Roz said, her voice quiet. "I guess we're talking about it."

"And the plan is…what?" Fitzroy lowered his voice as well.

"I'd ask Liam to ask his friend to poke around in some British government department emails. See if any extortion threat had come through."

Fitzroy paled and sat back. "You don't think I'd condone having anyone, let alone some U.S. hacker, poking around in Her Majesty's government computer system, do you?"

"Uh, no, when you put it like that. There has to be some way we can find out if any blackmail or extortion threats have come in. And for sure the government wouldn't want to advertise that they'd been threatened or hacked. Have you had anyone looking into this?"

She watched emotions—anger, frustration, fear—march across his face before he said, "Whether we do or not, I can't tell you, you know. Official Secrets Act. If someone hacked into our computer system, do you think we'd announce it?"

"Of course not. I'm trying to see what our next steps might be to trace the glass. And find whoever killed Ilic. And whoever might be trying to kill me. I do have a vested interest."

Fitzroy pushed his chair back and stood. "The weather's holding and it's a nice night. Would you like to look around? Maybe see the station for the railway?"

Quick change of topic, Roz thought. Was he hiding something? Aloud she said, "Yes, I'd like to walk off dinner a bit. Is it far?"

"Nothing in Dymchurch is far." Fitzroy put his hand in the small of her back and steered her out of the restaurant, raising her hackles until he said, "Things we shouldn't talk about in public."

What she had seen as a gesture of proprietorship, he meant as a caution.

The streets of the small village were deserted as they walked to the railway depot, a small white and green house set in a riot of flowers. The train was standing there, puffing away, and Roz realized what he meant when he said smallest railway in the world. The train and cars were little more than child-sized, the cars with open benches and windows for sightseeing excursions.

She knew she'd have to look up Thomas the Tank Engine after seeing the green-painted steam engine idling, the engineer standing taller than the cab. She sucked in a delighted breath.

"Oh, we *should* have taken the train."

"Not practical, I'm afraid." Fitzroy looked dour. "It doesn't run after dark, takes longer than driving and there's no privacy." He brightened. "It's charming, isn't it? Maybe when we have some time during the day, we can take it. The whole line is only about 13 miles long."

Tapestry of Tears

He tucked her hand into his arm. "Now, to the beach. We are tourists, after all. And the hiss of the waves will cover any conversation."

Out on the sand, Roz kicked her shoes off, the sense of similarity with home leaving a pit in her stomach. When she moved to Hamilton, it was to escape L.A., the horror and the frenetic pace of life. She never thought that one day she'd look at the Oregon coast as home. Now, standing barefoot on this stretch of sand on the edge of England, the coast of France so near she felt she could touch it, she shivered at a wave of nostalgia.

What was there about a flat expanse of sand sloping out to sea that made her homesick, made her yearn for a past? Had she moved to Oregon knowing that somewhere inside she had a memory of another beach, another sea?

CHAPTER TWENTY-SIX

"*I* didn't want to talk too openly about what we're hoping to do while we were in a public place." Fitzroy was watching her dig her feet into the sand and looked amused. "Do you do this at home, too?"

Roz turned to him. "No, at home I have a pair of shoes I wear for the beach because I take my dog running. It's too hard to run barefoot. What are you planning? And while we're at it, what did you find out about my late-night vandal?"

"Let's start with that." Fitzroy took in a lungful of the salty air. "Our forensic team did good work. There was a tiny fragment of the casing left undamaged and they were able to get a manufacturer's mark from it. It was made by a company in the States. The company sells a lot of these online, mostly to law enforcement and public safety organizations. They don't require much proof of certification so occasionally some get sold to individuals, unfortunately some to those vigilante groups you seem to have."

He stopped for a moment. "That's not fair, I suppose. We have some violent offshoots here as well. The world's gone mad, everybody wanting to blow up those who don't agree with them."

Roz waited for his free-association minute to be over before she said, "And this was sold to...?"

"Unfortunately, this was sold to a small local volunteer fire department outside of York. They bought a dozen of them to use in training their brigades to enter smoke-filled buildings."

"York?" Roz gasped. "Outside of York? That where Phoebe and Jocelyn are from."

"Have you ever been there?"

"No, not yet. I'm planning to head north before I have to go home." Roz didn't think Fitzroy needed to know her travel plans.

"York and Leeds, which is about 20 miles away, have a population of more than one million and are surrounded by so many small towns and villages you couldn't shoot off a cannon without hitting one of them. 'Outside of York' is probably equivalent to saying, 'outside of San Francisco'. The chance that the smoke grenades were shipped to the same place that those women teach is slim. We have enough coincidences and overlaps without dragging more in."

"You are going to check those women out, aren't you?" Not big on conspiracy theories, Roz wanted facts, and all facts pinned down. She'd been the victim of supposition when Winston was killed and was a person of interest for a few days when her neighbor in Hamilton was stabbed. She'd had enough of jumping to conclusions, though every coincidence had to be traced.

"Yes, we'll follow up on all that. And we're working with the multi-agency volunteer force that bought the grenades. It seems as though one of them can't be accounted for."

"You mean someone stole it?"

"No one is going out that far yet. They're checking all the movement in the facility where all the training equipment is stored. It's a long shot, but at least we have a path to follow."

He took a deep breath. "As to the hacking, that's another story. I can't tell you much, obviously, but know that we do have people looking into the possibilities. There are several facets to this. First, has there been anyone hacking in?

Second, is there any evidence of someone sending a blackmail or extortion plot?"

He was silent for a beat, then, "Yes, we've been hacked. But that's become an almost daily occurrence. Every time we find one hole and plug it, some clever kid gets in through another hole. This doesn't mean we've found anyone reading emails or searching for a specific topic." He stopped, stared across the Channel, now dark with a line of small waves breaking. His voice sounded distant. "I couldn't tell you if we had. You'll just have to trust that we'll keep you safe."

"Hal." His name felt awkward in Roz's mouth, as though this was a person other than a British detective. She started again. "Hal, I trust that I'll be safe, but I need to be kept appraised—in the loop, as we say—of what you're finding out. What if the next attack isn't just a warning?"

She wanted to ask about Ilic. About what connections he had in the world of fencing stolen art. Who his contacts were. Who he'd pissed off or cheated. Someone from the shadowy world killed him and she may be next on the list, except she didn't know what or who to look for.

Roz put her hand on Fitzroy's arm and felt a slight softening. His flinty stature seemed to belie a softer interior, and he responded by picking up her hand and holding it. They stood quietly together until he reached up his other hand, turned her head toward his and leaned in to kiss her. Lightly at first, then harder, deeper, his hand moving to caress her cheek.

He pulled back. "We should probably go. I didn't get much sleep last night and I suspect you didn't either. An early night may help both of us clear cobwebs."

"Yes, I could do with some quiet and a nice cup of tea." Roz pulled her hand away, turned and walked back toward the few lights of Dymchurch. When she hit the pavement along the esplanade, she leaned on his arm briefly as she wiped the sand off her feet and slipped into her shoes again.

"Thank you for dinner and for showing me this. It brings back comforting feelings of home." She didn't add that underlying those were questions about murder.

The short ride back to Hythe was silent. He pulled up to her apartment, helped her out and walked her to the door. As she put the key in the lock, he touched her face again.

"I enjoyed the evening. I'm sorry there're are pieces I can't share with you, but I'm going to continue on this case—and I hope continue with you." At that he gave her a light kiss, wheeled around to his car, calling "Goodnight" over his shoulder.

Inside, Roz dumped her purse, kicked off her shoes. Wryly looked at the sand she'd carried home with her. What did tonight mean? She'd hadn't learned much. Scotland Yard, or whoever Fitzroy was working with, were looking into hacking. And there certainly was hacking, that information he was open about.

They were also following what little leads they had on the smoke grenade. And she was given a not-quite-veiled warning about staying out of Her Majesty's Government's internal affairs and computer networks.

She had Hal's assertion that he'd "look up" Phoebe and Jocelyn, but he didn't seem too concerned.

Then there was the beach. What did she feel about it? If she'd kissed him back, or made any move to encourage him, would it have continued? Moved to another place? Did she want it to continue? She sensed an inherit danger to getting involved with the detective who was protecting her and working on a murder case that she'd stumbled into. Plus, he was involved with and knowledgeable about the missing stained glass. Would that overlap into her very reason for being here?

Enough. She slipped her clothes off, pulled on a sleep shirt and took her tea to bed with her Kindle.

CHAPTER TWENTY-SEVEN

*L*iam and Hal were seated at a computer, immersed in the dark web. Roz watched them as they clicked from site to site, mumbling to themselves. Why couldn't they see her standing right next to them? Men. If they were occupied, they lost a sense of their surroundings.

Didn't they even hear the birds?

Wait a minute, why were there birds?

Roz slowly swam up through layers of consciousness, the room, the computer, Liam and Hal drifting off into mist.

She rolled over and checked her phone. No calls and it was almost 9:00 in the morning. She'd managed better than eight hours sleep, felt rested and recharged. She stretched, showered and turned the kettle on. While the water came to a boil, she opened her laptop and started a to-do list.

Do a cartoon of one more panel.

Go online and look for glass. Check out some iffy sites.

Book a ferry ticket for another trip to Bayeux.

Check with Hal about the York connection.

She dumped ground coffee and boiling water in the French press, let it steep, poured her first cup.

A wisp of home came over her as she remembered the beach last night. She couldn't take her coffee out to the sand here, but she could go to the rose garden and watch the bees. She went out her front door, took the walk around the strip of apartments and found a bench by the colonnade where she sat. The scent of the late summer roses was almost too sweet, but the bees were drunkenly moving from flower to flower, picking up nectar.

A clink disturbed the solitude. She looked around. The beekeepers were here again, the clink was the sound of the smoke devices they used to calm the bees.

Up close they didn't look so much like eleventh century monks. Their overalls didn't flow like a habit, their heads covered by a hat with a strip of mesh covering their faces. They nodded to her, lit their smoke pots.

"It's a nice day," one said.

Roz thought he was speaking to her, so she smiled. "Yes. How long will this weather last?"

The second one, Roz realized a woman from her voice, said, "We should have at least a month before the winter rains set it. This will probably be one of our last collections. The bees don't fly when it's wet and we need to leave them enough honey for the winter."

The beekeepers practiced good husbandry, one of the underpinnings of a medieval society. Roz couldn't count how many church windows she'd seen with depictions of agricultural work and home crafts. Spinning, weaving, shepherding, planting, harvesting, all the crafts that kept people alive, clothed and fed.

She tended to gravitate to these scenes rather than knights, kings, battles. Those were about anger and war, but the homely ones of crafts illustrated the daily lives of the people and that survived. Here, in a quiet courtyard watching beekeepers and their charges, it felt more solid and lasting that most of the battles fought.

Roz shook her head. Was this escapism, day-dreaming of the past when she had contemporary work to do? She waved to the keepers as she turned to go back to her apartment and her lists. First and quickest, a ferry reservation and booking the hotel in Caen for tomorrow night.

Then, pulling out her sketching paper, she outlined a cartoon of a horse's richly covered bridle and saddle. This would get fitted in to one scene where Duke William's emissaries came to visit King Harold.

A rumbling stomach reminded her she'd only had coffee so putting her drawings away she headed over for lunch, today's a ploughman's special. The rough-cut bread, thick slices of Cheddar, pickled onions and cornichons filled her. She was taking the last bite when Phoebe and Jocelyn came in, spotted her and made a beeline.

No escape, she smiled. "I'm just finishing up. How was your day yesterday?"

"Good, good." Jocelyn pulled out a chair, sat, while Phoebe looked tense.

Roz watched them. "Are you OK, Phoebe? You look like you may be getting ill."

"I'm fine," Phoebe said. "It's just that I have no head for heights, and peering down at the beach yesterday for hours made me a little queasy. It's easing off, though."

Jocelyn tut-tutted at her friend. "We'll have to find other ways of doing research, you know. Maybe find a flat beach where we can imagine and reenact William's troops coming ashore. This section of coast has changed in the past thousand years, after all. Erosion, rivers and harbors silting up. It doesn't look the same as it did then, so we'll have to use our imagination."

"Have you seen Dymchurch?" Roz mentally kicked herself. They were natives and would probably know every inch of the coast.

"We know where it is but haven't been there. It's a bit farther west of where William landed. Have you been there?" Phoebe seemed to brighten at the idea of a flat piece of sand.

Well, in for a penny, in for a pound, she'd begun this line of conversation. Roz said, "Yes, DI Fitzroy and I went there for dinner last night. It reminded me so much of home."

"Home?" Jocelyn motioned for Phoebe to sit as well. "Aren't you from Oregon? I thought it was farms and forest."

"The interior is, yes. But there's about 400 miles of coast with some of the most beautiful flat beaches. A major highway runs along the Pacific with dozens of small beach towns." Roz laughed. "But nothing like the Dymchurch Railway."

One of the Altar Guild volunteer servers sat down two more plates of ploughman's lunch. "Can I get anything for anyone to drink?" she asked and then brought over glasses of water.

"Are you two heading out somewhere this afternoon? I need to get back to work, but maybe we can have a drink before dinner. Are you eating here?" Roz wondered if this sounded like a third degree. She hadn't talked to Fitzroy about any York connections yet, maybe she could ease around in a conversation, looking for coincidences.

Jocelyn had a mouthful of cheese and bread, so Phoebe said, "Probably just some research in the Hythe library. We may go as far as Dover. Although with the Chunnel, Folkestone and Dover are both impacted with traffic." She sighed. "If we could only have a time machine, go back and see what Harold and William saw."

A time machine? Roz thought this as well. Some people wanted to go into the future, but not her, she would have asked to be transported back to the twelfth or thirteenth century, to watch and work with the medieval glassmakers and window designers. Climb the scaffolding and fit the pieces of color into the patterns that would glow like jewels when the sun was just the right angle. Or walk along the stone floors bathed in a mosaic of color. She had a small taste of this in her studio at home, where she'd installed a floor-to-ceiling glass wall facing west to catch the setting sun.

Tapestry of Tears

She closed her eyes, let the feeling of longing wash over her. Then, "Off the subject, but you said you're from York? I haven't been there yet, but want to go before I head home. What would you suggest as the best places to stay?"

Phoebe and Jocelyn exchanged a look. "You'll want to see York Minster and Sheffield Cathedral. Both early stained glass. Do you think Harrogate?" Jocelyn waited for her friend to second the suggestion.

"Harrogate, yes, since you have a car. It's a spa town, has a Royal Pump House. Not as grand as Bath, but famous in its own right."

"Is that where you live? Where the school is?"

"No, the school is in Ripon, near the ruins of Fountains Abby. The place is littered with ruins and has its own cathedral. Dates to 672. Oldest Anglo-Saxon crypt in the UK."

To give herself a minute, Roz pulled her sleeve back and looked at her watch. She needed to talk to Fitzroy and relay these bits of information. Did he say where the grenade went missing? No, just that it was outside of York.

"I'm sorry, I have to run. Thanks for the suggestions, I'll look up Ripon and Sheffield and the cathedrals. The seventh century is early for stained glass, but I'd still want to check them out. See you about 6:00 for a drink?" She stood and forced herself to calmly walk out of the dining room.

CHAPTER TWENTY-EIGHT

"DI Fitzroy." Hal's voice was the epitome of British civil servant, restrained, helpful, questioning.

"Hal, its Roz. I just had lunch with Phoebe and Jocelyn and have something I think I should share with you."

Warmth crept into Fitzroy's voice as he said, "I'm tied up at the moment. Could you come by the office in an hour?"

What was he tied up doing? Roz felt a moment of irritation, then backed off. He could be working on another case or finding information on Ilic that he wasn't able to share—particularly over the phone.

"I will. Thanks." Roz hit the end button and stared for a moment. It was a small slice of time, not enough to dig into the dark web, nor enough to start lining up glass suppliers. But it was enough to do a search for an inn or B and B in the Ripon or Sheffield area. She happily spent three-quarters of an hour with maps, pictures and descriptions of the places surrounding York.

Fitzroy had said much like the area around San Francisco, but this was so different. The villages and towns were settled and established over years, when the fastest transportation was a horse and people seldom traveled. Many ventured only as far as the nearest market town, to buy, sell, visit the cathedral, so each spot developed its own identity. Not like California, where towns and cities sprang up almost overnight and often had the same bland atmosphere.

She bookmarked four possibilities, allowing her imagination to build a stay and immersing herself in the history and ambiance. Closed the Google search, slipped on a pair of flats and set out for police headquarters.

The constable at the front desk nodded to her and called DI Fitzroy, who came through the door from the squad room. "Right on time, come on back," he said and held the door.

Today the room was subdued. Two detectives scrolled through computers and one woman was on the phone. "Where is everybody?" Roz asked.

"This is our usual compliment." Fitzroy led her into his office. "We're more of a regional force so we have people who move from station to station as they're needed. Today, four people are assigned to Folkestone, working on a human smuggling case. Thirty-nine bodies found in a truck. Eastern European."

"My god." Roz sucked in a breath. "I thought with Brexit immanent people would stop trying to get into England. This is almost as bad as our border with Mexico." Then she was silent, until, "Does this have anything to do with Ilic?"

"No, not directly."

"Not directly?"

"Ilic was involved with theft and smuggling of primarily art and with money laundering. Smuggling people is iffier. If you have to, ditching stolen art or a suitcase of money is easier than getting rid of a truckload of people who will put up a fuss." Fitzroy wiped a hand across his face. "That is, if they're still alive. It's horrible and many times it's young women, destined for sex slavery."

Roz closed her eyes. How did she manage to get involved with the dregs of humanity? Theft was bad, murder was frightening, but pedophilia in the Church and sex trafficking had to be the lowest form of human actions.

Fitzroy interrupted her thoughts. "You wanted to talk to me?"

She pulled herself back, although her problems paled. "I wondered where the grenade went missing. Phoebe and Jocelyn are from Ripon. Their school is near there."

"Hmmm…" Fitzroy blinked his eyes. "Well, I can't tell you this, but it was near there. Harrogate, actually."

"Harrogate? That's one place Phoebe suggested I stay when I go up to York. "

"It's a nice small spa town, used to be very popular with the Russian crowd in the nineteenth century. Not in the same league as our Bath…"

"That's what they said. But Bath has a Roman history."

"Yes, and Harrogate has an Angle, Saxon and Viking history. Not in your area, is it?"

Roz stopped. Should she tell him her travel plans? Initially, she'd wanted to visit York because of its Viking and Anglo-Saxon history, which led up to King Harold and ultimately to William and the Norman invasion. History was so intertwined and convoluted. One pulled on a single thread and sometimes the whole weaving came undone with no clear-cut villains.

Fitzroy watched her, frowning. "If you plan to go up there, I trust you won't get involved with looking for a missing smoke grenade. There's no telling what happened, nor does it have anything to do with our explosion."

"But what if whoever stole it knew about me and that I was the one who found Ilic's body? What if they thought it was a good way to silence me?"

"Ms. Duke, Roz, that's too thin. I've always said there are no coincidences until there are. I think you'll have to let this be one of the exceptions."

She stared at him. He still looked tired, faint blue shadows under his eyes and furrows around his mouth. A nice face, attractive with soft brown eyes, fair hair. She hadn't asked how old he was, figured in his early forties from his revelation of his wife and child's deaths. A few years older than her own mid-thirties. Now exhaustion and worry added some years.

Fair, she thought. She'd keep Phoebe and Jocelyn in a side room in her mind. What she held back from Fitzroy couldn't hurt her. She needed freedom to pursue interests herself.

"Have you had any luck tracking down a hacker?" Roz' change in topic makes Fitzroy raise his eyebrows,

"No, we're looking, but I doubt MI-5 will share their results with us. Like your CIA wouldn't tell a local police force about one of their operations. Does your friend in Oregon have any other leads?"

Roz flashed back to her dream, Liam and Fitzroy bent over a computer. "No, I haven't heard from him. I was going to start searching myself, see what stained glass was available."

"Please be careful. People using the dark web can be dangerous. Someone, maybe Ilic's murderer, knows you're here. No sense sending up red flags."

"I will be careful." Was this the time to tell him she was heading for France tomorrow? Yes, it might buy her some honesty tokens.

"I also wanted to let you know I'm taking the ferry to Caen tomorrow with two overnights, probably in Bayeux."

"Thank you for telling me." Worry chased itself across Fitzroy's face. "I would have been concerned if I'd gone to look for you and you were gone. Please call me when you arrive and again when you're headed back."

"I will," she said to him. Fat chance, she said to herself.

CHAPTER TWENTY-NINE

This time the Channel crossing was rough. An early storm was moving in from the Atlantic, and the boat pitched and rolled. The passengers stayed inside, making the saloons thick with moisture and smells of wet wool and drenched bodies from those few who'd been tempted to hit the decks.

Roz braced herself in a seat using her pack as a bulwark and closed her eyes. She probably wouldn't sleep, but there was too much movement to read, so she made notes on a paper tablet. Coincidences? Too many?

Lympne. The church and the castle. Wait a minute, maybe start with Phoebe and Jocelyn. They'd been to Lympne many times.

York, Harrogate, Ripon. All places she'd visit before she went home. Find the school?

Flat beaches. Dymchurch. Any links?

The Invasion. This couldn't have any bearing on Ilic's murder, it was too overwhelming and ingrained in the psyche and DNA of the English.

The Tapestry. Again, too familiar, too important. A possible theft for ransom? No, it might be easier to steal the crown jewels.

Now to the missing glass. Was this at the crux of all the other events? Ilic? The grenade? The warning note? And did Phoebe or Jocelyn tie to the theft?

What if the women were just what they said, teachers on a sabbatical doing research for a book? In Roz' experience, teachers loved doing research. Then again, most of her experience with teaching had been Win and his colleagues, college professors who lived by the "publish or perish" rule, who always had some research gig. The teachers from Ripon were the opposite, seemingly reticent about publishing anything and chary about their research.

The storm hit as she drove off the ferry in Caen, her welcome to France seen in blurs through windshield wipers. Changing her mind about driving to Bayeux in the dark and rain, she went to her usual inn. At the small hotel, she and the manager exchanged comments and complaints about the weather, she checked into her room and sent a text to Hal. *Arrived, pouring rain.*

Downstairs, she decided on a glass of Calvados in front of a warming fire followed by a meal of pumpkin soup and sole almondine. As she said goodnight, she asked for coffee and a croissant before starting out by 9:00 a.m.

"Are you going to visit the Tapestry?" The manager was making conversation…wasn't he?

"Yes, I'll probably be gone the whole day," Roz said.

"Drive carefully. The roads get slippery in the rain."

"Thank you," she called as she climbed the stairs.

Tucked up under a down duvet, she called Liam to let him know she was back in France. He answered in a rush.

"Did I interrupt something?" She knew it was 2:00 in the afternoon in Oregon and worried that she'd barged into a meeting.

"No, no, I'm just finishing up some edits." Liam sounded as though he'd caught his breath.

"On a book? That's great…"

"No, unfortunately, a freelance piece about Oregon becoming the new foodie capital. For an airline magazine. Not wonderful, creative prose, but it helps pay for my apartment not here."

Tapestry of Tears

Not here. Roz remembered him telling her that "here" was Hamilton, where he had a house and "not here" was his apartment in Portland, where he spent a week or so a month.

"If you're in not here, where's Tut?"

"He's with me. He's enjoying being an urban dog, lots of new and interesting smells and sights. He doesn't get unleashed runs, but there's a dog park near here and he's making friends." A pause, then, "And where are you?"

"Not as urban as you. I'm in Caen. I was planning to spend a couple of nights in Bayeux but it's pouring rain so checked in to my usual inn here. I'll spend tomorrow at the Tapestry."

"Just called to give me your travel plans?"

Roz pulled the phone away and looked at it. Maybe she should have face-timed him so she could read his expression. He sounded a little testy.

Oh well, she plowed through. "I wanted to tell you about having dinner the other night at Dymchurch. It's a tiny village east of Hythe and reminded me so much of the Hamilton coast that I got homesick."

"You went there by yourself?" Odd question since she primarily traveled alone.

"No, DI Fitzroy took me. He wanted to talk a bit about the dark web, hacking, MI-5." She related the conversation, leaving out Thomas the Tank Engine, which felt less than a business topic.

"You saying the British cops are no further along in their investigation?" Liam sounded dismissive, although he didn't offer any information about his search either.

"They're still trying to link things. One small part, remember I told you about the two teachers from York? Turns out they're actually from Harrogate, a town outside of York, and the stolen smoke grenade went missing from the Harrogate fire agency."

"Does that pull the women in?" This piece of information seemed to wake Liam from his snit or lethargy or testiness.

"It's too early to tell, but I'm planning a trip north in a few weeks, as soon as I finish the cartoon for the commission." Then, "There's another interesting thing that just came up. Fitzroy is involved with a human trafficking case that blew in the other day. Thirty-nine people, Eastern Europeans, were found dead in the back of a truck coming through Folkestone."

Dead silence. "Are you there, Liam?"

"Yep, I'm here. We even heard about that discovery here in the colonies. Not quite like our immigration deaths, it sounded like these were people who'd been lured or kidnapped and were trafficked in. Maybe for sex slaves?"

"Fitzroy isn't saying a lot. I think he's looking at them more as slaves than as refugees. I wondered about the dead guy, Ilic, I found. He's from Eastern Europe. Hal, DI Fitzroy wasn't putting the cases together, necessarily, but it's pretty coincidental."

"That's interesting, but not a tight grasp. Let me know if any Ilic links turn up. I don't like the idea of traffickers thinking you're involved."

"I will. I have these waves of homesickness and need to talk to you, hear an American voice, get some news of normal events. I'll call again in a few days, when I get back to Hythe. Give Tut a hug and treat from me."

After a restless night's sleep, Roz drank a café au lait, downed a croissant with jam and headed out. The rain had slowed to a drizzle, leaving a drippy morning with low fog.

She got to the Tapestry Museum as it opened, spent happy hours looking at horses, colors, dead Normans in chain mail littering the bottom border. When she went out to grab lunch, the sun was gamely trying to make a dent in the overcast. Small patches of blue appeared and disappeared as wind hurried the clouds around.

Coming back out when the Museum closed, the sun had lost its battle and darker clouds were piling up. It felt like weather that invaders faced, so she headed for the coast road, the one tracing the edge of the cliffs Allied forces climbed during D-Day. She wanted the feel of embarking into the unknown. The gray of the sky matched the gray of the Channel. As she drove, watching the wind-whipped Channel, a heavy rain squall blew in, wind pushing her car out of its lane and water coming down so fast the wipers couldn't clear the windshield.

She slowed, said "Damn," and felt the car going off the road. Frightened, Roz tried to steer a car with no wheels firmly on the ground. With the steering wheel move freely, she sucked in a breath, increasing her panic. "Breathe," she thought, had an image of another car behind her, felt a slight bump. Then nothing but air as her car went off the cliff.

CHAPTER THIRTY

*T*oo much light. Bright white light leaked in around her closed eyelids. Roz thought she sent a message to her eyes to open, but before it got there, she lost consciousness.

Next time she was aware of the light, she forced her eyelids up briefly and heard, "There, she's coming around." Again, she lost consciousness before she could respond.

The third time she drifted back to awareness, she managed to open her eyes and lift a hand. This time the voice said, "That's better, she's responding."

She tried to turn her head toward the voice, but her body didn't listen to her brain. All she did was groan.

"Ah, she's waking up. Roz, Roz, can you hear me? If, so, lift your hand again."

Roz forced her mind to make her muscles act and her hand raised. Muscle memory or active movement? She decided active and pushed her eyes to open enough to see DI Fitzroy leaning over her.

"Ahhhh…" she said.

"Yes," he answered.

"What…?" she said.

"You were in an accident. Your car went off the road in the storm and you tumbled down one of the cliffs."

"Huh. Where…"

"Near one of the invasion beaches east of Omaha," Hal said.

"No, where is…" Her hand feebly motioned around.

"Where are you? In the hospital in Caen. Another driver saw the marks across the shoulder of the road, pulled over and looked. Luckily, your car didn't roll, just headed straight over the edge and by the time help arrived the heavy rain eased off. You've been unconscious for a few hours."

Roz closed her eyes again, and another voice said, "Stay with us." This voice had a French accent.

"Tired," she said faintly. "Sleep."

"No, Ms. Duke, please stay awake. You have a concussion and we need to gauge the brain damage," the French voice said. "Look at me. How many fingers am I holding up?"

"Three," Roz spit out. Why was she being subjected to this inane game when she was so tired?

"Good. Can you tell me what year it is?"

Again, with the stupid questions. "It's 2019."

"Good, good." The annoying French voice treated her like a dimwitted kindergartener.

"How bad?" She understood a concussion, but why did her body ache? Her chest hurt and every breath was painful.

"You have three fractured ribs and your ankle is broken. That's the pain you're feeling, along with one of the world's worst headaches."

Now Fitzroy. "You were fortunate, Roz. The fractured ribs are from the air bag and the seatbelt and the broken bones from you sliding down and your ankle collapsing. In that heavy rain, you probably hydroplaned and just slid off the road."

Did she? Bits and pieces came dribbling back. Happiness from the day with the Tapestry, watching the storm come roaring off the Channel, the massive squall dumping so much water that she couldn't steer, the slight bump… "Wait a minute, what about the other car?"

"What other car?" Fitzroy's voice sharpened. "We only saw one set of tire tracks going off the road."

Tapestry of Tears

Roz closed her eyes to concentrate. How did this happen? The rain was torrential, great gushes of water pouring down the windshield. No possible way wipers could handle that much. She was used to rain in Oregon, she remembered slowing down then a recollection of another shape, a car, glimpsed in her rear-view mirror through the water pouring off the roof. Then a slight bump. Did she hit a hillock beyond the shoulder? Or was it more of a jolt from behind?

Come to think of it, how did Hal find out?

"I don't know." Tears tickled the backs of her eyelids. Why couldn't she remember? "I just have this impression of another car behind me, too close behind me. I'd slowed down because my steering wasn't responding."

"If there was another car, they didn't stop. The man who found you, a delivery driver, thought you'd been off the road for maybe half-an-hour. Your wheel ruts were filling with water."

She lay back, not pushing her brain anymore. Answers would come, what she had to do now was heal so she could go home. Home! "Did anyone call Liam?"

"Yes, I did. I found your phone in your bag and called him as soon as you got to the emergency room. He's upset and wants to talk to you."

"Good, I want to talk to him, too. What time is it?"

"It's going on 3 a.m. It must have been about 6:15 in the evening when you went over the cliff. Why?"

"It's eight hours earlier in Oregon..." she began.

"He said to call him no matter what time. He's worried. Here." Fitzroy hit the speed dial for Liam and put it on speaker. When she heard Liam's voice, the dam burst.

"Oh, Liam," she said, her voice so choked with tears that she gurgled.

"Roz, oh Roz, I'm so glad to hear your voice! How are you? Wait, that's a stupid question, of course you're not OK.

DI Fitzroy told me the bare bones of the accident. What do you remember?"

The French voice, who turned out to be a young female doctor, handed Roz a handful of tissues. Once she'd wiped her eyes and blown her nose she was more in control and went through the story of slowing, the huge squall, losing control and then feeling airborne. "And I have a concussion, fractured ribs and a broken ankle." At the list of her injuries, Roz' voice choked up again.

"Do you want me to come over? I found a boarding kennel for Tut and checked on flights. I can be there day after tomorrow. How long will you be in the hospital?"

How long? She hadn't even gone down that road. Too much information was making her brain rebel.

"That's awfully sweet Liam, but until I know better what the next steps are, I think you'd better stay home. I don't know when I'll be released, don't know about walking. I have to deal with the car rental agency, let the church Guild ladies know. And I think I remember a car behind me, although Hal tells me I wasn't found for about half-an-hour, so if someone was behind me, they didn't stop and help."

"A hit and run? Are the cops looking for another car?"

"Mr. Karshner," Fitzroy's voice morphed into official cop-speak mode, "we're still not sure there was another car. And there's nothing we can do until daylight. The French will send an accident investigation team out in the morning, but we're not hopeful of finding anything. This was a fluke squall."

CHAPTER THIRTY-ONE

"When am I getting out?" Roz appreciated the care from the French medical team, but after two days, inactivity made her cranky.

"I think tomorrow." The doctor shined a penlight into each of Roz's eyes, nodded, said, "Uh-huh." She put her stethoscope on Roz' chest. "All your signs are good, once the ribs and ankle mend, you're back to normal. How are you getting home?"

How, indeed. Roz had no answer until she talked to Fitzroy. She might be able to manage the ferry on crutches but not with her purse, sketching supplies and overnight case.

"I'm not sure. Do I have to have a plan before you release me?"

The doctor smiled. "Not formally, but I would like to know you'll be safe."

"Is DI Fitzroy still in Caen?"

"I believe so. He left a message number from here in Caen."

Roz leaned over to a bedside table, picked up her own phone, hit Fitzroy's number. Got an "I can't come to the phone right now," so she left a voicemail.

"Can you give me the message number?" She punched in the digits as the doctor reeled them off. Heard the distinctive whrr, whrr of a French phone and a male voice, "Hallo, Caen Police," and a string of rapid French.

"Ah, do you speak English?" Roz, rudimentary in French, wasn't up to having a conversation with a French police department.

"*Oui*, yes," the voice said. "How may I help you?"

"An English policeman, DI Hal Fitzroy, left this as a message number. Is he there?"

"*Oui*. Just a minute." Then, "This is DI Fitzroy."

Relieved she'd tracked him down, Roz' voice wavered. "Oh, I'm so glad to catch you. The doctor said I could be discharged tomorrow."

She heard him suck in a breath. "Good, I'll wrap things up here and come by later."

"By the way, do you know where my things are?" Checking out of a hotel unceremoniously left dangling ends.

"I notified the hotel and they've packed things up for you. I'll swing by after I pick you up in the morning and we can collect them." He didn't specifically say he'd take her to the ferry, she could pin down those details when she saw him later that day.

She dozed off, waking with a start when she sensed someone in her room. The figure, a man, hovered by the door, indistinct in the early evening shadows. He wore a doctor's white coat, but something wasn't quite right. Under it he had on a black hoodie covering his head and wore a medical mask. She watched as he turned his head, heard voices in the hall and slipped out of her room.

The hall voices turned out to be Fitzroy and her doctor, who came in seconds later, discussing her release plans.

"Is it possible to get a wheelchair? I'm sure she'll be able to manage crutches, but boarding ferries, getting in and out of vehicles on her first day may be too much."

"Yes, I'd suggest that." The doctor came over. "DI Fitzroy already had a plan, so you'll be discharged in the morning. He's assured me he's arranged for an English

Tapestry of Tears

doctor to check you over and handle any further treatment you'll need."

"Thank you, doctor." Roz pulled herself up on her elbows and smiled. "I appreciate the care you've taken, but I'll be glad to start back into my regular routine." She paused, running her hand through her hair and adding a shower and hair wash onto tomorrow's to-do list. Maybe she wouldn't see anyone she knew, but facing the day clean and relaxed would help her cope. She added, "By the way, did either of you know that man who was here right before you came in?"

Fitzroy and the doctor exchanged looks. "What man?" the doctor asked. "I didn't see anyone."

"When I woke up, he was standing by the door. I thought he was on the hospital staff. He had on a white lab coat and a ..." She stopped, closed her eyes, continued "a medical mask. But why would he wear a mask? None of the other staff wear one when they come in my room."

Fitzroy jerked the door open, scanned the hall, then turned to the doctor. "Can you put this place on lock-down? Get your security staff to start a search?"

"*Mais oui.*" She spoke rapid French into her phone while Fitzroy was issuing orders on his own phone to some police entity.

Watching the reactions, Roz was now sure whoever the man was, he didn't belong to the hospital. The delayed knowledge hit her with a force of fear. Someone besides Fitzroy knew she was here and had come to find her. She began to shake.

"It will be OK, Ms. Duke." Fitzroy's calm tone allayed some of the worst fear. "Whoever he is, he doesn't know our plans, nor that you'll be returning to England tomorrow." He turned to the doctor, "Can we take her out a back door? Perhaps a staff entrance? We'll have an unmarked car delivered and I'll be the driver so we don't have a lot of police milling around."

Comforting words that only eased her fear slightly. After the smoke bomb, she understood someone was tracking her. This, though, was a physical assault, and the memory solidified the vague "bump" before her sail over the cliff into a certainty that another car pushed her off the road. She held this knowledge in, waiting to share it with Fitzroy until they were alone, in a private place.

The minutia of her discharge took up another quarter-hour, then the doctor left. Roz debated but asked, "What were you doing at the Caen police department? When I had to leave a message on your cell, I though you may have gone home." Not wanting to bare her fear, she thought, "Thank god."

A look of concern flitted across his face. Was he going to lie? Hold something back?

"I used this as an opportunity to fill the local force in on some of our cross-Channel cases. The human traffickers didn't leave from Caen, they took the Chunnel, but any of these ports with ferry crossings are potential transfer sites." He paused. "Then there's your case, the missing glass and Ilic. Not a big French connection, but the Sûreté works closely with Interpol, so they're aware of possible cross-border implications. Granted, the stolen stained glass was English, but the continent has buckets of it as well, so a possible market involves several countries."

A reasonable explanation. "Did you find anything out?"

"No, nothing specific. It's always good to meet other cops, though. Because Caen's a port, they watch for contraband, both coming and going. They don't get the traffic that Folkestone, Dover and Calais have, so people assume that customs checks are more lax." He grinned. "Not the case, either for us or the French, though. I love it when crooks think we're stupid."

Roz smiled back. "Are you going to pick up my things from the hotel?"

"Yes. I asked them earlier to pack up your room. When they went up to gather things, they thought you'd left the room in a mess."

"No, no, I left everything put away! For a quick trip like this, I don't bring enough to even unpack. The only things I left were the unmade bed and a wet towel hanging in the bathroom."

Fitzroy's eyebrows raised.

CHAPTER THIRTY-TWO

"*H*mmm. That's not good." Fitzroy was staring at an invisible spot on the wall.

"What, what?" Roz lost her earlier calm, and the dread slid back, weaving tendrils of fear along her nerve endings.

"If you didn't leave the room a mess, then someone else did. What was there?"

"Pretty much my clothes and bathroom things, cosmetics, shampoo, that sort of stuff. Why?"

"I didn't catalogue things, so don't know what was there or not there. What about your computer?"

Roz thought. "No, I had that with me. And my sketching things. They all should have been in the car. Did you look?"

Fitzroy looked chagrinned. "Well, I didn't. By the time I was notified and got here, your car was towed to a storage yard. I didn't ask the French if they went through it, they're treating it as an accident due to the heavy weather. All I've done is locate it and made sure it's safe. I haven't even contacted the rental agency yet, because you had a long-term lease for it."

"What does that have to do with my room at the hotel?"

"It's possible that whoever is stalking you—and I use that term—wants to find something you have. They knew about your accident, weren't able to get to your car to search it so ransacked your room instead."

"Can you go look at the car? I hope my laptop is still there…and my sketches!" Panic began to replace fear in Roz' chest. No, no, not her work. All her notes on the computer for ordering glass and supplies, all her sketches. The computer was backed up on the cloud, so replaceable, but a pain. Glad she'd left most of the completed cartoon in England, the recent sketches and drawings from this trip were finishing touches, but important, nonetheless.

"I will. I'm going to go back to the station, ask them to give you a guard outside your door until you can be discharged and get someone to take me over to the storage yard. I'll ask for a forensic tech or whatever they call it here to go with me and check the back of the car for any sign of a collision or bump. The weather was so foul that night, there might not be much evidence, but a dent or paint flake could turn an accident into a deliberate act."

A deliberate act? Roz took in the words, then it hit her what they meant. The deliberate act was to hurt her, maybe kill her. How had an innocuous trip to a place she loved, a day of working on an amazing project, a short trip along the coast turn into something that threatened her life? She had to hold it together, not show her fear to Fitzroy. She didn't need him trying to keep her safe and ending up having control over her.

"When you come tomorrow morning, would you bring my bag with you? I don't want to travel home in hospital clothes and what I had on when I went over the edge wasn't treated very well. I think it's toast."

"Toast?" The Americanism threw the English detective for a moment.

"Finished, ruined."

"Of course, I'll bring your things. Would you like anything else?"

"A big cup of coffee, café au lait, would be wonderful. This place doesn't have the best food, although being French, it's way better than at home." She stopped herself. A second ago she'd referred to Hythe as "home." Where was home?

Tapestry of Tears

Alone, Roz forced herself to stay calm. The hospital staff knew about a possible intruder, a French cop would guard her door, she was heading back to England tomorrow with a police escort. She lay back and wiped her mind of worry, pushing back to the last few minutes of her trip along the coast. Remembered the huge torrent of water. Remembered the feel of the wind, pushing her off the road, the realization that she couldn't control the car. The feeling of dread knowing she'd go off the cliff, then, the bump. It came from behind, she was sure because it made her glance up at her rear-view mirror. There. It wasn't a shadow, there had been a car. Maybe not a car, maybe one of those everywhere small white delivery vans.

She needed to tell Hal. It wasn't much to go on. Even if it had hit hard enough to leave a paint smear, there must be thousands of small white vans driving around the French countryside every day.

What the recovered memory did, though, made her certain someone in France wanted her dead. Was this tied into the smoke grenade, the threatening note, the scares in England? Or had someone followed her to France? If this was tied into Ilic, and he was part of the smuggling and trafficking ring, what had she stumbled across?

Too many of the pieces of this puzzle were missing. Come to think of it, she may be trying to put pieces from two or three puzzles together and they many never fit.

There was the fact of Ilic's murder

There was the fact that 30,000 pieces of medieval stained glass had been stolen.

There was the seemingly odd behavior of Phoebe and Jocelyn.

There was the note and the grenade in Hythe.

There was the deliberate hit and run in France.

There was the cross-Channel smuggling or trafficking that ended up with 39 dead people.

Did these all weave together, or was she trying to knit a three-armed sweater?

Too many questions, not enough answers, she needed to sleep before being discharged. The morning would bring enough of its own worries, like how to manage crutches. As she entered that stage of half-asleep, a thought bubbled up—how did Hal Fitzroy know she'd been in an accident?

*****

A gray, overcast day, the next morning Fitzroy arrived with Roz' overnight case. Happy to see her own clothes and toiletries, she asked for a nurse to help her shower. She had a few minutes of tricky dancing getting the cast that held her ankle together waterproofed. Managed, with the cast sticking out of the shower stall, to balance enough for a quick shampoo and body wash.

Her hair wasn't going to get blow-dried. She towel-dried most of the water out, then pulled it back into a ponytail. Clean and dressed in her own clothes, she felt up to facing a wheelchair and the rigors of learning to use crutches.

Hal wheeled her out to the curb where a French policeman waited in a car, ready to take them to the ferry terminal.

"I was impressed that I had an English police escort," Roz said. "Now I see I'm international."

"He's escorting us to help you get settled on the ferry." Fitzroy smiled at Roz and carefully transferred her from the wheelchair to the car, tucking her cast leg in. "A constable will meet us in Portsmouth to get us off and back to Hythe."

"You didn't bring a car?" Roz was appreciative of the planning and help, but disliked being fussed over too much.

He climbed in the back seat beside her. "No, I figured I could just impose on the locals to get me around. Besides, I took a helicopter over."

CHAPTER THIRTY-THREE

A helicopter? He must have been in a hurry to get to France. Now the half-asleep thought came back, and she said, "How did you know I'd been hurt? You aren't on any of my documentation to be notified."

"Ummm..." he began. "Well...I sort of..."

"Sort of?" Roz frowned. "Were you having me followed?"

"No, not followed. I just, well, asked the Caen police to notify me if they came across you in any danger. Didn't anticipate this."

A spurt of anger welled up. Why were cops always around her nowadays? Then she tamped it down, knowing she felt safer with Hal near. "I guess it's a good thing, the way this turned out. I admit, I wasn't looking forward to trying to board the ferry alone and on crutches."

"I hope you'll be happy to learn I vetoed medical transport—an ambulance and a gurney." He glanced at her, gauging her reaction and relaxed when he saw her mouth twitch.

"Eternally grateful. I would have been mortified with all that."

A spate of French from the driver as they pulled up to the terminal and Fitzroy said, "Thanks."

"What for?" Roz was uncomfortable, not understanding.

"He's arranged with the ferry crew to let him come aboard to help get you settled. We'll take up a row of seats, so I hope it won't be crowded."

It wasn't, and they snagged a row of four seats by a window. Roz was able to put her cast leg across a seat between her and Fitzroy, then changed her mind and switched so she sat next to him, her leg angled away. The ferry was loud, and she didn't want to shout a conversation.

"Did you go and look at the car?" she said.

"I did. I picked up your laptop and a roll of papers, but that's all I saw. The paramedics who transported you to the hospital had your bag, so I think we got everything. Oh, and I found the rental agreement in the glove compartment, so I grabbed that, too."

"Thank you. Where is it?"

"In my bag." He gestured to a large backpack at his feet. "Do you want to see it?"

Roz shook her head. Either it was intact or not but she couldn't do anything about it now. "I remembered that I was hit. I have a feeling it was one of those small, white vans that delivery companies use. Did you see any dents?"

"No, but I wasn't looking." He blew out a breath that ruffled the short hairs around Roz' face. "This puts a different slant on it. We haven't been treating it as evidence of a crime. I need to tell the Sûreté that. Anything else I should ask the French forensic people to check?"

"I don't know what. You said there were no witnesses, no other tracks. For damn sure there aren't any CCTV cameras along that stretch of coast." She closed her eyes and laid back against his shoulder. Were there any other tiny glimpses of memory? They'd have to surface in their own good time.

She was dozing when Hal said, "We checked out those two women. No connections to anything other than their school. They don't even volunteer for first responder duties in any of the tiny villages around Fountains Abbey."

"Thank you. Probably I'm paranoid, seeing conspiracies. Life was so much simpler before I found Ilic."

Tapestry of Tears

"Finding a body or getting involved in a murder can do that." Hal reached over and took one of Roz's hands. "I can tell you we're putting a lot of effort into finding Ilic's killer and now finding whoever is after you. I'm not taking this lightly."

How should she interpret this—the handholding and comforting words? Was he becoming another complication? He did kiss her after their dinner trip to Dymchurch, but was that loneliness, interest, friendship? And he hadn't made any other moves until now.

Also, what was her interest in him? She was glad and grateful he was involved with the case, appreciative of his concern and his professional dealings. Then again, there was helping her close up her apartment outside London, a few lunches and dinner, showing up after the grenade incident, the kiss after Dymchurch, coming to France and spending three days making sure she was safe.

Beyond the danger, she was aware of him as a man. An attractive, caring, funny, intelligent man who'd opened parts of his life to her. She didn't think he told any other crime witnesses about his wife and child's death or his parents' background, personal things about him that drew her in. Was she getting involved? What did that mean? She wasn't from here; she had a complete life eight thousand miles away. With another attractive, caring, intelligent man.

Too much. Too much emotion, exhaustion, turmoil, pain. Just let the hours wash over her, accept Hal's caretaking, let her body and mind heal and not rush to make decisions. There would be time for those later.

In Portsmouth, the reverse of the French leave-taking meant two constables boarding the ferry to help her navigate the crutches and carry her things. They piled into an unmarked car, drove to her apartment in Hythe. Mrs. Lewes, the head of the church Guild, was there to welcome her, and

Phoebe and Jocelyn hovered nearby, asking if she needed help.

"I'm fine, truly," Roz said as she sidled through her door, watching where she placed her crutches. "It's going to take me a couple of days to get used to these," she waved a crutch in the air, "but all my bones will heal." Turned to Hal. "Have you made an appointment with the local doctors about any continuing care?"

"I did. I thought you'd prefer to come directly to your place first, but tomorrow I'm taking you to the hospital to get checked and see if there's any home help we can find."

"Home help? I don't want anybody here fussing over me."

"Not a 24-hour person, just someone to help with meals, bathing. Come to think if it, the bathroom doesn't have any grab bars. Does it?"

"No." The Guild woman shook her head. "We've never thought to have any installed, but I'll call tomorrow and sort it out. Even if Ms. Duke hadn't been hurt, it's probably a good idea for all our units." She was quiet for a pause, then, "I think I'll have a disability person check us for any dangerous things. Maybe shower mats as well as grab bars."

Roz sighed. She hated to make waves, but knew she couldn't manage on her own, at least for a few days. Once she got the hang of crutches, she'd be fine, so she let Fitzroy lead her into the bedroom, trailed by the young constable who'd driven from the ferry carrying all her things.

"Wait," she said, "Just leave the backpack and my purse here. Put the papers and my computer on the desk in the sitting room." Sat on the bed, her leg in its cast elevated. "Thank you all for helping me, but I think I'd like to just rest quietly." Turned to Mrs. Lewes. "Would it be possible…"

"Of course, the woman said. "I'll have someone bring dinner over to you. And some coffee and a pastry in the morning, if that's alright."

Tapestry of Tears

"Wonderful, thank you so much. I'm afraid my presence has thrown a wrench into your peaceful routine. I'll pay for any work that needs to be done."

"Not a worry." The Guild head waved her hand in a negating movement. "It's probably something we should have thought of ourselves and will make our units more attractive as rentals."

The welcoming committee left, and Roz sighed again. "Hal, would you mind at least putting all my shampoo and things away? I don't think I can manage on crutches to unpack my toothbrush and toothpaste." She felt a little squeamish about this much intimacy. Then again, he'd seen her at her worst in the hospital and he'd packed all the things up in France. It wasn't like he was a stranger. Was it?

CHAPTER THIRTY-FOUR

The Hythe hospital was small. Probably anything requiring advanced care would be handled at a regional center like Folkestone. Roz waited with Hal in an outpatient room, something like urgent care at home, she thought.

The doctor came in, said "Hello, DI Fitzroy, what have we here," and turned to Roz. "Are you having any pain?"

"Well, my ribs are still sore and achy, but my foot and ankle are less painful."

"It looks as though the French put you together pretty well, what can we do for you?"

Fitzroy took over, said, "I'd like x-rays of her ribs and ankle. If her ankle needs to be recast, I'd like that done. The hospital in Caen gave her some crutches. She's visiting from the States, planning to be here for a few more weeks, and I wondered if she should have some home health care."

What Roz needed right now was some deep breathing, so that she didn't light into Fitzroy. Who died and made him god?

The doctor's raised eyebrows let Roz know she wasn't the only one taken aback. "What's your interest here, DI Fitzroy?" he asked.

"Ms. Duke is a witness to a murder in the small church in Lympne, and she's had a few threatening incidents. Her current injuries are from being run off the road in Normandy. We haven't gone so far as to put her in protective custody, but we do want to make sure she stays healthy. If she can be approved for a home health caregiver, even for a few hours a day, it means we don't have to assign a constable to watch her."

Roz closed her eyes. Oh lord, she hadn't put all of this together, thought Fitzroy was only being solicitous when he came to France to fetch her. They were going to have a conversation when the medical people were finished with her.

After Fitzroy's explanation, the doctor ordered x-rays, took the cast off and manipulated her ankle and pronounced that French medicine did all the right things. "I don't think the ankle is going to require surgery, it's a fairly clean break, but you'll have to have a boot on for probably six weeks. And I don't want you putting any weight on that foot for at least four weeks. After that we'll see. You may be able to walk on it, but still in the boot. The ribs? They'll heal on their own, but don't lift anything heavy and move carefully. Don't overuse the crutches for at least two weeks. Are you here on holiday?"

"No, kind of a sabbatical," Roz said and gave a brief description of who she was and why she was here.

"Hmmm, interesting," the doctor said. "Well, don't plan to go tromping around any old churches for the next few weeks. I'll check you again in a month. And I'll send in the social worker."

Once the social worker took all her information and heard the story, Roz was given the name of a woman who'd come in for four hours a day during the week to help her shower, dress, fix simple meals, get to the Guild dining room. She'd never had anyone else in her living space after Win was killed but was determined she'd be compliant for the short time while she healed.

Fitzroy drove her home, got her settled at her desk. "I'm increasing the frequency of patrols at night," he said, texting into his phone. "A technician is coming to install another CCTV camera to cover the sidewalk in front of your apartment, with the ability of close-up on anyone who approaches your door."

"Thanks for all you've done and are doing." Roz was grateful, but she wanted to clear up her position as a "witness" and Fitzroy's interest. "Why'd you tell the doctor that I was involved in a case and all but in protective custody? I thought you just wanted me to quietly look around for mention of the missing glass."

"That's what I started out thinking, but the warnings, the grenade, the 'accident' of being run off the road have upped the stakes. Now I'm beginning to believe there's a larger presence interested in you." He moved to the kitchen area. "Would you like a cup of tea?"

"You British seem to think that things can be patched together with a cup of tea." Roz smiled to soften her words. This wasn't a criticism, more of an observation, but a cup did serve to give pause and decrease building tension.

Fitzroy busied himself with the kettle and cups. "You're probably right, it gives us a chance to marshal our thoughts."

"Are yours marshaled?" Roz didn't want him to dodge the question of where she fit into his case, let alone into his life.

"As well as they can be when the picture is still murky." He brought a cup over to her desk. "We added a few things together and came up with a probable scenario. Do you want to hear it?"

"Of course I want to hear it, I seem to be in the middle of it and I don't even know what 'it' is." She nodded her thanks as Fitzroy moved a wastebasket under her booted foot to keep weight off it.

"When I first met you, you remember? At the Lympne church and Ilic's body?"

Roz stifled a sigh. "Yes, it's pretty well stamped on my memory."

"At that point, we only had a murdered immigrant. When we identified him, we thought we were uncovering an international art theft ring, lucrative but not usually violent." He stood and strolled to the window. "Thinking about your knowledge and interest in early stained glass, it seemed a logical idea to have you be on the lookout for any black market in glass. Easy and safe. Then things began escalating."

Escalating. Roz thought a simple word for the fear that began building after finding the threatening note on her doorstep. Surely too calm a word for the smoke grenade.

"Well, what now? Is there enough money or interest in smuggled art or artifacts to try to frighten me away? Let alone try to kill me, I suppose." A frisson of fear rippled from her skin and shivered the tea in the cup in her hand, making her glad that Fitzroy's back was to her.

"Now, there's more chatter and talk linking the dead immigrants in Folkestone to a well-established smuggling ring. It's looking as though they'll move anything—art, people, goods, animals…" He stopped at her look of astonishment.

"Animals?"

"Some alive and whole, some dead and in pieces. Exotic animals are one way some super-rich show off their wealth to one another. You can't display them openly anymore, though."

Roz thought of home and how the tenor of things changed when PETA began their campaign against fur. Some of her very well-off clients were switching their spending to her designs rather than another sable coat.

"I can see that. The exotic makes things valuable."

"And even worse, the trafficking of humans is a lucrative money-making business. To use as slaves in sweatshops or dangerous factories. Or as sex slaves and in the porn industry. If you smuggle in a piece of art and sell it on the black market, you can have several thousand euros or dollars of profit. But if you buy a young woman, kidnapped and smuggled in and put to work as a sex slave, you have a machine that makes you money every hour of every day for years."

Now the frisson became an all-over shiver. This was too dark. Roz' mind was not accepting that she had become an inadvertent witness to such horror.

CHAPTER THIRTY-FIVE

"I've distressed you." Fitzroy had turned away from the window and watched Roz as she paled. "I didn't mean to, but I want you to know why I'm so concerned—and insistent about your security."

She took a deep breath. "I can see that, but I'm still not sure where or how I fit in."

Fitzroy took a chair next to her and reached to hold her hand. "I've acted somewhat off the cuff until now, keeping an eye out for you but trying not to spook you. All that changed with your 'accident' in France. It's clear now that 'they' whoever 'they' are, think of you as a direct threat. Probably think you have more knowledge than you do. And this puts you directly in the path for elimination."

Elimination. There was no softness, no misunderstanding of that word. The edge of a panic attack hovered in her chest and her hands got clammy.

"Breathe," Fitzroy said. "I'm sorry I've frightened you. Breathe in for a count of 10, hold it, then breathe out to the count of ten."

Roz closed her eyes, breathed, and felt the tightened spring in her chest relax.

He stroked her hand, and she felt a little of the tension seep out. "I wanted to tell you the worst. I'm afraid you've thought of me as bossy, pushy, ordering you around because I can. That's not the case. The threat against you has been inching its way up and I'm trying to put barriers in place to keep you safe, but I don't want those barriers to be visible to them—the ring, the criminals, the dangerous men."

"This is why you followed me to France, then. Why didn't you just tell me you thought I might be I danger?"

He held on to her hand. She knew he was tethering her to him while telling and realized there may be personal reasons, as well as business one, that he needed to make clear. "We couldn't let you get frightened and run, or to cancel your plans. It must look like you were just doing what you wanted or needed to do. If we'd told you all this before your trip to Caen, it may have tipped them off."

"If I'm understanding this, you're using me as bait, right?" Roz' tone was frosty, but she didn't pull her hand away.

"Bait's such a crude term." Fitzroy raised his other hand and touched her cheek. "We're watching you closely but not interfering, so they'll think it's only happenstance we're near you."

At this, Roz lifted their entwined hands. "And this? Is this just more disinformation?"

Fitzroy jerked as though hit with a live wire. "No, no...I, umm…"

Ha, she'd caught him out. Let's see him worm his way out of this, she thought.

"When I responded to the call of a body in Lympne church and met you, I was responding as a copper doing his job. When I got to know you better, and when the ID came back on Ilic, I realized there was more there than a tourist who'd stumbled over a body. You had skills and a career that made you a valuable asset to help us with our theft case." He moved his hand from her cheek and put it over their coupled hands. "Then I saw there was an attractive, woman under the carapace of your professionalism, a woman who seemed to be vulnerable. As I heard the story of Winston

Tapestry of Tears

and watched you trying to fit pieces of information into a puzzle, I knew there were unresolved questions."

"What do you mean, putting pieces together? You think I'm fraught with conspiracy theories? That I jump to conclusions?"

"There, that's part of it. You're quick to make a decision. Not full-blown conspiracies, just using a perspective of assuming the worst."

Roz didn't jerk her hand away, but Fitzroy felt it grow flaccid between his. He must have hurt her, downplayed her fears or interests.

"You may be right." Now she pulled her hand back. "After Winston was killed, I lost a part of the essential me. I began to mistrust people, to analyze every action, pick their words to pieces. It might look as though I mistrusted them, but it's a method of keeping my thoughts and feelings buried."

She looked down at their hands, separate now. Hers were slim, nails short and unpolished, nicks and small scars lacing her fingers, a result of working with glass. His were larger, fingers long and supple. She picked one of his up and turned it over. The palm had old calluses and defined lifelines and felt capable and honest.

Could she trust him? They were thrown together in this horrible situation. She wondered what she'd have thought of him if they'd met under different circumstances.

After Winston's murder, Roz had no interest in any other men, then Liam fell into her life, also in a bizarre and dangerous way. What did she feel for Hal? In her mind, she called him Fitzroy, as though not using his Christian name kept them a degree apart, but she was beginning to recognize a pull, a warmth when they were together and when he touched her.

"Hal," she began, and at her using his name, he glanced up. "Hal, I think I haven't seen the full extent of this problem, this case. It gives me the shivers when I think about what's really going on. Those poor people, being jerked from their homes, used as slaves."

"You say people, but it's usually young women, almost children, really. So many of the ones we've rescued are younger than eighteen, some of them as young as thirteen. And many of them end up being killed when they're no longer useful."

"What does that mean?"

"Ahhh…if they end up pregnant, usually. Or if they try to escape." A sorrow from deep in his soul washed across his face. "I went into police work to right wrongs and help keep people safe. I had no idea that we'd come to this callous disregard for human life, particularly the abasement of women."

Now Roz took his hand and kissed the palm. "It took me by surprise to realize what this case was about and how you wanted me to be involved. I was angry and frightened when I thought you hadn't told me everything, been honest. I see that it's affected you in ways you've kept to yourself and whatever I can do to help, I'm in."

"Thank you." He leaned over and kissed her cheek, then his lips slid to hers and he kissed her, hard. Leaned back, then cupped one hand behind her head, pulled her toward him and kissed her again, this time his tongue working between her lips.

She responded.

CHAPTER THIRTY-SIX

Rain driving against her windows the next morning matched Roz' mood.

She wasn't in pain, although her ribs were uncomfortable if she twisted the wrong way and the boot made it awkward to get around. A feeling of general malaise attuned with the wet, drizzly day, wind and rain coming in gusts. Not a day to venture out, not enough decent light to post her cartoon and continue work on the design.

Adding to her aura of discontent was last night. Hal's kiss was sweet, warm, and she responded to it. And kept responding as it shifted in intensity. Her body seemed to take over in ways she hadn't felt since Winston.

She'd been at her desk when he leaned over, she thought for a good-night kiss. It had deepened, she'd responded, and then, what? Not trusting her reactions, she pulled back, still holding his hand. Had she subconsciously given subtle signals? Was he reading more than what was there?

"Hal…" she began.

"Have I overstepped?"

"No, not…overstepped." Roz closed her eyes. What was it then?

"I'm not ready," she said.

"Because you've been hurt?"

"That's probably part of it. My confidence, sense of self, is shaken."

"Do you feel as though I'm taking advantage?" He pulled his hand back and seemed to withdraw into himself.

"No, not taking advantage. I haven't been involved with anyone since Winston."

"Not Liam?"

She looked at him, curiously. Was that a jealous statement? "Liam and I are friends, nothing more."

"Ever?"

"I don't know. I don't know that I can get involved with anyone until I answer questions about Winston. Why was he at the mall where he was killed? Was he meeting someone? Mixed up in buying something that he didn't want me to know about?"

She rested her elbows on the desk, head in hands. "Did he have some secret life that I didn't know about? I trusted him with everything, my love, my future, my life. Was it misplaced? Until I can understand some of these questions, how can I ever trust again?"

Hal reached down and touched her shoulder. "Those are hard questions: they affect a lot of survivors. Both victims who made it through and those left behind when violence turns into death. So many people wonder if there was something they could have done. Some hints they could have seen. Even survivors of horrendous, traumatic events have a kind of guilt. 'How did I live, and they didn't?' Some never get over it. The death of one they love can bring about their own internal death."

Roz raised her head and looked at him. "How do you know that? Is that what you felt after your wife and child were killed?"

"Somewhat, yes, although my brain took over. I'm a policeman, a detective. I deal with sudden, violent death more than almost everyone and understand and acknowledge the randomness of it. It's not easy, but to keep your own sanity you may have to let go and just accept.

"I am interested in you, personally. You're intelligent, quick, talented, *very* attractive. You're challenging, I love your grasp of history, your curiosity, your seeking knowledge. I'm sorry if you feel I rushed you."

"Thank you for that, I'm going to have to use that old canard, 'It's not you, it's me.' This is something that I'll have to come to terms with if I ever want another person in my life." She took his hand again. "Our story isn't written yet."

At that, Hal gave her a quick goodnight kiss and opened the door to leave, almost running into the home health nurse who'd come to help Roz get to bed.

The woman was a little too cheery for Roz' taste, bustled around picking things up, unpacking and calling her "Love."

"Do you want to take a shower, love," she called from the bathroom. "I've set out towels, your toothbrush. Do you use cream at night? Did the hospital give you any prescriptions? Are you on any other medications?"

"No," Roz had responded. "If you'd leave a glass of water for me, I can manage. The doctors said just aspirin or Tylenol for pain if I need it."

"Tylenol?" the woman frowned, then her face brightened. "Oh, you mean paracetamol. I'll set a couple out next to your water."

She whisked back to the kitchen area, rinsed cups, got water and waited while Roz undressed and pulled a sleep shirt on.

"There you go, love, I'll swing by in late morning tomorrow and see what you need. Help showering or dressing, I daresay. Sleep well, I've left my card on your nightstand."

After the trip to the hospital, the conversation with Hal, the cheeriness of the nurse, Roz was exhausted. She'd managed to find a comfortable middle ground living by herself and realized that being with people was tiring. She'd slept soundly for a couple of hours, then woke with her brain spinning. Men chasing her, people—women and children—with wasted faces groping at her, pleading with her to save them.

She lay in her bed, focusing on her surroundings and the past few days. Events were chasing her, but was she frightened? Maybe not frightened, certainly disconcerted and feeling off-kilter. She took the pills, drank half-a glass of water and picked up her Kindle to read herself back to sleep.

After her restless night, the rain added to her mild discombobulation, and she settled in for a quiet day of research and notetaking.

Mrs. Lewes brought warm scones, the cheery nurse made coffee, Roz showered and dressed in comfortable clothes, glad she'd packed some loose, drawstring pants intended for lounging but now fitting over her boot.

Sitting at her desk, laptop open, boot resting on the overturned wastepaper basket, she began cruising for any mention of stained glass, old glass for sale, theft of stained glass. The same sites popped up as had in her previous search. She shifted her search to Bishop Odo of Bayeux, idly paging through the story of the Conquest and the Tapestry, looking for a tidbit she hadn't uncovered before.

The phone chimed, and an unknown number popped up. It was a call from the States, a 608 area code. Roz stared, not placing it until she recognized it as a code from Wisconsin, where the school she was doing the commission was located.

Now what, she wondered. She wasn't late on anything; she hadn't promised them a sample for another six months. Probably just checking to see how it was coming.

"Hello," she said, expecting the voice to be the Dean of Humanities.

Instead, it was a guttural male voice, accented with some Slavic language consonants.

"Ms. Duke? Ms. Duke, this is another warning. France wasn't an accident and next time we won't leave."

CHAPTER THIRTY-SEVEN

Roz stared at her phone, now hearing only dead air. How did they call from Wisconsin? Did they know about her commission? Who were they? She checked the phone number online and discovered it was from the university, although didn't find which department.

Could they have someone working with them? Was that how they knew about her commission and university involvement?

She hit Hal's cell number and waited through four rings until his voice mail picked up.

"Hal, please call me. I got a call from the States that has me worried." Then called the Hythe police, found he was out and left a message with the duty officer as well.

She'd done what she could. Couldn't even pace with the boot on. Trapped in a web of horror, her fear built. Maybe her dream of being chased by terrifying men wasn't just a dream, but an omen. Maybe her subconscious knew she was in more danger than she felt during waking hours.

Her mind was a hamster wheel, spinning endlessly. She needed to stop and take charge.

First step, call the Dean of Humanities. She hit the number then realized it was 4:00 a.m. but left a voicemail anyway, asking her to call back when she came into the office.

As she contemplated a next move, she jumped at a knock on her door.

"Who's there?" Without a peephole, she knew better than to simply open the door.

"Mrs. Lewes sent me." A voice Roz recognized as belonging to one of the young women who served meals.

Roz grabbed her crutches and gingerly made her way to the door, opening it to see the woman holding a napkin-covered tray.

"It's lunch," the young woman said. "A quiche. And soup. Where should I put this?"

"On the desk." Roz carefully swung around, closed up her laptop and moved papers to clear a spot. "That way I can watch for a let-up in the rain, although I won't be getting out today, I don't think."

"Right, it's a good day to stay inside," the teen said. "I'll come pick this up later."

The warmth and smell of the food reminded Roz she hadn't eaten much over the last few days. She was grateful for the Guild staff and their cook, it felt as though they'd made special dishes for her convalescence.

Roz' phone chimed as she ate her last bite of quiche and she saw Hal's name pop up.

"Hi, thanks for answering my messages," Roz swallowed a sip of water causing Fitzroy to ask if she was eating.

"I'm just finishing lunch. The Guild sent it over. I've been well taken care of."

"You left a message to tell me that?" Roz could hear a trace of humor in Fitzroy's voice.

"No, that's just conversational glue. I have to tell you I received a call from the university that's commissioning my Tapestry window."

"Is there a problem?"

"Well, yes. It wasn't the Dean on the phone, it was an anonymous voice with what sounded like a Slavic accent. I was told that the next time, they would stick around and make sure the accident killed me."

Tapestry of Tears

"What!" Fitzroy's shout made Roz pull the phone away from her ear.

"It wasn't the university, someone had hacked their phone. On top of everything, the call was at 4:00 a.m. Wisconsin time." She was silent for a few seconds. "I assume a phone can be hacked?"

"I know a number can be hacked to send text message, so, yes, it can. They may have hacked into the university phone system, found your number and called, thinking you'd answer from that number."

"They were right. Without thinking it through, like the time difference, I answered it. If they could do that, is anything I own safe? My computer, my email?"

"We probably have to assume that they're in all your electronics and devices. I'll get the Yard's tech people on it right away. We may be able to track back through and find the hackers, and in the meantime, I'll get you a complete new cyberspace identity."

"Does that mean a new phone number? How will anyone get ahold of me?"

She could hear keys clicking, Fitzroy reporting the hacking. "There are small companies and programs that can trace every call and where it originated from, then backtrack," Fitzroy said. "There will be a trail from the university number back to where and when the call was placed. That will give us a location. All this may take a few hours, so for now, don't use your phone or your computer. I'll come over and give you your new identity when it's installed."

"Wait, if they've hacked into everything, did they hack into my bank and credit card information?"

"Probably. I'll come over right away and we can begin shutting down all your financial accounts. You can use my phone to report things."

Roz felt naked and vulnerable. It was frightening enough that they'd managed to take on the university's identity, now she realized they could almost eliminate her in the world of electronic transactions. She could lose her client information, possibly her assets.

"Thank you, Hal, this is scarier than I thought. I'll see you in a few minutes?"

"It may be slightly longer. I'm in Dover, meeting with international people, Sûreté, Interpol. I'm going to tell them about what's happened to you and that you'll be incommunicado for a day or so until we can get you a new identity. Expect me in about an hour and in the meantime, don't answer your phone, use your computer or answer your door."

Hal clicked off and Roz looked around. She'd thought this a safe, peaceful spot where she could pursue her harmless passion for medieval history and stained glass. Instead, she was now in the middle of a horrendous twenty-first century net of kidnapping, slavery, stolen goods and people, computer hacking and identity theft. She was working on a stained glass piece that would describe the revolution of power and peoples that brought about modern Britain. Which would ultimately lead to the largest empire ever seen and change the political culture forever.

Roz had thought the world of Harold and William was dangerous and violent. Little had she known that more quietly lethal and violent events would be unleashed through a technology that could change the world at a stroke of a key.

And now she was a victim of that technology and could lose everything she'd worked for and wanted. Not to mention, she was now a kind of prisoner, unable to continue her work, talk to her friends, interact with the world around her.

Tapestry of Tears

Wait a minute. She mentally slapped herself. Knock off the drama. She'd sat here not long ago watching the beekeepers, imagining herself in the medieval garden, working with the monks. She'd leaned toward understanding what it meant when all work was done by hand and travel was at the pace of a walk.

Not able to time travel, she could at least entertain herself and do some work without the crutch of electronics, so she pulled a book from the edge of her desk and began to read a translated contemporary account of the Conquest.

She jumped at the knock, called out, instantly relieved to hear Fitzroy's voice.

CHAPTER THIRTY-EIGHT

"Just a minute, it takes time for me to get to the door these days." Roz pulled herself up, balanced on one foot until she had the crutches situated, and opened the door.

"That was fast," she said as Fitzroy came in.

"Less traffic. And," he looked a little sheepish, "I hit the emergency lights a couple of times. Not something I usually do, I leave that action stuff to the pandas."

Pandas? Roz gaped at him, picturing…what? A zoo? Roly-poly black and white…ahhh, black and white! British standard police cars.

"I'm glad you're here." She stretched out an arm to brush his sleeve. It felt good to touch him, so solid and warm. Tears began to tickle, and she turned, crutched her way to her desk chair and sat, smiling at him. "I find that sitting in a harder, straighter chair like this makes it easier to function. Please, pull the other chair up to the desk and show me what you've done."

"We haven't finished anything. You're still completely off line and won't be back until you have a new identity." He sat, leaned his elbows on her desk. "Even with everything new, and your old identity erased, you'll have to be careful until these guys are caught. Hackers can backtrack through ISPs and link old and new. For instance, if you continue to use the same sites, browse for the same searches, they may be able to trace you again."

Roz paled. "You mean I'll never be able to buy from the same vendors, chat to the same groups? And what about my online business of selling kits? That's what keeps bread and butter on the table."

Although her international reputation was built on the big commissions, a sizable chunk of Roz' income came from her sales of kits that allowed people to make their own small pieces. Van Gogh's *Irises* and scenes of the beach behind her house in Oregon were stand-bys.

"We'll have to figure something out. My biggest hope is that we can track these people down shortly. Once we have them in custody, we can take down all the fake and hacked sites and get yours reinstated."

Roz' phone interrupted them, and she glanced at the number. "It's a Wisconsin area code and I think the university number. Should I answer it?"

Fitzroy nodded and mouthed, "Put it on speaker."

"Is this Rosalind Duke?" The woman's voice was business-like but warm.

"It is. Is this Dean Longe?" A wave of relief washed over Roz as she placed the voice

"Yes. I got your message, Ms. Duke, what can I do for you? You said our phones were hacked?"

"I think so. I answered a call from your number about five hours ago, only the speaker was a male with a Slavic accent. That's when I realized it was 4:00 a.m. your time and certainly not your office."

"What did the caller say?"

"Dean Longe, this is DI Fitzroy of the Hythe constabulary. I'm with Ms. Duke and we've been working with her on one of our troubling cases. Because she's doing a commission for you, you've apparently been pulled into the net as well."

"Net? What case is this? How are the English police involved?" The Dean's voice lost its warmth.

Roz took over and gave a thumbnail description of the stolen glass, the attempts to frighten her off, the discovery of

Tapestry of Tears

human trafficking and the recent attack on her life. "So, you see," she wound up, "I'm immobilized in my apartment on Hythe and the phone call this morning from the university scared the wits out of me. I was gobsmacked when I understood that whoever this group is, they're clever, intelligent, well-funded and ruthless."

"We're narrowing down the search." Fitzroy's calm tone, designed to ease fear, was a balm to Roz. "We're working with Interpol, the Sûreté, Scotland Yard, your FBI and NSA and liaising with some EU and NATO committees. This has gone from a theft of some of our national treasurers to kidnapping and human trafficking on an international scale."

"This is distressing." The dean's flat American accent brought a sense of omen to the discussion. When she repeated the charges that Fitzroy laid out, it sounded like plain, unembellished fact. "What do you suggest as our next steps?"

"The first thing you need do is get your IT team to trace the hack, change what you must and get back behind some security. Our immediate concern is Ms. Duke, but as you're an American university, I don't know what other sensitive projects or programs you have that may be vulnerable to hacking and a ransomware attack."

"Thank you, Det. Fitzroy." Dean Longe's voice now was brick and full of business. "I've texted IT as we're talking and set up an immediate meeting in my office. I think I need to bring the Chancellor in, as well as our security people. This is Ms. Duke's number, correct? Is there a better number where I can reach you?"

"Yes." Fitzroy looked at Roz and raised his eyebrows. Dean Longe was no usual bureaucrat but a woman of action. "After we hang up, this number will no longer be valid. Ms. Duke is going to be dark until we can tie this up." He rattled off his cell number along with the number of the department in Hythe. "Just in case," he said, "here's a number for the

Art Theft Unit at Scotland Yard, as well. They should be able to find me if neither of the other numbers work."

They ended the call and Roz sat back. "What do you mean, this number is no longer valid? I have to have a phone."

"You do," Fitzroy said and pulled a burner phone out of his pocket. "You'll be able to use this for maybe a dozen phone calls, then we'll get you another one. Tell me who you might want to talk to, I'll send them a text from my phone telling them to go buy a burner phone and text the number to me. Once I have some numbers, I'll give them to you the old-fashioned way, face to face."

"Are you sure all this is necessary?"

"The problem is that we don't know what's necessary. So much information floats around in space and the cloud that one can never know who's listening. Or who's paying attention. I think we need to treat this as quarantining your information because a virus may get hold of it." He paused and touched her head. "I'm so sorry this is happening."

Then the tears broke through. "No sorrier than I am." Roz wiped the corner of her eye on her sweater sleeve and nodded at Fitzroy as he handed her a handkerchief. She gave him a slight smile, and he took her hand, leaned over and kissed her forehead.

That was enough for her to crumble. She laid her head on his chest, snaked an arm around his back. "I am frightened. I'm away from home, not able to connect with my friends, in a foreign country, now on crutches—what have I done in a past life?"

CHAPTER THIRTY-NINE

*F*itzroy leaned back and looked her in the eye. "Why do you think it's something that you've done? You think of yourself as having psychic powers? The ability to wreak havoc?"

Roz had to grin. At Hal's words she pictured herself as one of Macbeth's three witches, stirring a caldron in a cave and muttering incantations. "No, it's just that maybe centuries ago I wronged someone and the karma is now showing up. Or maybe I had such a charmed life with Winston that I'm paying for having had happiness."

"Those are pretty dark thoughts. I don't always believe in coincidences, but I believe in the randomness of life, or at least the perception of it. We'll never know about that butterfly wing, or the ultimate causation of events but why do people say they've done something bad in their past? Why couldn't today's happiness be caused by the past as well?"

"Be an optimist?" She smiled. That's what I planned to do when I moved to Oregon, she thought. And look what happened, a grisly murder. Granted, the victim was a pedophile who'd gotten away with his crimes for years. And now the body of a smuggler and human trafficker threw itself in front of me. I'd be a ninny to ignore warnings.

"Be happy? It's pretty simplistic, but you can change your reaction to things." He gave her a wry look. "At least that's what I've heard. I still can't find any happiness in my family's deaths, but just keeping on has helped to lessen the constant pain."

That brought Roz up. What a dolt. Wrapped up in her own miseries, she'd forgotten that Fitzroy had a black hole of his own.

"I must have had blinders on. I usually can see the bigger picture." She gestured at her immobile leg. "This threw me, I've never had a broken bone before or felt this physically limited. I need to keep reminding myself that it's temporary."

She shook herself like a dog coming out of the rain. "What are our next steps? How long will I be cut off from the world? Thanks for the burner phone, when will I get my laptop back?"

"I'd expect our IT guys to finish with it in a day or two. Do you have any work you can do without it?"

She squirmed in the straight chair, looking for a comfortable spot to rest her leg. "I have a few books here. I can do more research, but I'm really at a place where I need to search for glass. And the easiest way to do that is online." She stopped, wrinkled her nose. "Hmm, that's also the only way I can help track down any sub rosa stained glass sales."

Hal stood. "I've put your laptop as a rush, so we can get it back to you and trace the hacker's trail. Right now, I'm going to call your friend Liam, advise him on our progress and ask him to go buy a burner phone. It might make you feel more in control if you can talk to someone at home."

Home. Interesting. Hal must think of her as a visitor. Was she? Of course she was. Even though she had settled in here and planned to be around another couple of months, Hal's comment brought her to a different reality.

"Thank you, Hal, you've been more than helpful." With a fine irony, she wondered if the kiss was in the helpful camp or somewhere more personal, more intimate.

Fitzroy must have called Liam as soon as he was back at the department because it wasn't more than half an hour before the burner phone chimed and a 541 Oregon area code popped up. She answered with just a "Hello," and was relieved to hear, "Roz, is that you?"

"Yes, it's me, and I'm so glad to hear your voice!!" Not usually a gushy person, she was on the verge of tears to be in touch with the familiar.

"I know from the cop that you're physically OK, but the whole business of having your phone, computer, life hacked must be terrifying."

Roz took a deep breath, let it out slowly. "Did he tell you about the call from the university?"

"No, he just said their IT people were cleaning up and changing all your electronics. What did the university say?"

She closed her eyes. "Well, that's the thing, it was the university's phone number, but it was the hackers. They said the next time they would make sure I was dead before they drove off."

Liam's voice exploded and Roz jerked the phone away from her ear. She let him slow the vent down, then interrupted. "Liam, Liam. Wait. Fitzroy and I talked to the Dean, and that's how we figured out how deep this hacking went. And the police here, all the way up to Scotland Yard, are on the alert. Hal has given me a string of contact numbers if I hear anything from the …the…I don't even know what to call them. Smugglers? Traffickers? Thieves? Just plain nasty, bad guys?"

"I don't know what or who they are either. I thought you'd stumbled across a group of international art thieves, but this is vicious crime on a massive level." She could practically hear the gears in Liam's mind shifting and meshing.

"Have you talked to Sam again? Has he found anything on the dark web about the stained glass?"

Liam muttered something, then Roz realized he was talking to Tut and a tsunami of longing washed over her. When would she be home again to walk with him and have his warm body curled up with her? How could a project begun with such innocence and high hopes have disintegrated to this?

"He hasn't found a lot." Liam's voice jerked her back from the well of loneliness. "He found one guy offering some pieces of medieval glass, but when he asked to see a sample, the guy went silent. I think we have to assume that it's being offered for sale, but whoever has it is being cagey. And he hasn't found any indication of asking ransom for it. I think your English sources would be a better source for that."

"You're right, but with everything else going on, I haven't pushed Hal for information about it. I'll let you know if I find out about."

She heard Liam clear his throat. Was this ominous?

"Enough business, how are you?"

There was silence, with only a faint sound like the surf.

"I'm trying not to overwhelm you or interfere, but it's hard being a continent away and knowing you're hurt. That someone is planning to murder you. I know you don't want anyone thinking you're a damsel in distress and need to be rescued, but I also don't want you hurt."

Was Liam trying to tell her something? She was still unsure about Hal's intentions, and now should she add Liam into the mix? She knew she had to concentrate on getting well, finishing the sample window, wrapping up her stay, helping Hal find the thieves and possible murderers. That was plenty on her plate without adding two interesting, attractive men to the equation.

"I appreciate your concern." She made her voice go low and warm, letting him know she was interested in him as a man in addition to a friend.

"I'm concerned about Tut, too. He misses you and won't be happy that you're having to extend your stay, for whatever reason."

Roz laughed. "That's right, blame me if poor Tut ends up attaching himself to you!"

"No matter what, I'm not letting him forget you."

CHAPTER FORTY

*T*he thin edge of homesickness worked its way into Roz' thoughts. She'd been building a practical life, stepping from project to project since Winston's murder. First, get away from LA and everything that had been familiar. Then, establish herself in Hamilton, form a new community, until discovering the horror of the archbishop's pedophile ring. Next step, challenge herself with a job no one had done before, translating a historic work of art into a stained glass window.

Methodically, she'd followed a plan for a sabbatical of research, enmeshing herself in one of her favorite periods and happily spend time in rural England, some of which hadn't changed much over the last 900 years. Then, a misstep. Finding a 21st century body in a 10th century church. The juxtaposition was jarring, and if she were being honest, probably more upsetting that the original invasion had been for the locals.

The Normans' arrival had meant a complete overhaul of society, but she was looking at it through the long lens of history. On a practical level, the invasion couldn't have had a major impact on the immediate daily life of most people. Like her, no doubt they went about their business, coping with frustrations and changes and wondering what the future held.

She thought she'd known hers, now maybe a reassessment was in order. What if Dean Longe felt there it was too much danger in being associated with her? Having to revamp the university's computer systems had to be expensive. If they canceled her commission, she'd lose the months and money she'd spent living in England. True, much of the research was interesting and she'd learned from it but it didn't bring in paying work.

On a personal level, should she, could she, choose between Liam and Hal? Much hinged on where she thought was home. She'd had no intention of leaving Oregon, moving to England, and still considered the States home, but the more she grew to lean on Hal, the more she appreciated the calmer, more human-sized pace of life here in Kent.

Plus, Tut.

If Kent was long-term, she'd have to begin procedures to bring him into England.

And there was the small detail of being targeted for murder.

If she gave up her stay in England and moved back to Oregon, would the threat go away? She thought not. She couldn't unsee the body, couldn't stop the investigation that Hal was heading up. It went far beyond her involvement, far beyond the theft of the stained glass. Her discovery was such an iceberg tip, so miniscule as to almost be meaningless, except it had focused a laser on the smuggling ring.

Enough, she told herself. All the "what ifs" were beating her brain up with no solution. Start one task, one day at a time. Piling her sketch supplies into a backpack, she maneuvered her way out the door and around to the garden, hoping the few autumn bees would keep her company.

She was engrossed in sketching the details of a horse's harness when the sound of a step brought her back. She saw one of the beekeepers headed toward her, his smoker can smelling wrong, somehow.

"Hello. Are most of the bees holed up for the winter already?" What Roz knew about beekeeping didn't allow for an in-depth discussion.

"I don't know." The voice from the mesh hood wasn't English. It held an Eastern European accent. And one of the man's hands moved to wave the smoker in Roz' face. The smell hit her, sweetish, not oily as she expected, and she felt dizzy.

"You're not one of the regular beekeepers, where are they?" She struggled to stay awake, stay upright.

"I'm taking you. The boss is tired of you interfering in our business."

Roz pulled back from the man, raised her had to wave away the cloying smoke. Her arm wasn't working right, and her hand weighed a ton. "I'm not going anywhere."

The fake beekeeper grabbed her arm, trying to pull her upright. "Yes, you are," he said as he tugged at her, finally getting her standing, wobbly on one leg. "Come on, you can walk."

Her head cleared for a second and she focused on the small silver gun glinting in his hand, the smoke can now dangling. Think, think! With one hand pulling her and other with a gun, he was as off-balance as she was. Fighting an instinct to pull away, instead she leaned forward, putting her weight on her cast and reaching for a crutch. She managed to swing it, catching one of his knees, just enough to cause him to let her go, windmilling his arms to stay balanced.

She used her sudden freedom to spin on her leg cast and started to take a step away when he grabbed her ponytail, jerking her body, causing her to stumble and go to her knees.

"Well, bitch, you did it now." His snarling voice sent chills through her and panic rose like bile. She had to get away, she had to find someone. Her phone. Through her fog she remembered putting it in her backpack, now out of reach on the ground by her chair.

The only weapon she had was a crutch, but as she went to pick it up again, he snatched it away. Now completely off balance she tipped to the ground, sending flames of pain licking through her leg. And her head! He'd wrapped her hair around his hand and tried to pull her up, the pain so bad she felt consciousness oozing.

"Stop, stop," she moaned. "Why are hurting me? What did I do to you?"

"You talked to that cop." The voice was low, menacing, a growl. "I told them that killing Ilic and not getting rid of his body was a stupid idea, but they said no one ever goes into the old church. It would be weeks before he was found. Even then, people would think he died of exposure." He shook his head and jerked her hair again. "Couldn't just drop him off a boat in the Channel. Wanted to make an example of him."

Keep him talking, she thought.

"But I'm not even from here! I'm American, not European. I'm not interested in your affairs." Even in her own ears, her voice was weak, pleading, her excuse nonsensical.

"We don't care if you're from outer space, you found him and ratted us out. And then, you started working with the cops to find the stained glass."

Roz' mind whirled. Was this really all about the glass, not the other smuggling and human trafficking? That wasn't good, but theft wasn't as serious as the other crimes. Maybe she could bargain a way out.

She reached up to pull her hair out of his hand, causing him to jerk it tighter. The pain brought tears to her eyes but she gasped out, "I didn't find out anything! I haven't told the cops anything because I don't know anything."

"Doesn't matter, too late." He began walking out of the garden, trying to drag her behind him.

"Wait!" She was on her knees, starting to move. "Let me stand up so I can walk."

He slowed, watching as she managed to get a shaky footing. This brought her close to his own height and eased the pressure on her hair, lessening the fierce pain. "Let me get my crutches," she begged, thinking that something, anything, in her hands might be useful.

"You don't need them." He motioned with the gun, impatient to get her out to the street.

Without her crutches, Roz barely inched along, the adrenaline of fear keeping the pain in her leg at bay until she was able to take a deep breath. Then the pain came roaring back, sucking breath out of her and causing her leg to collapse completely.

As consciousness left, she felt the first kick.

CHAPTER FORTY-ONE

Pain. Gravel biting into her cheek. Her hip on fire. As she came to consciousness, she tried to catalogue. Her head throbbed, even her hair hurt. Her hip shot off streaks of pain, Her face stung. Oddly though, her cast leg wasn't a major source of pain.

"Roz, Ms. Duke! What happened?"

She slitted her eyes and saw Phoebe's face leaning over, with Jocelyn standing behind, looking stricken.

"Somebody…somebody…" She closed her eyes, tried again. "Somebody grabbed me."

"What somebody, there's no one else here." Phoebe's forehead creased with worry. "Did you fall? Did you try to walk on your cast and fell?"

"No, a beekeeper…wait, not a beekeeper…"

"You're not making sense." Jocelyn's no-nonsense voice clanged making Roz' ears hurt. "The beekeepers have gone, they'll only come back one more time this winter."

"Dressed like a beekeeper." Roz blinked her eyes, wanting to tell this right. "A man, dressed like a beekeeper, came at me. He was swinging a smoker but it smelled wrong, sweet, not smoky. It made me dizzy."

Phoebe turned her head and exchanged a glance with Jocelyn. "Better call Mrs. Lewes. And maybe that constable, what's his name?"

"DI Hal Fitzroy." Roz was able to get his name out. She didn't want him to see her in this helpless state, but he had to hear about the not-beekeeper with the Slavic accent.

Joselyn took off to the office to find Mrs. Lewes and call the police department, Phoebe took Roz' hand.

"Lie still, we don't know how you fell, you may have hit your head, your cheek is scraped and bleeding. Trust me, I've seen this kind of thing before with the girls who take a tumble. Usually nothing breaks and all's well, but it doesn't do to take things too lightly." At her plain-spoken games-mistress voice and calm advice, Roz felt some of the dread seep out.

She took better stock as the pain eased. She was lying on the gravel path away from the bench where the man grabbed her. Why was her hip on fire? Then a memory of a kick before she faded into nothingness. Why did he kick her? Maybe she was moving too slowly with her bad leg and he began dragging her. That could be why her head throbbed, from being dragged by her hair. And her face? Scraped from the gravel path.

Mrs. Lewes came rushing into the garden as Roz moved to sit up.

"No, no, please stay down," the Guild lady said. "I've called that nice Detective Fitzroy and an ambulance. They'll only be a minute."

Roz groaned. Why was she being a distressed damsel in front of Hal again? Then again, this was the first person she'd seen with ties to the smuggling ring. Think, she told herself. What was there about him that would help with identification? And where did he go? The appearance of Hal followed by three paramedics with a gurney stopped her thought process.

"Roz, I'm so dreadfully sorry." Hal was leaning over her, worry and caring etched on his face, his brown eyes sorrowful. "If I'd thought you were still in any danger, I'd never have left you alone here."

She couldn't answer, the paramedics were going through their lists of questions; what day was this, what month, what was her name, where was she? She answered but this was a litany she was heartily sick of.

They carefully rolled her over on her back and fastened a cervical collar around her neck, even through her protestations that she was fine.

"All of her vitals are good, no indications of broken bones," here the one young woman paused, "other than her leg. Because of her prior injury, I think we need to transport her to A&E."

"I agree," said Hal. "I'll follow you." To Roz, "I know you don't want to go to the hospital, but I think it's best. Plus, we can watch you easier there. And now we know you need watching."

As the paramedics hefted her onto the gurney and headed toward an ambulance, Roz saw some SOCO's pull up and begin unloading their equipment. When they began to pull on the white cover-ups she gave a shiver.

"There, that's what he looked like." She pointed to the techs. "I thought he was one of the beekeepers, he was wearing one of those white suits and had a beekeeper's hat and mesh mask on. Now that I see the techs, it could have been one of these suits. Can anybody buy them?"

Hal eyed the techs. "I suppose so, I've never thought about it. They're just there in our stores unit."

"Maybe if you could track down a few sales? He could have bought it online. Probably untraceable." The medics put in an IV and wanted her to stay still.

"I'll tell them to find out when they're finished here. I suspect there's not a lot of evidence lying around. Once you're settled, I going to have a couple of officers take a statement."

As she was rolled away, she saw Hal head over to the little group of women clustered near the bench. Phoebe and Jocelyn were watching the SOCO techs while Mrs. Lewes was on the phone. With who? Would this latest stunt get her evicted for being too disruptive? That would be all she needed, not even having a place to stay after she'd given up her flat outside of London.

Mercifully, the ambulance didn't use light and sirens. She'd had enough fuss already. The medic riding with her kept up a line of chat, inane comments about how the weather was changing, getting ready for fall, asking if she'd bought her fall wardrobe, did she have any plans for Guy Fawkes Day?

She said no, she was American and didn't celebrate Guy Fawkes Day.

It wasn't until she was in a bay and a doctor asked some of these same questions did she realize the medic had been keeping her talking so she didn't lapse into a coma.

Hal showed up, another constable in tow, and held off his questions until she'd been x-rayed, poked and prodded. Then he introduced another officer, this one a woman with a large portfolio case.

"She's our police artist. She'll work with you to get an idea of your assailant," he said.

"I told you, I didn't see him, really. He had one of those mesh beekeeper hats on…" she began and he interrupted her.

"I know we won't get a good likeness, but I suspect if you concentrate, you'll remember details that will help. We've been surveilling some of the gang for a while and may be able to pin down an individual." He stood and paced into the corridor before coming back to the side of her bed. "The puzzle is getting more clear. We thought we'd been dealing with separate groups of people, some thieves, some smugglers, some sex traffickers. Now we believe it's all the same group, probably out of Eastern Europe, maybe run by the Russian mafia."

"Russian mafia?" Roz had heard stories about Russians moving in and taking over syndicates in the New York area.

They were reputed to be even more ruthless and vicious than the Sicilians. "Why would they care about some medieval stained glass?"

"They don't care. They're only after money and power. Some of them work for the oligarchs, some are associated with the Chechen gangs, a few even free-lance."

"Why would they be interested in me?" Roz frowned, causing her hair to feel on fire.

"Because you found Ilic."

CHAPTER FORTY-TWO

"That was a pure accident..." she began then pursed her lips. "Wait, he did say something about how somebody was upset because they'd left Ilic in the church instead of dropping him in the Channel."

Hal nodded. "He was a loose end. A low echelon thief and gofer. He thought he'd pull a fast one, steal the stained glass, then sell it on the black market. The big bosses wouldn't even notice."

"What happened?"

"There had been a fair amount in the tabloid press about the discovery of the glass, 'England's History Discovered' sort of thing so when Ilic highjacked a truck moving it from Westminster the honchos took it amiss. Dealt with him then sent a ransom note."

Roz fought the pain medication to stay awake, then, "Wait a minute! You didn't tell me about the ransom demand!"

"No, I didn't." Hal's voice was sheepish. "It just came in two days ago and I didn't want any word to get out about it."

"This is just great! I'm still like the staked-out goat, Liam is putting himself in danger with his friend Sam trolling the dark web, and you wanted to keep it a secret? For how long?" Her fit of pique made her head throb despite the meds. Right now, she wanted nothing to do with any man. "Just go away."

"I'm sorry I had to keep it from you, I thought it would put you in more danger. Little did I realize they'd already begun their moves." He leaned over her. "I'm going to ask the doctors to keep you overnight at least so that we have a quiet place to work. I know you're angry—you have the right to be—but the fact remains that you've been attacked. And you're the only one who's seen any of them. Your information is valuable."

As much as Roz wanted to maintain her head of anger, the pain meds were taking over. She though a short nap would clear up some of the fuzziness.

When she opened her eyes again, she was in a hospital room. A cone of light from a reading lamp illuminated her but beyond her bed all was shadowy and the window showed night.

"Ah, you're awake." A nurse was fussing with a blood pressure cuff. 'I'll just pop out and tell that nice Detective."

Roz started to say "No, wait…" remembering that she was ticked at Hal, but he was next to her, then, "Do you feel better? Can you help us now?"

She sighed. "Hand me some water, please. Then I guess so."

He poured from a bottle and handed her the cup. "Good. I'll go call the artist."

The woman must have been near. She came in, pulled a chair up inside the spill of the light and took out a sketch pad.

"Let's start with how tall you think he was." Hal stood on the opposite side of the bed.

"I don't know, I'm not a very good judge…" then she remembered. "Wait, when he pulled me up, I was almost the same height. I'm 5'7" so he isn't very tall."

"And his build?'

"It's hard to tell under that suit. When I hit him with my crutch, it felt as though it was hitting muscle. Not squishy like fat, or bony."

Tapestry of Tears

The artist was making notes. "Probably 170 cm, about 13 stone," Hal told her.

Then to Roz, "Would you say stocky?" He wanted to pin her down.

"Yes, I'd say so. He was bigger than me, muscle, not fat. He seemed strong."

"OK, now his voice. This won't help the artist much, but if he had a Slavic accent, he may have slightly Eastern features." Hal was ticking things off an imaginary list.

"I don't know so much about Slavic, but it sounded just Eastern European to me. Guttural, I couldn't tell Polish from Lithuanian from Ukrainian. Kind of a 'Fiddler on the Roof' accent."

Hal stared at her. "That's Russian-Yiddish but I think I understand. I know you people in the States don't have the same ear for accents as we do. Was he wearing gloves?"

Gloves. She had to think. "No, I know when he grabbed my hair, I saw his hands."

"Anything remarkable?"

"No, no...wait. I remember he was missing part of a finger."

"Good. Which finger?"

"The top joint of his little finger. Left hand. He had the gun in his right hand."

"How about his face?"

"No, it's a blank. I told you he had one of those mesh hat things on." She knew her voice was reaching into the peevish timbre but she was tired of beating up her brain.

"You're doing fine." Hal nodded at the artist. "Can you do a sketch of his hand, another one of a stocky man with a beekeeper's outfit on, maybe one of a slightly Slavic-looking face, probably jowly, maybe dark beard?"

"A beard!" Roz was back in the garden, looking at the man, "He did have a beard. Dark. Not a neat one, all messy as though he hadn't shaved for a month or so. Didn't even look combed."

"Good, good, how about a mustache?"

Roz closed her eyes. "Yes, no, not exactly a mustache, just all the bottom half of his face was covered in hair. Dark hair. Maybe black."

"Thank you, Roz, I know you didn't really get a look at him, but this will be helpful. Particularly the missing finger joint. That's a typical torture method for the Chechens, slowly snipping off finger joints until they get the information they want. This guy could have run afoul of some of the gang in a previous venture. They could even have used his earlier malfeasance to intimidate him into becoming a hit man."

He turned to the artist. "Do you have enough to get started.?"

"I do. I'll come up with a few and you can get the team started on matching the sketches with known Russian mafiosi." She slid her pad and pencils in her portfolio, grabbed her purse and left.

As she headed out, a doctor headed in. "Well, Ms. Duke, I've had a good look at your x-rays. No damage to your hip, although you're going to have a doozy of a bruise and be sore for quite a few days.

"I am concerned about your leg, though. By being forced to stand and walk on it, you've damaged the original break. I'm afraid it's now going to require some surgery. Trim the ends of the bones, put in some pins, maybe a rod to hold it. You may set off airport metal sensors in the future."

Roz groaned. "This doesn't make me happy. When do you want to do this?"

"I think first thing in the morning," the doctor said, far too cheerily.

"And after the surgery?"

"We'll want to keep you for two days, see how things go. Then when you're discharged, it needs to be some place where you can be looked after. Maybe a rehab facility? You'll need some physical therapy."

Just great. One top of everything else, she likely had no place to go. She needed to call Mrs. Lewes and smooth things over there, ask someone, who?, for a recommendation for rehab.

She couldn't stop the tears.

CHAPTER FORTY-THREE

With her leg pinned and recast, Roz was restive after two days in the hospital. The pain had lessened, true to the doctor's prediction she had an ugly huge bruise, purple edging towards yellow, on her hip and she hadn't washed her hair, her scalp still too tender.

Hal came by every day and even Jocelyn and Phoebe stopped by, the women bringing a note of heartiness and outdoors with them.

"I'm so sorry this happened," Jocelyn said one afternoon. "The weather is perfect, a hint of crispness in the air, but sill sunny and warmish. Everything can change here on the coast in a flash. We don't want to complain and tempt fate though. A storm swept the Armada away and even the Germans faced nasty weather in 1940 in the Battle of Britain."

Phoebe nodded. "We do get tired of clouds and rain. The usual caricature of an Englishman is in a suit with a rolled umbrella. Facetious but sometimes accurate."

"We've had some nice rambles and were able to do research. I think we have a solid idea of the lay of the land in 1066, even with almost a thousand years of change." Jocelyn paced the room, picking up and putting down a cup of water, a book. "We think the best place to visualize the true invasion is probably at Dymchurch, the beach there is still flattish and you could pull light boats up on the sand to unload. Other places erosion has worn cliffs down and ports have gotten silted up. Some don't even exist anymore."

Roz closed her eyes. As nice as it was to have some company, the women's voices melted together to a drone of background noise. She didn't have to respond so she nodded, then came back from where her mind had drifted. "Does this mean you're headed home?"

"Yes." Phoebe answered and Jocelyn nodded in agreement. "We're planning to head home in two days. That will give us the weekend to get settled before the next term starts."

"Do you live alone?" A germ of an idea was floating, looking for a place to land and grow.

"Well, yes and no. We have lodgings at the school, each of us has a flat." Jocelyn glanced over at Phoebe. "She's fortunate. Her family is from Ripon and left her a small cottage, so she spends most of her nights off campus."

Phoebe grinned. "And Jocelyn comes over when she needs some peace and quiet. There are about 250 girls at the school and chaos reigns when they're in full cry."

"Do you teach anything besides PE?" Roz watched the two faces screw up in questions, then realized her mistake. "Sorry, I meant games. PE is our word for it, physical education."

"Ah." Jocelyn beamed and said, "We don't teach anything else, but we do have teacher's duties. Getting them down for meals, bed check, general supervision in chapel, things like that."

"And we're responsible for such sex education as they get. It's a subject of much hilarity and embarrassment for the younger ones. Those are the ones who come to visit us in our flats and ask questions one-on-one." Phoebe pinked up. "It's also a bit clinical, neither of us is married. There's always the odd girl or two who asks point blank how many men we've been with."

A question that curious young girls would ask, Roz thought. And now she wondered.

She'd subconsciously thought the women may be lovers but hadn't asked. None of her business. What she did glean from the conversation was that they had some living space that wasn't in use full time.

"Do you suppose," she began as Phoebe said, "Where are you going when you're discharged?"

"I don't know." Roz shrugged. "The doctor said I'll probably need some physical therapy and suggested a rehab facility."

"Has he booked you in at one?" Phoebe was exchanging glances with her friend.

"I don't think so. I was going to ask Hal when he came this afternoon." Roz felt the hook get taken.

"Well, that's sorted then," Jocelyn's voice filled with a no-nonsense teacher's authority. "You come home with us. You can stay in Phoebe's rooms at school and she'll move her stuff to the cottage."

"I couldn't put you out!" Roz' protests got overridden by both the women. They'd taken the bait without a hitch.

"You're not putting us out at all. We move back and forth any way, this will just mean that Phoebe may have to give up some of her one-on-one student hours." Jocelyn smiled at her friend. "Not something she'll regret."

"Besides," Phoebe chimed in, "although we're not licensed physical therapists, we do have a lot of training and we know a therapist in town who could oversee your exercises. Plus, the school has plenty of equipment to build strength and muscle."

"If you're sure, I certainly appreciate it." Sharing a living space with an acquaintance at an active and busy girls' school wasn't high on Roz' wish list, but it was a sensible move. She had limited options.

"I'll ask the doctor to be discharged day after tomorrow. I don't want to make you change your plans any more that you already have. Can we swing by the church and pack a few things?"

"Of course, that's not putting us out at all." Jocelyn's voice was gruff. Emotional? Snitty? Then the woman smiled. "Besides, you'd said you wanted to visit York before you headed home."

Home. It was such a safe, comforting word. Roz was leery of putting too much emphasis on the future, she was barely able to deal with the present. Home was a day at a time right now.

"I don't know how much sight-seeing I'll be able to do at this rate." Roz waved her hand at her cast. "The doctor said I'd be in this at least three weeks before I can even think about a walking cast."

"Are you able to use crutches?" Phoebe gathered up her purse and sweater. "There are lots of thing you can visit that wouldn't involve stairs. You could manage those with crutches."

"We're getting ahead of ourselves," Jocelyn said. "Let's let her heal here until we're ready to go." Turned to Roz. "I'm so glad you've said yes to our plan. We'll come by tomorrow and see if the doctor will release you to our custody." She giggled. "Sounds a little like getting out of prison."

The women closed her door as they left and Roz used what passed for silence in the hospital to begin a list of what she needed to pack. Ringing phones, doctors being paged, carts and trays rattling was a background noise that decreased at night but it was never truly silent.

Her mind went through her small apartment, picking and choosing. Most of her tops, maybe two dresses, two or three pair of drawstring pants. Maybe she could impose on one of the women to stop and buy a pair of wide-legged pants to fit over the cast. Her toiletries. Her new laptop. Her sketch book and rolls of cartoons that she'd finished. How many books?

With her eyes closed as she inventoried the books and belongings in both her living space and the adjacent apartment where she'd stored things after moving from London, she felt a frisson of fear wash across her skin.

Someone was in the room.

CHAPTER FORTY-FOUR

"Just what the hell are you playing at?'

Roz recoiled at the menacing male voice. Her assailant?

Her heart began to pound. She threw her hand over her eyes and peeked out between her fingers.

Not any assailant, Hal. She'd never heard him use that voice before, like something he'd use to stop a criminal.

"Playing at? What you talking about? And why are you yelling?"

"I'm not yelling…although I should be. I ran into those two women in the lobby and they told me about your harebrained scheme. Move up to Ripon? Stay at a girl's school? Have no police protection? Did the medications affect your mind? You're not…"

"Just wait, you jerk!" Roz stopped the flow of rant with her own sharp words. "I'm not what? Am I under arrest? Have you read me my rights? What do you think gives you the ability to dictate my movement?"

They glared at each other, he standing at the foot of her bed, her leaning up on her elbows to add emphasis to her voice.

"I don't think so. I'm a grown woman, an American, not your subject. And have no criminal history, haven't done anything wrong. I'm free to go and do what I want with whoever I want."

He watched her, then, "You may have those rights, but I have a duty to keep you safe. And a duty to find whoever is running that group, that gang of traffickers. For starters, didn't you stop to consider what some human sex traffickers would think about you hiding in a girl's school? Just because we so far found girls and young women from Eastern Europe who have been kidnapped and trafficked, doesn't mean girls in Britain are safe. Every year there are hundreds of girls who go missing. Unless we find them, or their bodies, we have no way of knowing they haven't ended up in some brothel or being sold to some group of pimps.

"When you stumbled across Ilic's body, none of us had any idea what that might lead to. We looked at you as an asset because of the missing glass. Then we watched as the full impact of the enterprise unfolded. It grew like fungus after a rain. But we were hopeful that you'd work with us. When it was clear you were in danger, we knew the leaders were getting nervous, were targeting you to not only keep you quiet but to get rid of our best lead into their schemes."

The silence when Hal stopped was deafening.

He'd hit on important points but what really stopped her was the comment about the girl's school. She hadn't thought about that, moving into a situation that might put a lot of innocent lives in danger.

She couldn't know how badly the gangsters wanted her. Was there a possibility they'd kidnap a student or two and sell them to sex slavers? Or maybe hold them for ransom? After all, a private girls' school assumed parents who had money.

The pause to think took her boiling blood down a few degrees but she was still pissed about his highhandedness and moves to control her.

"That's true, I didn't work that through." She took a deep breath, then, "The fact is you plowed over plans that we were making. I'm at a standstill. I have no safe place to go after I get out of here, and I can't stay here much longer. I'll be crawling the walls."

Tapestry of Tears

She stopped. She was on the thin edge of anger and fear and wouldn't let Hal see her slip over. Tears of anger and desperation pricked at the back of her eyes, but she tamped them down. He'd never know which they were and might assume weakness. She couldn't give in.

"There's still the issue of staking me out like a sacrificial goat. Now that the stained glass will be recovered, why am I important to them? To you?"

Hal opened and closed his mouth a couple of times. Finally managed to get out, "Were you hearing me? You were initially in involved because of your expertise, but when our search for the glass and Ilic's killer ramped up, the enterprise started to have a bigger footprint. Ilic was only part of the skeleton. He was stupid and unimportant and his ineptitude caused his death and began a path that led to the traffickers."

"How?" Roz had calmed enough her brain was working the puzzle like a rat's maze. "I know you linked Ilic to an Eastern European mafia, but what connected that to the dead bodies in the truck at Dover?"

Silence. She watched emotions flitter across Hal's face until he said," Well, there are one or two things I haven't told you."

CHAPTER FORTY-FIVE

There was a standoff. Which one of them was angriest? Probably Roz.

What was there about all cops that made them so smug, so reluctant to share information? First the detective in Los Angeles who kept her in the dark for months until she finally gave up and moved to Oregon. Winston was murdered at a place neither she nor he frequented, so the LAPD felt she was a Person of Interest, because who else would know where he'd been going?

Then the police chief in tiny Hamilton, Oregon just because one of her caming knives was the murder weapon when her neighbor's body was discovered.

Now DI Hal Fitzroy of the Hythe Police Force was lying to her because she had the rotten luck to stumble across a body in an unused church.

She eyed him, pulled up her iciest voice. "Any just what have you *neglected* to tell me? Or was this a sin of commission?"

She watched as Fiztroy visibly shook his anger and irritation into a safe place. "Once we got a ransom demand for the stained glass, you didn't need to be involved in internal British affairs. And after we discovered the smuggled people dead in Dover, we were able to glean some information from the truck driver." He held up his hand as she leaned toward him to ask a question. "I'm not telling you anything more about what we found, except that it led us to a young woman who'd been trafficked and managed to get away. She's living in a safe house now, undergoing intensive therapy and will be a star witness when we roll up the gang."

As he paused, Roz said, "Why did you feel you couldn't tell me that?"

"Because if we couldn't protect you, we didn't want you to have any knowledge that you'd have to lie about. We felt, and feel, that it would be much more dangerous for you."

"You want to protect me? How about you left me alone in that French hospital until somebody came in my room? What about the fact that one of the gang's guys was able to try a kidnap attempt in my garden? What happened to all your talk about having a guard for me?"

A slow bloom of color was climbing Fitzroy's face. Embarrassment? She hoped so. He should be embarrassed at their small-town flounderings. But the minute he opened his mouth, it wasn't embarrassment, it was rage.

"Let's just slow down here, Ms. Duke. We moved you from London to be able to keep an eye on you. When the smoke bomb hit, we felt it was a warning, but installed cameras. When you went to France on your own, I alerted the French police and followed you at a distance. I admit that had we kept closer tabs we may have been able to prevent them running you off the road, but in that huge storm, they might never have been seen anyway.

"Now, back in Hythe, I doubt you've noticed it, but we've had a person with you. Apparently, the gang has noticed him, even though you haven't, and set up a fake emergency to pull him away from the church long enough to allow them time to kidnap you. When you were attacked, your guard was fifteen miles away, mopping up after a traffic accident. And now? I came because the guard we have here at the hospital said those two women had been in with you and left in rather a hurry. That's how I ran into them in the lobby."

He stood and slammed his hand down on the bedside table, causing a plastic teacup to fly off to the floor. "We are always short-staffed, but you and your safety have been a high priority. Especially since you've been targeted. Possible for murder. And you're a solid link to our finding the traffickers."

The red wash ebbed. Fitzroy washed a hand over his face and his eyes took on sadness. He leaned over, picked the teacup up, found a paper towel and mopped up the mess.

"Ms. Duke, you try my soul. From the moment I saw you at the Lympne church, I was interested. Couldn't decide if it would be good or bad to get too close to you. Were you part of a group we'd been trying to watch who we were sure were smuggling along the coast? Or were you an absolute innocent, just wrong time, wrong place.

"Then, things began happening to you, so I put you in the 'wrong' category." He stopped, another bit of pink in his cheeks. "And I found myself attracted to you. A no-no, regardless of what your true nature was. Even if you were simply a witness, I could jeopardize our case if we were involved."

Roz's lips were glued together. What could she say? How could she have missed all the signs? Not figured out the danger of being involved with the detective? Was she so self-absorbed that she'd put some of those around her in peril

She closed her eyes, took a deep breath. No apology, but she had to recognize his feelings and efforts to keep her safe.

"Detective Fitzroy, I haven't been as aware as I thought. I didn't know there were people watching out for me, didn't see any guards, didn't think about luring gang members to a girls' school. The fact though, is that by keeping me unaware, in the dark, you've allowed me to make unsafe decisions, to push me into making quick and possibly wrong moves."

Roz hated that she'd misread the situation so badly. Was part of it that she was in a foreign country, operating with different rules? In her haste to find a safe place to stay and recuperate, to start working on her physical recovery, she'd felt alone, adrift in an unfamiliar culture. It may have been rash to so quickly cobble together the plan with Jocelyn and Phoebe, although it felt so right. A place away from here, where she'd be incognito and allowed to heal. And the fillip of having time to investigate an area of England she didn't know well.

"I'm still unhappy that you've so cavalierly changed my plans and made the offer to stay in Ripon looks suspicious. If not there, where? I don't feel safe going back to my flat at the church." She paused, rested her head on her hand. "And I'm not sure Mrs. Lewes would have me back. I've been a lot of trouble."

Fitzroy looked at her, understanding that fear—fear of the unknown, fear of the future—had underlain what seemed like a frivolous, too-quick decision.

"I wouldn't worry about Mrs. Lewes. She's told me that your troubles have knocked her out of her complacency. The church and the Guild have been operating as though it's 1930, 'safe as houses,' in a gentler time. Having you as a guest jolted them into the 21st century. More violence, more danger, brought them into the wider world where few things can be taken for granted any more.

"She's thankful that a CCTV system has been installed, they'd had a break-in or two and now can record who comes and goes. Your difficulty in getting around with your crutches made her realize they'd have to make all the flats, the grounds and the church accessible for the handicapped. In an offhand way, she told me you're the best guest they've had in years, even called you "a breath of fresh air'."

Tapestry of Tears

Roz tried to hide a grin. It was a fine irony that she'd come here for the past and ended up dragging people into the future.

"Thank you for telling me that. I still don't want to go back there, too many bad memories and the gang know where I am. Plus, I have to arrange for some rehab, maybe a physical therapist to come in a few times a week. "

"Remember where you are. This is Britain and the NHS will have already set your rehabilitation in motion."

Her shocked expression told him that she hadn't considered it, was still working on the model that all the decisions and responsibilities were hers. "That's good to know, I'd've worried about finding some place. This still doesn't answer where I'm going, though. To a rehab facility?"

"No, they'd track you down there. You're moving into my house."

CHAPTER FORTY-SIX

"Your house? Oh, I don't think so!"

Fitzroy whirled to the window. Roz could see his shoulder shaking. Was he going to lash out at her again?

When he turned back to her, the laugh lines around his mouth were deeper and his eyes gleamed. "I don't think you understand. That wasn't an invitation. It was an order."

"You're ordering me?" Roz gasped. After their fight, conversation, frustrating argument, he had the audacity to order her? And to order her to stay in his house?

"Yes. I've spent the last bit of time going over every step we've taken to keep you safe and it still hasn't worked." He held up his hand as she opened her mouth. "It's no good, the only other thing I can do is ship you home to Oregon. I don't want to do that because once you're out of Britain, I have no authority or means to follow you, track your movements, watch who comes toward you. The other is, I'm sure you can heal just as well at home, but I do feel responsible for your health and would be happier to see you completely well."

What if she flatly refused? Did he have any power to keep her here? To keep her in his house? What was the worst that could happen if she were to go there? She would be guarded and know the gang couldn't touch her. She could finish her work and ship the sample window home

The alternative wasn't appealing. Even though the airlines would accommodate her and her cast, it would be a long, uncomfortable trip with probably two plane changes, then a couple of hours in Liam's car, not to mention at least two hours to Heathrow from Hythe.

Right now, she wanted some quiet, a room of her own, a walk-in shower with shampoo, loofas, fluffy towels. Space to spread out and work, put up her cartoon and finish cutting the glass. Barring a light table, a large, flat surface to begin assembling the window.

As she mentally listed her wants and needs, the idea of a safe, comfortable space to enough time to heal won out. Aware she wasn't bargaining from a point of strength, she asked, "And what's at your house?"

"You'll be in the master suite with an en suite bath. Shower, not bathtub. There's good light, it looks out on the back garden, there's room to move some of your supplies and work needs. It's on the ground floor so no stairs."

"And where will you be?"

"I'll move to one of the upstairs bedrooms There are two with a connecting bath. Probably the one that my son was in. I'm going to have a constable move into the guest room so that you're never alone."

She didn't have a choice, but a small part of her longed for what she thought was a peaceful setting of a girls' school, all mellowed brick and ivy, companionable women with interests much like her own, the slow pace of academia. Then it hit her. She'd be with maybe three hundred other people, students, faculty and staff. Noise, bells, voices, bodies rushing, yells. Even at a university, Winston used to complain that he had to do much of his work at home, at school was just too distracting.

"Alright then. When can I get out of here?" It wasn't a graceful give-in. She knew it was inevitable. Now to make the best of it.

"The doctor will release you tomorrow if it's into my custody. A physical therapist will be here to help you with the move, get you set up in my house. Two of my constables will pack up both your flats at the church and move everything. You can spend a day or two arranging it to fit your needs. I do have a cleaner who comes in twice a week, but I'm going to arrange to have someone in daily for cooking. I'm not much of one and you can't stand long enough.

"I'll go make the arrangements with the doctor and see you in the morning. It's for the best and I really don't bite."

Roz' dreams that night were of being locked up, hearing cries and moans, chains rattling. She woke claustrophobic, the chains the sounds of breakfast trolleys, the moans the voices over the PA system.

Hal arrived as she was finishing a cup of coffee, all her roiling stomach could handle.

"Are you ready?' This morning he was less demanding, more solicitous, aware this wasn't her choice.

"I think so. I didn't take a shower or wash my hair. I was hoping I could do that at your house?"

"Of course." He waved a hand at someone standing in the corridor. "This is Sarah Lightener, the physical therapist assigned to you. She'll help you with bathing and get you settled today then tomorrow begin some exercises."

Sarah was a youngish woman, perhaps in her mid-thirties, with flaxen braids and the body of a Saxon peasant, strong and competent.

"Hello Ms. Duke. I'm to help you, but I expect you to do the real work." Her smile lit up her eyes and Roz felt herself warming to the therapist. Maybe this wasn't so much an intrusion as assistance.

They made a small parade traipsing out of the hospital. Roz in a wheelchair as required by the hospital, Detective Fitzroy carrying bags with her clothing and the few books Jocelyn had brought, and Sarah pushing her.

Mercifully, they left through a back entrance, out by a loading dock next to the ambulance bay so the entire hospital didn't watch. The car waiting wasn't a police issue, but a small Range Rover so Roz was comfortably slid into the passenger seat, with Sarah following in her own Cortina.

Hal lived just outside of Hythe proper, in a converted farmhouse with extensive remodeling. The bones of the nineteenth century building were still visible, yellow brick and stone, masses of roses climbing the front. It looked comforting, safe. She wouldn't admit it to Hal, but it was a perfect place to recuperate and recharge. And the added enticement of another officer there at all times.

Roz waited until Sarah came around to help her out of the car and steady her over the paving stones leading to the foyer. As she looked up from carefully placing her crutches on the slate floor, she sucked in a quiet breath. Hal didn't exaggerate, the view out of the French doors to the back garden was lovely. More massed roses in beds, a footpath meandering down to a strea, lined with reeds and water lilies. Beds of perennials and bulbs, now browning in the lead-up to winter, that would be explosions of color in the spring.

"This is beautiful and peaceful, Hal. Thank you for suggesting—ordering—it. Are you the gardener?"

He was wrestling her bags inside and grunted. "No, my wife was the one who laid out the gardens. I just try to maintain them, though I do have someone who comes in a few times in the spring and summer to trim and neaten. Back here is your room."

She followed him down a short hall into a large room with a bed, a desk and a chaise under a floor lamp for reading. This room, too, overlooked the garden with deep casement windows that could be opened to catch a breeze.

"We can move the desk to the other side, closer to the windows, so you can get enough natural light. I assume that's how you prefer to work?" He dropped her bags by the closet as Sarah busied herself gathering towels and toiletries to stock the bathroom.

Footsteps echoed on the slate and a voice called, "Where do we put this?"

Roz turned to see three young constables carrying boxes of her glass and tools, her rolled cartoons and a new laptop.

"On the desk?" She glanced at Hal. It was his house.

"The desk is good. Jeremy," Fitzroy motioned to one of the constables, "help me move it under the windows."

The constables brought in two more loads of Roz' clothes, books and all that she'd left behind.

"That's it," Hal said. "Did you see Mrs. Lewes?"

"We did." The constable called Jeremy stood straight. "We told her, and those two other women, that Ms. Duke was being moved into 'protective custody' at a place we weren't able to disclose."

Protective custody? Well, Roz thought, it was as good a euphemism as any other.

CHAPTER FORTY-SEVEN

*I*n all the crime novels she'd read, Roz imagined protective custody as being locked in a third-rate hotel room with guards on the door who brought cheap sandwiches for all three meals.

This wasn't that. After a long shower and hair washing, helped by Sarah who was proving to be even more helpful that she first seemed, Roz changed into soft yoga pants with the side seam slit up to accommodate her cast and a cotton long-sleeved tee. Lunch came in on a tray, a bowl of thick vegetable soup and slices of homemade bread with butter.

Hal stuck his head in as she was eating. "Is everything alright? I asked Belinda, a friend who usually works at the pub, to come in and fix a couple of meals a day. Will she be OK?"

"OK? If this is protective custody, I may have to get used to it. The soup is delicious, and I haven't had homemade bread for ages." She took a sip of water, put down her spoon and took a deep breath.

"I think I own you somewhat of an apology." This was going to be hard. Roz spoke her mind and didn't usually feel she had anything to be excused for, but maybe she'd judged Hal too harshly. "I underestimated what you were doing to keep me safe and the lengths you were going to to find the traffickers. This is wonderful, Hal, and will make the rest of my stay in England memorable. Thank you."

Fitzroy nodded. "We help each other out. I'm off now, not sure when I'll be back. Belinda will come over and make dinner, Sarah will be back to get you ready for bed. I hope I'll see you in the morning." He spun around and headed out.

For the balance of the day, Roz arranged her working tools, sorted out her rolled cartoons for the stained glass panel and set up the desk, using the office chair as a surrogate wheelchair. She was going to have to start using the crutches if she wanted to venture outside the bedroom but wanted Sarah's help and tips on maneuvering.

Dinner, fish and chips with mushy peas, came on a tray as well, this time carried by Belinda who introduced herself with a cheery, "Hiya, I'm Belinda, not a true chef but I can do pub meals, hope you like this, how about a curry?"

"Hi Belinda, this is fine. It's a treat being served meals. I'm hoping to get up and around better so that you don't have to come over twice a day."

"Not a bother, I used to watch DI Fitzroy's son occasionally when his mum was busy so I'm familiar with the house." A shadow passed across the young woman's face and Roz understood that Hal and his family had deep roots in this small town. The accident affected him and his life more than Hal let on.

"He told me the bare bones of the accident that killed his wife and son, but I don't know any more than that. What were they like?" Not too invasive a question, after all Belinda brought it up.

"She was a wonder, had her own architecture firm that she ran from home so she could spend time with her son. Designed the renovations here." Belinda scanned the room. "In fact, she had a set-up much like yours, although what she called her office was what's the guest room. DI Fitzroy changed the rooms upstairs. Probably couldn't bear the constant reminders."

Everyone dealt with their grief in different way, Roz thought. She ran to a small town more than a thousand miles away from Winston's murder, Hal stayed but changed his surroundings. "How long ago was the accident?"

"Just over two years ago. Do you want a glass of wine?"

"No, thanks, I don't want to mix alcohol with my meds." Roz tried not to show her surprise at the swift change in subject. Had she stepped on hurts or crossed some boundary? Now she looked more carefully at Belinda. The woman in her late twenties, pretty in an unremarkable way, dark brown hair pulled into a ponytail, dark eyes full of good humor, easy to talk to, probably a good pub employee. Did she have more than a passing friendship with Hal?

"D'you mind if I look at your drawings while you eat? That way, I'll take your dishes away when you've finished."

"Not at all. Has DI Fitzroy told you what I'm working on?"

Belinda shrugged. "Not completely. He said you're a stained glass artist working on a commission for some university in the States. Pretty much all I know about stained glass is what I see in churches."

"That's where an awful lot of it ends up." Roz took a bite of her breaded fish. "This is really good! So much of what we get at home is from one of the chains and not very tasty."

The young woman's smile reached her eyes. "Thanks, I make the batter myself with beer. It's popular on our menu."

They chatted while Roz finished her meal and she learned that Belinda was born and raised in Rye, just a few miles down the coast from Hythe. She'd met a man who worked for the National Park System in South Downs and moved to Hythe. When the relationship soured, she'd stayed on, taking the job at the pub and settling into the community.

"And that's the story," Belinda said, gathering up Roz' dishes. "Nothing exciting, but Hythe has more life than Rye did and I enjoy meeting the tourists. A lot of them seem to be wandering around looking for William the Conqueror."

"I guess you could count me in with them," Roz said. "The commission I'm working on is to translate some of the Bayeux tapestry into stained glass."

Belinda politely nodded as she picked up the tray full of dishes. "I've never seen the tapestry, just some pictures in school. Only been to France twice on the ferry. Used to go with pals to drink cheap wine but they got so rowdy I quit going. I think the cleaner will bring you tea," she stopped, "or maybe coffee in the morning. I'll be back later to bring lunch."

Cheerful Belinda was pleasant company, but Roz was glad when she was replaced with Sarah. It had been a long day and she appreciated Sarah's help getting ready for bed. She and the therapist worked out a schedule for two exercise sessions, morning and afternoon, and practice using crutches. Sarah was confident that Roz would be moving well with crutches in a week and once that happened, she, Roz, could manage the garden for the last of the good fall weather.

In bed, Roz opened her Kindle and chose a recent bestseller to read herself to sleep. As she drifted off, she wondered if Hal had come home when she heard a door close and soft footsteps up the stairs. She was planning a conversation with him, laying out how the next six weeks would go and subtly digging into any relationship between him and Belinda. Did he know that the young woman might be interested? Was Roz interested herself? There was an attraction, but she didn't feel confident in her ability to read the signs and she wasn't even sure she knew how to flirt any more.

Well, she wasn't going anywhere, so she had plenty of time to practice.

CHAPTER FORTY-EIGHT

"It's good to hear your voice." Liam's American drawl filled Roz with homesickness.

"Thanks, it's so good to hear you, too. I love England but it's becoming clear it's just not home. How are you?"

A light laugh, then, "I think the question is really, how are you?"

"I'm much better, now. I'm in 'protective custody' which is different than I expected."

"Yeah, I got a call from Hal. Not much choice, he ordered you to stay at his house. Is it comfortable?"

Roz was quiet for a second. "It's more than comfortable. Fitzroy has given up his bedroom so I don't have to climb stairs and I'm working at a desk I think his late wife used. It's a little creepy."

"He didn't tell me that. Have you talked to him about it?"

"No, I don't want him to feel that I'm ungrateful. Plus, I've barely seen him in the last two days. Mostly I see Sarah, my physical therapist and Belinda, a woman from the pub who brings my lunch and dinner."

Now Liam did laugh. "Are you getting spoiled, being waited on?"

"What Sarah does is hardly being waited on. She's pushing me to use crutches, making me exercise twice a day to build up core muscles and the muscles in my thighs so that I don't walk crooked when the cast is off. I had no idea that I could baby my leg and possibly end up with a limp because I was unbalanced."

"When Hal told me he was moving you into his house for safety and rehab, I have to admit it made me uncomfortable. I wondered if he had other plans."

"I wouldn't worry about that." Roz felt the smile in her voice. "I think Belinda from the pub may have prior dibs."

"A hotbed of romance in the heart of the English countryside. If I wrote romance, I could weave a tale."

"Don't put too much into it, this is just my guess. I can't ask Hal because I haven't seen him, and I don't know Belinda well enough to broach the subject."

"Are you sorry you didn't come home?"

Was Liam curious or was there a note of disappointment there? "There's a tinge of regret, yes. You know when you're not feeling well, there's no comfort like home, all the familiar things. I am better off here, though. It's quiet, peaceful and I feel safe. I haven't put you in a position of taking care of me, I haven't had to navigate the rehab situation, let alone pay for all the care. I miss you, I miss the diner, I miss Tut dreadfully but I know when I do get home it'll be on my own two feet."

"Sounds like the Roz I know. How's it going on your project? Are you able to work?"

How was it going? Would she ever be able to look at the finished piece and separate it from all the danger and pain she'd gone through? "It's coming along. There's a large window overlooking the garden and I've taped a copy of my cartoon up to lay out the colors and cutting for the glass. In a week or so, as soon as I'm strong enough to move around easily with the crutches, Hal said he'd rig up a plywood table I can use to cut the glass and assemble the piece."

"You're not doing the whole thing are you?"

"No, I'm planning on something about three feet by maybe five feet. I want to have a sample to show Dean Longe as well as a springboard for the finished piece. The clerestory window space is five feet tall and runs 50 feet along one wall. This won't fill all the space, I think the tapestry part will be about 30 feet and the rest I'll fill in with large pieces in a random pattern." Enough. They were stuffing chatter into the void, not talking about what needed to be said.

She took a breath. "I guess you've talked to Hal about the ransom call for the glass?"

"I did. And I'm glad. We weren't coming up with anything. Even Sam and all his contacts didn't have a lead. I told Hal that the British government sites were dang good, not easily hacked. In hindsight, that's another reason for you to stay where you are."

"You think they'd be able to hack me easier at home?" Roz wasn't following that logic.

"Not hacked, your safety. If they traced you here— probably pretty easy to do—there'd be no protective custody. In fact, no police presence at all. Hal's got good connections in Europe, I think not so much here."

"You and Hal have gotten quite pally." Roz fought to keep the snit out of her voice, but Liam picked up on some.

"Not pally, we both have an interest in keeping you safe and alive. Hal because he wants to catch the bad guys and me…" Liam's voice dribbled off like a sudden rain in the desert.

CHAPTER FORTY-NINE

"*J*ules' is going to renovate this winter, they've already closed off the back room." Liam's abrupt change of topic spun Roz' brain around like a spin cycle. Was he uncomfortable with revealing too much to her, telling her how he felt?

"That's sensible, using the down time." She closed her eyes and saw the popular diner packed to overflowing during the summer tourist season with lines out the door. "Are they expanding?"

"Yep, they bought the next-door place, where the empty store was?"

A safe discussion, it brought waves of memories. She felt centered in Hamilton now and vested in the small town's events.

"I guess there'll be some changes when I get back. I hope it's not being gentrified." Roz remembered a trip to Mendocino with Winston a few years ago when cars were sporting bumper stickers with "Don't Carmelize Mendocino," a jab at the chi-chiness that overcame the former artist's colony by Monterey.

Liam laughed. "I don't think so, we're a working town, loggers and fishermen and will keep our roots. Summers, well, that's not who we really are. Stay here in January and you'll see our bones. Can you see Jurgen getting frou-frou?"

"No, no I can't," Roz said, picturing the giant Scandinavian who owned the Fisherman's Friend, Liam's second favorite restaurant.

"I like that you're talking about changes when you come home." She heard longing in Liam's voice and warmth bloomed in her stomach. Maybe she needed to concentrate on the unspoken message, though not being able to watch his face, his body, for telltale clues to his emotions made it difficult.

"I don't know how long it'll be." Roz propped the phone up against her laptop as she struggled to find a comfortable position. "At least until I can master the crutches. I'll work hard." Then, "Is Tut there? I haven't heard him."

"He's asleep in your bedroom. We came over to your house and had a long run on the beach. I'll give him a love from you. I know he misses you, too."

Too? "I miss you guys. I need to get back to work if I'm going to head home soon. I'll call again in a day or so."

******

Roz stared out at the waning day beginning to shadow Hal's garden, her eyes unfocused, her mind on the Oregon beach and the soft hiss of the flat Pacific waves. When she arrived in England, she felt a sense of coming home. The land felt familiar, the expanses of rolling hills, the tidy fields, the green, everywhere the green. The light was tempered, not as harsh as the Southern California sun, not as damp as the coastal Oregon mist. The pace of life in the small towns and villages comforted and didn't challenge like the hectic LA heartbeat.

She wasn't sorry she'd taken this leave. It had been good work, good research, solid craft and she'd stretched her abilities. The South Kentish coast was lovely, hills dotted with sheep, the downs in the distance, the now-small towns and villages that played such an outsized role in the history of this land. Maybe it was time, though. As much as she'd enjoyed her personal time with Hal, it wasn't what she knew she needed for the long term.

Tapestry of Tears

A tap on the door and Sarah stuck her head in.

"Are you ready to tackle your evening exercises? I know it's early yet, but if you get them over with, you'll have time to relax before bed."

"Yes, you're right. I just got off the phone with my friend in Oregon and he was asking how much longer I'd be here. I told him I was going to work extra hard at getting it together. I discovered I miss home and him and my dog."

"You have a dog? What kind?" Sarah was setting up chairs and exercise bands to strengthen Roz' balance and arms for the crutches.

"He's a rescue greyhound, he'd been bred for dog races and the training was abusive. He runs like the wind, but he's a big softy inside and want mostly to curl up with me. Here." She leaned over to her laptop to pull up a picture of Tut on the beach then, "Oh, lord, I forgot. The police have my old laptop because it was hacked. I only have a few of my design files on this one." She sighed. "And my phone as well."

"I can imagine him." Sarah came over and helped Roz to balance on her good foot while tucking crutches under her arms and straightening her spine. "That's it, let your arms take the weight, not your shoulders. Now use your hips to swing your body forward a step."

Roz managed about twenty minutes practice before she fell back into the chair. "I know I have to keep at it, but just gaining my strength is hard right now." She reached over for her phone. "I have an idea. No one knows this phone number and my friend, Liam has a burner phone as well, I'll ask him to take a picture of Tut on the beach and send it to me."

"Don't go to all that trouble for me." Sarah wound the bands up.

"It's no trouble, besides, I need to have a picture of him! I forgot they're all locked up in my hacked computer." She tapped a message to Liam, waited for about ten minutes then heard a ping.

"Here he is." Liam had taken a picture of Tut on Roz' bed and another shot of him on the back deck leading out to the beach. He was alert, his head cocked as though saying hello.

Sarah oohed appreciatively. "He's a beauty. And is this your house?"

Roz nodded, a lump forming in her throat. "Yes, my back deck faces the ocean. There's a flat, smooth beach that runs for about four miles along that part of the coast. Hal, DI Fitzroy, took me to dinner in Dymchurch and the beach there it reminded me of home."

"I can see why you want to get home it looks like a lovely spot. I'll stay and help you get ready for bed and then see you in the morning?"

"Thanks, Sarah. I'm tired tonight. Do you know if DI Fitzroy is home? I'd like to talk to him."

"I'll go ask when I leave. Is it alright that you're ready for bed when he comes in?"

Roz smiled. "Oh, I think so! He's seen me in the hospital both here and in France, so I don't think there's much he hasn't seen."

When Hal tapped on the door, Roz was propped up in bed, her leg elevated, wearing a long sleep shirt.

"I'm glad to see you in bed and resting." Hal came in the room, moved over to the bed and sat on the edge. "I've been busy so sorry I didn't check in on you. Is everything alright? Are you comfortable? Is the food OK? Is Sarah pushing you?"

"Yes, yes and yes." Roz answered with a grin. "You've been more than hospitable. I talked to Liam earlier and said if this was protective custody, give it to me any day."

"Good. And I'm happy you talked to Liam. Did he tell you the news about the ransom?"

Tapestry of Tears

"He did. He said that he and Sam had gotten no where and your security was probably better than ours."

"I don't know about that, but we spent a lot of years playing spies during the last half-century so we've learned some things." He grinned again. "Just look at James Bond and John LeCarre."

"Yes, but those are fiction."

"Fiction built on some facts. We did have a few spy scandals in the 1960 and 70s. We tightened things up a lot after those. I don't have much new to report. Jocelyn and Phoebe have packed up and headed out and I'm eternally grateful I stopped your travel plans with them. We're keeping watch."

"Keeping watch? On Jocelyn? Why?"

Hal picked up Roz' Kindle and scrolled through some pages.

"Are you avoiding me?

He looked up. "No, not avoiding. There's just something about those two that makes me curious. You remember your movie about the hapless character, Forrest Gump? The dim guy who always seemed to be in the middle of events through no fault of his own?"

"Yes, but do you think those women..."

"I don't know what I think. They seemed to always be around when anything befell you then were on the spot when it came to giving you a 'safe' place."

"But that's just coincidence. After all, we were staying at the same place, looking at the same things. Had similar interests in the Conquest and the Tapestry."

"True, but then things are coincidences until they aren't."

"Do you have any specific reasons to doubt them?"

"I'm not sure I 'doubt' them, they just bear watching for a bit. We still have a major trafficking ring to deal with. This isn't going to get put together tonight, maybe not this week, but hopefully soon, we're putting a lot of resources into it. I have a few constables taking shifts in the guest room. They have orders not to bother you, but if you get nervous, call on them. I'm going to be in and out for the next few days."

"Where are you going?" Then Roz put her hand over her mouth. "I probably shouldn't ask you that."

"No, you shouldn't, but I'm going to Europe to meet with some people." Hal stood. "I'll check in when I get back. I may have some good news about your 'protective custody'."

CHAPTER FIFTY

The next few days moved like a placid river, falling into a rhythm of exercise periods, hours of intense glass cutting and work, good meals, an hour or so when Sarah would help Roz out to the garden to practice using crutches on irregular surfaces.

As the bruises on her body and soul began to heal, Roz started looking forward to finishing up the panel. Hal had asked a police carpenter to put together a large, flat plywood surface for Roz to assemble the glass, cut the cames and commence soldering. The plywood would become part of the wooden box the panel would get shipped home in. Once home, the panel would get framed and taken to the university committee responsible for letting the commission.

Now that she was on the downhill side of the window's construction, Roz spent longer and longer standing, fitting and soldering, wanting to finish and see if her vision was true. After her evening exercises, which helped relieve the stress of standing and leaning over and strengthened her arms and shoulders, she fell into bed at night. Worn out but elated with her progress.

She talked to Liam twice more, checking-in phone calls, keeping up her headway on work and recovery, but not mentioning Hal's "protective custody" comment. If the traffickers were arrested, she'd have even more reason to head to Oregon. She told Liam she had a doctor's appointment the next week where they'd monitor how she was doing and maybe move on to a boot. And once she was in a boot, even though the doctors still wanted her to use her crutches as much as possible, it would be time to start toward home.

With a plan and an aim, Roz felt more centered than she had since she stumbled on Ilic's body in the Lympne church. That was fading in her memory. It was unfortunate, but the fool had brought it upon himself, trying to pull off a side deal with his handlers. Particularly, she thought, by getting involved with the theft of a part of England's heritage. What possessed him to think he could double deal the mob as well as the British government?

One afternoon Brenda came in early with dinner, tonight's a shepherd's pie full of lamb, veggies, piled with whipped potatoes and topped with cheese.

"I am exercising, but not enough to work that off," Roz said eying the dish which smelled glorious.

"Eat what you want." Brenda brought another plate and dished up a serving. "This is good for the pub as well, it won't go to waste. I came a bit early because Sarah has been telling us about your work here and how wonderful it is. I'm wondering if I might have a peek?"

"Of course." Roz crutched over to the sheet of plywood. "At home, I'd have it in a frame and put it against a west-facing window so the colors would come alive. But you'll have to imagine some of it."

Brenda carefully moved over to the plywood sheet as Roz pointed out some of the horses, the boats, the Normans gathering supplies, the comet over Westminster and King Harold on his throne. The young woman sucked in a breath.

"I've never known how stained glass got put together. It's like a giant puzzle, isn't it? How do you know what goes where?"

Roz unrolled some of her cartoons, showing Brenda how the drawings became the cutting patterns for the glass, how the colors worked to make the piece vibrant, how to cut and fit the cames to give strength and solidity to the piece.

"I always heard about the Conquest, but I had no idea what it really was. It was just a big battle in a small village. Funny how little things like that can make huge changes." She laughed. "Rather like me running off to live with the Ranger then ending up here as a cook and barmaid. Life treats you in strange ways."

"What do you think you want to do with your life?" Roz felt Brenda had begun the topic, so she wasn't being too prying. Maybe she could suss out any interest in Hal.

And Brenda bit. "I'm taking a course in Police Science at the community school."

"Do you want to be a police officer?" Roz stared at the young woman.

"I'm not sure, but I thought it would give me more things to talk to Hal, DI Fitzroy about." A blush rose into her hairline.

"Ah, you're interested in him?"

"Interested? I suppose. I was crazy about his wife and son. She was so alive, so creative and she was such a good mom. I saw how destroyed he was when they died. I've been thinking I could maybe ease his sorrow." She stopped, reddened. "Not to replace his wife, I've never be able to do that, but to give him some solace."

Solace. That's what she missed with Winston's death. Learning who shot him helped. Knowing it was an accident—wrong time, wrong place—helped as well. But true peace and consolation wouldn't come until she understood why he'd been in that wrong place and time.

"I think that's admirable, Brenda. My husband was killed as well, in an accidental shooting, and I still ache in the middle of the night. Has Hal indicated he might be interested?"

Brenda shook her head, closed her eyes. "I'm too nervous to approach him. He's always perfectly polite and asks me for small favors like bringing your meals, but it's been very gentlemanly." She went silent, then, "I wondered if he was getting interested in you."

Roz sucked in a breath. "I don't know. There were some indications—and he did kiss me once—but once he and my friend Liam began talking, I felt Hal pulled back a bit."

"So, is Liam your boyfriend?"

Was he? Good question. "I don't know. We're good friends, enjoy each other's company, have curiosity in common. He's crazy about my dog…"

"You have a dog? Where is he?"

Roz went through the tale she'd told Sarah and whipped out her phone to show Brenda, who oohed at Tut. "He's a handsome boy. I'd like to have a dog, but my landlady has a strict no pets rule. Enough people bring their dogs to the pub that I do get some time with them, but it's not the same as your own." She glanced at the time on the phone, said, "Oh, I have to run, get ready for the dinner crowd," picked up the dishes and left with a "Ta, see you tomorrow."

There were skeins and skeins wound around this small English town. Roz was appreciating the similarities with Hamilton and understood people had more in common than differences, yet there still needed to be a home. And as much as she felt comfortable here, it's wasn't home.

CHAPTER FIFTY-ONE

The panel was nearing completion. Roz estimated another two weeks would finish it, then she'd have to find some specialized shippers to construct the wooden crate it would travel in to Wisconsin. At home, she'd done some research and had three companies she used to move either partial or completed pieces, but here she narrowed it down to calling the British Museum for recommendations.

There was a firm in Canterbury. She called and made an appointment for someone to come, check out the panel and give her an estimate. Their estimator was available in a week, she set the appointment and got back to work.

Between Sarah's exercise routines and Roz standing for longer and longer periods, leaning over the plywood, fitting and soldering, she was gaining strength and balance. One day Sarah drove her to a doctor's appointment and, after an ex-ray, was pronounced "healing well" and told she'd be able to be in a walking boot in three weeks.

With her commission wrapping up and her physical state improved, she was nearing the end of her sabbatical and began focusing her thoughts west. The panel was only one of the things she needed to get ready to ship. All of her tools, extra glass, books, drawings, personal items had to be gone through and sorted. Would it be sensible to ship everything home? No, of course not, so there were two days spent with the bedroom in a clutter of piles, some things already in boxes, some waiting for packing.

She was rolling and unrolling cartoons of her original designs, choosing which ones might make a good display of the art of stained glass making as an extra exhibit for the university when someone tapped on the door.

"Come in," she called, assuming it was Sarah, when Hal's voice brought her up short. She whirled around.

"You're back!" Good one, Roz, she thought, point out the obvious. "When did you come home?"

"We took the Chunnel, got to Dover about noon, stopped at the office. It looks like something exploded in here. What are you doing?"

She cleared a spot on the bed, sat and patted a place next to her.

"I have an almost 'all clear' from the doctor so I'm beginning to pack up. In a couple of weeks, I'll be out of your hair." She paused. "That is, unless I'll still be in 'protective custody'?"

"I don't think so." He smiled. "My trip to Europe was productive, we've wrapped up most of the ring, arrested about twenty of the traffickers, shut down the Eastern European end. There are still a few loose ends, two guys we think living in England who are out in the wind, but we have enough description that it's only a matter of time until we have them as well."

"That's wonderful. I haven't heard anything on the news about it."

"And you won't until we have the last few. We'll probably only announce we found and charged the people who were responsible for the deaths in the truck outside Dover. We want to keep a low profile because there are so many enforcement agencies and so many countries involved. No one is taking the lead on this."

"What about the stained glass?"

He looked at her blankly, then. "Ahh, the Westminster glass. That's the catalyst that got us involved in this, but it turned out to be more of a red herring. Yes, we're going to announce that the glass has been found. It never left Britain and was, in fact, being held for ransom. Her Majesty's government didn't pay the ransom but was able to recover the glass."

Roz looked at him. "That's a bit of a white lie, isn't it?"

"It may be, but we think these ends justify those means. We didn't do a media blitz when the glass went missing, so we're not blasting it's recovery." He grinned, she said "What?"

"We're also not going to blast that we're working with the church to beef up security. This was just a warning theft. They own enormous treasures, not to the level of the Catholic church, but riches nonetheless. A stolen piece of church art may not be able to be sold, but the idea of ransom lights up some people's eyes."

"Are you home for good, then?"

"Back in England, yes. I may not be home in Hythe yet, though. Depends on how successful we'll be tracking down the last few of the gang. The ones on this end were the ones who made the placements for the women, and children, to be sold as sex slaves."

He stood and walked to the window, taking in the peaceful garden. "Those are the ones I want to get. They deserve more than we can do to them. The dregs who view people as commodities. There's no punishment too bad for them."

"Are you ready for your room, your home, back? I could move back to the church for a week or two until I can actually leave."

"No, no, that's not necessary. I have a place I can stay when I'm in the area and we may have rolled up the bulk of the traffickers, but there are still a few around, so I'm more comfortable with you being here, and in 'protective custody'," he glanced over at her, "until we have everyone. "

"Roz, are you ready? I've brought dinner." Brenda's voice came from the hall.

Hal and Roz came out of the bedroom and Roz said, "Brenda, look who's come home. Do you have enough to feed him? We can eat in the dining room. There's not a place to set a dish down in the bedroom.

The young woman's face split into a wide grin. "Welcome home, Inspector! Yes, it's a curry and there's more than enough. I'm never sure how much Roz will eat, so I err on the side of plenty. Let me put this in the kitchen and get the table set up, you can eat in a sec."

As she bustled around, Hal followed, asking what she needed help with, and Roz stood balanced on her crutches, smiling. A comfortable group for a meal.

"Have you had any problems with the constables I've assigned to you?" Hal handed Brenda plates and utensils while she took lids off bowls of steaming curry and rice.

"No." Roz felt surprise wash through her. "I'd forgotten there was even one here. I've never seen or heard him, or her." Then she remembered the soft steps on the stairs, which she'd assumed were Hal. Maybe it was the constable, heading up before she was asleep and leaving before she was up in the morning.

"Good. I told each of them they weren't to disturb you. Tomorrow I'm assigning Jeremy, you met him when he moved you in."

"I did and he seemed like a nice young man. I'll make it a point to say hello." Roz pushed her chair back from the table. "I have to stop eating so much of Brenda's meals! I'll gain weight and never be able to haul this body around on my crutches."

Hal watched her. "I doubt that will be a problem," he said, and smiled.

CHAPTER FIFTY-TWO

"That's great news." Roz could hear the excitement in Liam's voice and smiled to herself. Good, someone besides Tut wanted her around.

"It is." She knew that by making this call and telling Liam she'd be coming back she made her choice known. Now all she had to do was to figure out how much she wanted Liam in her life and discover if she wanted an intimate relationship.

"I'm assembling the panel now. I have a shipper recommended by the British Museum coming the first part of next week to talk about building a crate and give me cost estimates."

"That's going to be expensive." Liam sounded worried.

"Probably, but the university is paying the freight. Assuming they'll commission the final window, this can be part of an interactive display about the research and background that goes into producing a historical exhibit."

"Does this mean you'll go to Wisconsin instead of coming home?"

Home. She closed her eyes and stepped into the warmth of the familiar. As much as she loved England, Oregon was her home now. "No, I'll be flying into Portland. It will take longer to ship to panel back, so I'll fly to Madison when it gets there and help uncrate it. Probably plan to stay a few days." She paused to take a breath. "Is there someone who can pick me up?"

A low chuckle. "Are you playing the coy game with me now?"

"Well, maybe a bit."

"You know full well Tut and I will be there to pick you up. With a brass band."

"Thank you, although you don't have to bring Tut if that's an inconvenience."

"He's going to be more excited than me to see you. Of course, I'm bringing him."

Roz felt warmth climbing up her chest. This man knew some of her buttons and pushed the positive ones. "I haven't looked at flights yet, but I'll try to book something that gets in in the afternoon."

"Don't worry about it. If it's an evening flight we can stay in my condo. Tut's familiar with it now and there's an elevator if you'll still be on crutches."

"Thank you. I may be in a boot, but the orthopedics guys here want me to keep as much weight off it as I can, so, yeah, I'm thinking crutches."

She could almost hear Liam thinking. "Hmmm, it may be a good idea to stay in Portland for a day or two anyway, get you to a doctor here, figure out any rehab. Do you want me to start looking around?"

"Thanks. I doubt I'll find a top-notch ortho guy in Hamilton." She paused. "What will I find in Hamilton? Anything different?"

"No, the big news is Jules' expansion and I already told you about that. We're just plugging away. Life doesn't move at jet speed here."

Now Roz chuckled. "I know, and I'm looking forward to it!"

By the time she got home, Roz would spend close to six months in England on what was initially planned as a three-month trip. She'd left Oregon in late spring, missed the massive influx of tourists and was returning in the fall. In time to celebrate the traditional American Thanksgiving holiday. She wrapped her mind around cooling days, pumpkins, turkey, spiced lattes.

Liam did a precis of what their friends were up to, Roz brought him up to date on Hal's search for the last few gang members and they hung up, her to picture home before she went to sleep and him to write ten pages on his newest novel in progress.

As she drifted off, she heard soft footsteps up the stairs. Probably Hal, she thought to herself.

*****

Roz woke to rain. Sarah came in peeling off a damp Macintosh and put a takeout- coffee and bun on Roz's desk.

"The wet weather held off for quite a time this year, but we're in for it now. It's what keeps things green, but I do get tired of slogging season." She went to the mud room behind the kitchen, hung up her wet things and took off her Wellies. Roz smiled. Wellies were year-round but came into their own in the winter.

"I talked to my friend in Oregon last night," Roz said. "He's planning to pick me up and is checking out orthopedic and rehab doctors in the Portland area. Will there be any problem in getting my records, X-rays and stuff sent home?"

"I shouldn't think so. I'll call and get things started on this end. When are you planning to travel?"

"It might be another week or ten days. I have a shipper coming next week for sending the panel to the university. Then a few days to construct the crate, I imagine."

Steps sounded in the hall and Roz looked up to see Hal shaking off an umbrella.

"Oh, I didn't hear you go out," Roz said.

"I didn't go out I'm only just coming in." Hal stuck his umbrella in a stand, came into the bedroom. "It's a nasty day out, started raining in the early hours."

"You were out in it? I thought I heard you heading upstairs last evening."

"No, we were out watching a warehouse. We'd had a tip that they brought children there before sending them off to the 'buyers'." Hal had a slight frown. "You heard steps?"

"I have a few times. I always assumed it was you. Maybe it's the constable who's staying here?"

"It must be but going upstairs to their bedroom shouldn't be a bother."

"They haven't been a bother, most times I forget they're here." She waved her hand at the plywood panel taking up room next to the desk. "I'm getting to the end. Would you like to see?"

He nodded and walked over to the panel. "I'm not sure I can picture this with light behind it. It looks impressive and I'm amazed at how you're piecing it together, like a jigsaw puzzle. Will it ship?"

Roz went over the arrangements, then, "Museums and galleries do this all the time. The Egyptian Tut exhibit was a logistical nightmare. It's a bit spendy, but doable."

"I'll let you get back to it." Hal's attention roamed around the room, taking in all the signs of packing up. "It seems you're making progress towards leaving."

"Some. I still have to sort some things out. Not sure how much glass I want to take home. I'm still at the point of 'pick it up, can't decide, put it down again'."

He glanced over at her. Did she see a scowl?'

"Remember, you're under protective custody until we get the last of the gang. The ones out in the wind are the ones more dangerous to you. One of them is the guy who attacked you in the church garden."

"If you have the bosses, why would the men here want to harm me? Ilic is dead and his murder is solved, I wasn't a witness to anything else they were doing, how can I be in danger?"

"Your attacker confessed to you. We may know now who killed Ilic, but that doesn't mean we're disinterested in arresting his murderer. Your description is helping us find him as well." He paused, then, "I've been up all night. I'm going to take a shower and sleep for a few hours. Maybe I'll drop in before I head out again."

His footsteps on the stairs sounded different from the others she'd heard.

CHAPTER FIFTY-THREE

Roz leaned over to unplug the soldering iron and almost lost her balance when Hal said, "I'm off. Hope I have some good news when I see you next."

She leaned on the edge of the desk, careful not to jostle the plywood. "Are you going back to the warehouse?"

"Yes, unless some other, better lead comes in. We've had reports of strange goings-on, trucks coming in at night, voices and shouts. It's supposed to be abandoned, no one around." He came over and touched her shoulder. "Have a good night, see you tomorrow probably."

The brief exchange left her feeling awkward, slightly out of sorts. He hadn't stepped over any boundaries, yet she felt something was unsaid. She stared at the door for a few seconds, shrugged and went back to putting her tools away.

Coming out of the bathroom, she heard a cheery "Hello" in the foyer and followed Brenda into the kitchen.

"What do we have tonight? It smells wonderful."

"I made goulash. Even managed to find some Hungarian paprika to spice it up a bit. Some of the regulars don't like it, say it's too 'foreign' but visitors eat it up." The young woman was bustling around, finding dishes and utensils. "Is himself going to join you tonight?"

"Himself? Oh, you mean Hal, no, he's working, out..." Roz stopped. She shouldn't say that Hal and his team were keeping watch for the rest of the traffickers. She finished with, "He said he'd see me in the morning."

"Just you then. Do you want to eat now?"

"I have a few more things to put away. I'll eat later and watch some news. I haven't kept up with anything that's going on in the world."

Brenda wrinkled her nose. "Not sure there's a lot. Usual squabbles in Parliament over that stupid Brexit and a big storm is headed up the Channel. They're cutting back the bus schedules for the winter, not so many tourists and people on holiday." She looked at Roz, "You maybe wouldn't like it here in the winter, not much to do, some shops closed, not much traffic,"

Roz grinned. "Oh, I suspect it's much like home. Where I live, it's crammed with tourists in the summer, empty during the winter. We like the peace the winter brings, but so much of the town depends on the dollars the tourists spend. It's a mixed blessing."

"Same here." Belinda nodded. "Better get back, there'll be some early diners. I left enough in case the Inspector comes in later. See you tomorrow."

Dinner was delicious when Roz warmed it up and ate while watching television news. Brenda was right, not a lot going on and not a word about the arrest of the trafficking ring, but warnings of heavy rain, wind and possible coastal flooding.

Hal's house withstood the wind, only an occasional gust that rattled branches against the windows. Roz watched rain battering the back garden, pulled the drapes closed and got ready for bed. Sarah had cut back her exercise workouts to only one in the morning, saying if Roz was planning to head home she needed to be independent.

She was drifting off when she heard footsteps on the stairs, not Hal, probably the constable. Why was he coming in so late during the storm?

A huge thunderclap crashed her awake and she lay there hearing pounding rain. Reached over to turn on the bedside lamp, but no, no electricity. Scooted to the edge of the bed, grabbed her cell, hit the flashlight and made her way to the window. Rain was coming down so hard she couldn't see beyond the roses lining the house that were being flattened by the storm.

A massive bolt of lightning lit the room in an eerie blue wash and she screamed. There was someone here.

The man moved toward her and she saw he had a uniform on. The constable. She relaxed.

Then he reached out for her phone. The cell flashlight beam hit his hand as he grabbed at it and she saw that the tip of his little finger was missing.

"I'll take that," he said, his voice guttural.

"Jeremy? Constable? Which one are you?" There were several who took turns staying at the house and she hadn't met all of them.

"Ha. That fool is upstairs in the bedroom. Didn't even hear me when I hit him with the needle. Now it's your turn."

Roz had hopped from the bed to the window, not wanting to bother with crutches, and stood, leaning against the side of the desk. Trapped. She couldn't run, for sure couldn't hop fast enough to get away, threw her hands up in front of her to push him away.

It wasn't happening. He slapped her hands down and she saw a gleam from a hypodermic needle lit by the cell's light. Tried to turn away from the needle but he was too fast, and she felt it jab into her arm. Woozy, she was unable to stop herself sliding to the floor, then felt his arms pulling her up.

As she lost consciousness, she felt him lift her up, carry her out the bedroom door.

******

She swam back to awareness, her arms aching. Wanted to move them but couldn't. Her mouth was dry, her tongue seemed swollen and left her unable to make a sound. Found she couldn't open her mouth at all and realized it was taped shut. Wiggled her fingers, pulled at her arms and felt them plastic zip-tied to the back slats of a wooden chair.

That's when she opened her eyes. She was in a room, maybe an office with a desk and two chairs besides the one that held her. Along one wall a window glowed with a faint light, showing a larger space, absorbed by the gloom. The door to the room opened, letting in the man with the missing fingertip.

"You're awake. Do you know where you are?" He grinned. "Oh, forgot you can't talk." He walked over and ripped the duct tape off her mouth, taking a layer of the skin of her lips with it. Tears instantly filled her eyes from the pain, but she wouldn't give him the satisfaction of watching her cry.

"What do you want?" Her scratchy voice startled her. She cleared her throat and tried again. "Who are you?"

"Who I am doesn't matter. And what I want is for your boyfriend to stop trying to arrest us." The accent jarred her memory. This was the guy from the garden.

"I don't have any ability to call him off." Roz had read a lot of crime fiction books and knew the conventional wisdom said he'd go easier on her if she kept him talking. Pretending an interest in his plans.

"Nice try." He squatted down in front of her. "We know who you are and that you're famous. There are people here and in the States who will pay for your safety. You shouldn't have stuck you nose in our business."

Kidnapped? Were they planning to ask for ransom?

Her Majesty's government said they'd pay a ransom for the Westminster stained glass, but that was a piece of British heritage. And Hal said they didn't pay it, anyway. Was that why the thugs who were out in the wind, daring the cops to catch them, so angry?

What was she? A noted artist with no family, no patron. She had some money from Winston's killing but could she get to it? It was tied up in investments and still in the States, not easily accessible. The British government wouldn't pay, neither would the American one. Liam had no money to speak of.

If they asked for a ransom, how would anyone pull it together? And what if they didn't?

CHAPTER FIFTY-FOUR

Roz had difficulty making her mouth move, her lips were on fire though the intense pain eased.

"I'm thirsty," she croaked.

"So?"

"Please, can I have some water?"

Her kidnapper grunted then went out to the area beyond the office. Roz strained her vision and saw that the open space was a vast empty building. An abandoned factory? She couldn't see any machinery, just a few rows of stacked boxes lit by windows high at the tops of walls.

Light. This must mean it was day. She cast her mind back to pull fragments of memory. She'd been asleep when the huge thunderbolt woke her and she discovered the electricity was off. Hopped to the window to watch the pelting rain and flashes of lightning and felt there was someone in the room with her.

Not the constable Jeremy, but this thug with the missing fingertip, the one who'd attacked her in the church garden. He'd said to go ahead and scream, no one would hear her and jabbed a needle into her arm as she tried to fight him off. Then, nothing.

He came back with a bottle of water, tried to hand it to her and laughed.

"I guess you can't open it. Or hold it."

Raz hoped this meant he'd undo the zip-ties. No. He opened the water and held it to her mouth, grinning when she gulped and spilled it down the shirt she'd been sleeping in.

"Don't want to waste much of this, there's not any more where this came from."

She gingerly ran her tongue over her torn lips, the coolness of the water easing the burn slightly.

"What's your name?"

"Why would you want to know that?" The man stared at her and Roz felt like a specimen on a glass slide, about to be dissected.

"I just want to know what to call you. Can't keep saying 'hey you'."

"You can call me Josef."

"Josef? Is that Polish or…"

"Doesn't matter. It's not my real name and you'll never know where I'm from. Trying to get some identification? Thinking you'll be able to tell someone?"

Roz' heart constricted. Was he meaning she wouldn't be ransomed? After all this, he'd just kill her? Keep him talking, her rational mind said.

"What do you mean?"

"We're sending a note now, not a phone call, too easy to track."

"A note? For what?"

"How to get you back. Keep you from being killed." He laughed again.

"What do you want?"

"To get out of this blasted country."

"Why'd you come here if you hate it?"

He made a face, picked up an old telephone from the desk and threw it against the wall where it shattered. "The boss thought it would make us more money. When the EU formed, there weren't any borders anymore. People moved around wherever they felt like and the labor market changed. People from middle Europe, the former Soviet states, moved to the richer Western countries and undercut our market for cheap slave workers. We used to charge a lot to get people into France, Germany, Britain on false visa and work permits, but those weren't needed any more. You didn't like it in Bulgaria? Wages too low? Pack your bag and move to Germany where unskilled workers were needed."

She'd had him pegged as a brainless thug, now she had to rethink. He was articulate, seemed knowledgeable about the politics of the EU and his speech was educated.

"So what changed?" Roz didn't care, anything to keep him talking.

"Brexit."

"I don't understand. I'm American and don't know what that meant."

He gave her a look of disdain. "You Americans, you think you're so superior and you're just a bunch of stuck-up snobs who don't give a shit about the rest of the world."

Roz didn't feel like she needed to carry the flag, she needed to get away. "Well, why did Brexit make a change?"

"Eastern Europeans stopped moving here and companies that depended on cheap labor were desperate. The British didn't want to do farm work or clean toilets or sweep streets, they were too good for this. So our workers were in demand again."

She watched as his eyes went vacant, then, "As we were bringing workers in, we realized it didn't have to be just those kinds of workers. We could bring in women, children, rent them out by the hour for sex, not sell them to a factory."

Roz' stomach rebelled, and she threw up the sips of water, continued until there was nothing to bring up but bile.

Josef watched impassively. As her retching slowed, he threw the remains of the water at her. "Does that bother you?"

She nodded, too wrung out and stunned to respond any more than that.

He walked out into the large area again and she heard him opening something then close it with a slam. He came back in with another bottle of water.

"We haven't had our usual amount of traffic since they arrested the boss and all the others. We did have more water." He uncapped it, threw some at her mouth to wash off the vomit, then poured some in her mouth.

She gagged, swallowed and ahhhh, through her foggy brain, Roz understood where she was. A place where they brought the new women and children who they'd use as sex slaves. This was a holding place. And a sudden insight. Was this the warehouse that Hal and the others were staking out?

CHAPTER FIFTY-FIVE

*J*osef whirled around and ran into the warehouse when a loud bang reverberated through the building. Roz heard him yelling at someone in a guttural language and the someone answered. She didn't understand the words, but the tone was clear—the two men were pissed at each other.

The shouts reached a crescendo then became slaps against flesh and a woman moaned. Someone was beating up a woman. One of the sex slaves? It had to be a woman who'd been trafficked earlier because the authorities managed to shut the ports and entries after their roundup in Europe.

The male voices were louder, still arguing. Nearing the office? Then Josef came through the door, dragging a young woman by the arm. He threw her into the office, she landed, hard, against the wall and slid down.

Behind him, the other man had a younger woman, a girl, by the hair. She stumbled as he pushed her into the office and fell against the first woman.

"These two will keep you company until we move everyone out." Josef said something to the women in a different language, then continued the argument with the other man. Whatever they were quarreling about, it was clear from the tone that Josef was the boss. The second man fought back verbally, then turned and grumbled his way out of the office and back into the gloom.

Roz watched Josef, wondering if he was the one who'd hit the woman. He may be higher up, not just hired muscle as she'd originally thought, but the facts remained he'd attacked her in the church's garden, dragging her by the hair, and kidnapped her from Hal's house, drugging her rather that beating her. Either way, she was his prisoner, tied to a chair, unable to move.

She didn't speak until he, too, walked back into the cavernous warehouse and she head his footsteps recede until even the echoes tapered off.

When she was sure he was gone, she whispered "Who are you?"

No answer.

She spoke louder. "Tell me who you are. Have you been kidnapped, too?"

The first woman, who Roz saw was little more than a girl herself, whispered back in the same guttural language that the men spoke. Roz squinched up her forehead and shook her head. "I'm sorry, I don't speak that language," and the young woman nodded.

"We came to work but not." Her voice was quiet, her English spoken with a heavy accent.

"Where are you from?"

"Romania." The woman scooted across the floor and cradled the girl in her arms, talking softly in Romanian.

"Do you know her?" Roz wanted to get as much information as she could. If she ever got out of here, maybe she could give Hal some leads.

"She my sister."

"Oh. How old is she? How old are you?"

"Eighteen." The older one pointed to herself. "My name Stefka. She Bettina. She fourteen." Gestured to the younger girl in her arms.

"You're babies! What happened?"

"Not babies, women. We sign up to come work in England, no work in Romania. Supposed to be waitress at fancy hotel or nanny to rich people. Got here and were forced to go with men." Here she put her hands together and mimicked intercourse. Roz thought her English didn't stretch enough to know the words.

The girl looked at Roz. "Bad men. I didn't like. They beat me." She turned, pulled up her tattered dress and Roz saw yellowing bruises and fresh marks from a belt or a cane on the backs of her thighs.

"Oh no, I'm so sorry." Roz was fighting back tears. She felt angry and helpless, but she was older, more sophisticated, stronger and in a familiar place, speaking her own language. She couldn't wrap her head around what these two young women had gone through.

"Why did Josef and the other man bring you here?"

The sisters spoke to each other rapidly, perhaps, Roz thought, figuring out what to say and wondering if they could trust her. They were silent for a few seconds, then the older one said, "Bettina pregnant," stroking her younger sister's hair.

"She's pregnant? But she's only fourteen…" then Roz remembered some of the statistics of teen pregnancy at home. Of course it was possible, particularly if you were being raped by how many men a day?

"Wouldn't they take care of her?"

"They try to make her get rid of it. She's too scared. Mortal sin. We're Catholic."

The picture was becoming clearer. Two young women, possibly not the youngest ones ever trafficked, probably answered an ad or found a "recruiter" who promised them and their hungry families money and a chance at a better life in England. The girls, or perhaps their father, signed papers that they work to pay off their transportation costs and when the debt was paid, a part of their wages would be sent back to the family.

This never happened. Roz had read some stories about this trafficking but never thought she'd end up in the midst of it. Some of the older women who were lured into this scheme did end up working, but at non-skilled sweatshop jobs where they were locked into their dorms at night and locked into the factory during the day. If they were lucky, they'd get two meager meals a day.

"Did you ever get a job here? Did your father sign the papers for you to come here?"

"No." Stefka shook her head. "They put us in big room with other girls and men come in and point at the girl they want."

Hal had told her that the younger ones, both girls and boys, were rented to pimps who'd set them up in deserted houses or decrepit hotels. They'd be locked together in dorms where maybe each had a mattress and a box to keep clothes in, then as men showed up, they'd be taken out to spend hours being raped, sexually abused, sometimes beaten, depending on the customer's desires.

Even though Roz knew about these horrors, somehow she'd thought this abuse and degradation was being erased. Now, it was in her face.

"When Bettina refused to get an abortion, did they bring you here?"

"No, they say they kill her. If she's pregnant or has baby, she doesn't bring in money for months. Other girls we know, they get pregnant and disappear. Bad men say they get sent home, but I know different. I watch one night as they take a pregnant girl outside, beat her with a bat until she's dead, drag her body off into the woods."

Bile rose in Roz' throat but she had nothing to throw up. She closed her eyes as tears welled up.

"How did you get here?" she asked.

"We ran away. One night, we go out a window and climb down a tree. We get to a big road and hope to get ride, but the only car that stop was one of the bad men. He force us in and bring us here, then fight with the other man. They will take us somewhere and kill us."

And probably me as well, thought Roz.

CHAPTER FIFTY-SIX

The sisters wound themselves together and started softly talking in Romanian, then Stefka began singing in a low voice. From the sound, Roz figured it was a lullaby or children's song, the sister's way of trying to help Bettina get back to a place of safety.

Despite her discomfort—her arms ached, her legs were numb from sitting upright—Roz dozed. A light voice waked her.

"Lady, lady, I think they're back."

She opened her eyes and the gloom in the warehouse had deepened, no light came in the clerestory windows. It was night, but what time—near midnight or the wee hour—she didn't know.

She listened and thought she heard sounds of things being moved. Boxes, machinery, furniture? Oh, please let it not be the scurrying of large rats!

There, a beam of light slashed across the far end of the space. Someone was out there, then the light went out, silence returned.

Roz and the Romanians were quiet, wrapped in their own fears and assumptions. She couldn't touch them but tried to send comforting thoughts.

A door crashed and beams began crisscrossing the warehouse, limning the few remaining pieces of machinery.

Josef and his partner must have rounded up some helpers to move everybody out and they didn't care who heard or saw them. This was not a comforting omen, they must believe they were safe.

Then a loud boom and voice. "Armed police! Throw down any weapons."

Police? Maybe this was what she'd hoped, this was the warehouse Hal and his force were watching.

Another boom and acrid smoke began filling the far end of the space. Tear gas?

Then yells and scattered gunshots. A voice screaming "Armed police. Throw down your weapons."

Two male voices shouting in the guttural language she'd heard earlier, seemed to be coming their way. If the traffickers got to them first, they'd use them as shields to get out safely.

She had to do something

The only weapon she had was her voice.

She began screaming "Don't shoot! Don't shoot! We're trapped." Then her eyes began streaming and her throat clogged up from a trace of the tear gas drifting in the huge open space.

Small mercies, the gas also seemed to stop the traffickers' progress toward the office. She could hear them choking and coughing while trying to argue with one another.

Apparitions loomed out of the smoke and gas and resolved themselves into armed, masked and vested police carrying large guns who yelled "Armed police! Drop your weapons! Down on the floor! Now, now!"

Although Josef and his partner tried to fire back, the gas disabled them. They collapsed on the floor, groveling to get away.

More noise, shouts, movement, then a gas-masked figure poked a head in the door of the office and yelled, "There are women in here. Maybe prisoners."

"Oh god, please help us!" Relief flooded Roz' voice and her body slumped against the restraints.

Tapestry of Tears

The officer edged into the room, carefully checking for any other shooters. Saw the room only held Roz and the two Romanian women and went to Roz.

"Are you the one who shouted?"

"Yes, yes, please get me loose! I don't think I'll be able to walk." Her lips were slightly healed but talking broke the skin again and she felt blood oozing. "Do you have any water? All of us are dehydrated."

"I'll go check." The first officer went out into the warehouse and Roz heard him shouting, "Water! Anyone have water! There are three women in here."

He came back, with another officer in tow. "Who are you?"

"My name is Rosalind Duke. I'm an American. And these two are Romanians who were trafficked and used as sex slaves." With safety so close, Roz felt salty tears mixing and stinging with the blood. "I know the younger one is Bettina, the older one is Stefka. They're sisters."

The second officer pulled off the gas mask and Roz saw it was a young dark-haired woman who went to the sisters.

"Do you speak English?"

"I do," the older one said. "Bettina, my sister, not so much. Will you help us?"

"I will," the policewoman said. "Are you injured? Do you need a doctor?"

"Not injured, just beated." Stefka pulled up her dress as she had done for Roz, to display the bruises and scars. "And my sister, too. She's pregnant."

The policewoman whistled. "She's just a kid. How did this happen?" then snapped her mouth shut releasing how it happened. Turned to the man who was cutting the ties on Roz' arms and legs. "We need a medic and maybe an ambulance. Have someone to call."

Freed from the chair, Roz gingerly moved her arms, pushing her shoulders forward and swinging her hands to her chest. The movement of the frozen joints and muscles sent jolts of fiery pain and she clenched her hands, trying to bring circulation back.

"You have an injury to your leg." The officer looked down to where Roz was slowly moving her boot. "Did they do that?"

"No, this was prior." She grimaced at the ache in her knee. "I'm still supposed to be on crutches, but I'm sure the kidnapper, Josef, didn't bring them when he grabbed me."

Another constable, this one not armed, came in with bottles of water. "I've called for an ambulance, they're three minutes out. I checked with the medics and they said not to drink the whole bottle at once because they didn't know how long you'd been without water."

"A few hours for me," Roz said. "Josef did give me some. I'm not sure about the girls, though." She took the bottle with both hands, not yet able to grasp it in one hand, and poured it in her mouth, trying to avoid putting her stinging lips on it.

"How did you come to be here?" the constable pulled a small notebook from a pocket under her vest, then paused. "You said your name is Rosalind Duke?"

Roz, nodded. "Yes, I go by Roz."

"Are you the one who's been working with DI Fitzroy?"

Roz smiled, picturing Hal, a calming feeling washing over her. "Yes, I was staying at his house. That's where I was kidnapped from."

The constable blanched, said, "Oh my," clicked on her shoulder radio. "Tell DI Fitzroy that we found the Duke woman."

CHAPTER FIFTY-SEVEN

Paramedics guided a gurney past the two thugs, sitting handcuffed with streaming eyes, outside the office door and came in.

"Are you injured, ma'am?" the first one through the door asked Roz who was braced against the wall on one leg, her booted foot behind her.

"Not really, I'm woozy from whatever was in the shot he gave me and the pins and needles in my arms will go away. I could use a pair of crutches, though."

"Sorry ma'am, we don't carry them, I'll have someone find a pair. Is there anything else you need? You should sit down again."

Roz leaned against the man as his partner moved a chair over then carefully sat down. The pins and needles were easing off and feeling coming back, leaving her with a dull ache in her shoulders.

A third paramedic, a woman, was softly talking to the Romanians and gently probing for broken bones. She turned to Roz. "We're going to call for another ambulance, the girls seem uninjured other than bruises, but we need to get them to hospital to check for concussions. I can't feel any breaks in major bones. Do you think you need to be seen in A and E?"

"No, I've had enough of trauma centers and hospitals for a lifetime. Do I need to sign something that I refused further treatment?"

The paramedic who helped her into the chair was checking her eyes and reading from the blood pressure cuff he'd slapped on her. "All basic vitals are fine, so you don't need to sign anything. We still need another ambulance, one of our constables was shot in the leg. I'll ask them to bring crutches."

A spate of conversation outside the office caught her attention and she heard someone say, "Yes, Guv, she's in there." Hal's familiar face appeared at the doorframe, worry wrinkling his forehead.

"Are you alright?" He strode over and gently touched her shoulder. Her heart lurched at his touch and presence. Safe, she felt safe again.

"Yes, sort of. He didn't injure me, just tied me up. My shoulders ache, my hands are tingling, and I need to find a bathroom, but no more damage than before."

Hal laughed and ran his fingers down her cheek. "I'm glad to see this horror didn't undermine your spirit."

Roz nodded over to where the paramedics were loading one of the Romanian's onto a gurney. "I'm more worried about them. They're been badly misused, beaten, raped." She lowered her voice. "And the younger one is pregnant, only fourteen."

Hal closed his eyes in silent understanding. Then business took over and he asked the paramedics if the girls were being taken to the hospital in Folkestone.

"Yes, Guv," the paramedic said. "They have the most complete A and E in the area, we can get them CT scans and whatever else they need. Although," she looked down at the younger one, "probably ultrasound for her."

Roz was quiet, relishing the calm the police and paramedics worked in. It was good to let go of responsibilities and fear and focus on her own situation. Once everything was secure and people were where they

Tapestry of Tears

needed to be, she could ask Hal to take her to his house and revel in peace.

She opened her mouth to ask when he said, "I'm going to get Jeremy to take you home, well, my house. I have to get those two," he waved at the two men on the floor, "to the station and begin questioning. And I need to have a constable go to the hospital with the girls."

Seeing the sense in this, Roz said, "I'll wait until the next ambulance comes with some crutches then go with Jeremy. Bu the way, was he the guard that got a knock-out shot too? Josef thought he was so smart he bragged to me."

"He was." Hal sighed. "He's feeling guilty that Josef was able to give him a shot while he was half-asleep. He feels he should have been wide-awake because he was on duty, protecting you."

"The storm was so loud, I doubt he'd have heard Josef. What did you find when you got there?"

"A window at the back of the house was broken out. Josef came through, went upstairs, found Jeremy dozing, stuck him and took his uniform. It didn't fit well, but it was enough to fool you in the dark into thinking it was a constable. Jeremy was just rousing when I came in, found you gone and raised holy hell."

One gurney was wheeled out while another one came in, the new paramedic handed Roz crutches, the second young Romanian was loaded up. Hal said, "Jeremy, take Ms. Duke home," and Roz got handed off to an embarrassed policeman.

"I'll see you later. Take care of yourself, I'll call Sarah to come over and help. When I get there, we'll have to have a debriefing, but I don't want to bring you down to the station for it."

Roz tucked the crutches under arms, soreness bringing tears to her eyes, and led Jeremy out through the warehouse. The police had brought in lights and Roz got a look at where she'd been kept. There were big pieces of machinery, maybe drill presses, down one aisle and crates stacked against the wall where a roll-up door showed night, lit by red and blue emergency vehicle lights. Jeremy went to a small panda car, opened the passenger door and Roz slid in, lifting her leg to tuck it in the well.

******

Sarah waited at Hal's, gave Roz a gentle hug, led her to a hot bath. "Brenda brought some soup for dinner, I'll go heat it up and you can eat at the desk. Do you have any injuries I need to look at?"

"No, but I could use a massage. My shoulders were pulled back for hours." Roz groaned as she slid into the bath, resting her booted foot on the tub's edge. A bit awkward but she relished the warmth soaking into her hips and shoulders.

After the bath, after a massage, after she'd dressed in clean, soft sweats, after she'd eaten Roz felt she could face whatever debriefing Hal intended. She was sending a longish email to Liam when Hal tapped at the door.

She looked up and sucked in a breath. "You look in worse shape than I do," she said, motioning him to sit next to her on the bed.

"Hmmm..." He swiped his hand across his eyes and grimaced. "At least I'm not injured. Just close to 48 hours with no sleep, not enough food, too much coffee. This'll pass."

"What happened?"

"Thanks to you, we have witnesses."

"I didn't do anything except get drugged and kidnapped. How did that help?"

"If Josef hadn't grabbed you, hadn't taken you to the warehouse, we might never have found you. I told you we were watching a warehouse that we thought might be their base of operation for transferring the victims to the buyers. Not only did her take you there, but his partner, who doesn't have brains, brought the two girls there. They were planning to drop both of them in the Channel. Once the younger one turned up pregnant, they had no use for her and meant to eliminate both of them from ever talking."

"They told me that." Roz was silent, remembering the fear on their faces. "They were sure the men were going to murder them."

"And so they would have, and you, too. It was just dumb luck that Josef's partner brought them to the warehouse. That was the argument the girls heard before they threw them in the office with you."

"Where do I fit in?"

"You being in the warehouse bought them a few more hours. They left the three of you there while they went to find a large enough boat to take you all out. If you hadn't been there, the two girls would be dead already. We probably would have found you, but we never would have found two witnesses. Those girls will tie the entire scheme together."

Hal was silent for a beat. Roz watched as emotions, questions, plans flitted across his face.

"We may have a chance to round up some of the buyers, now." He sighed. "It's liable to haul in some of our well-known, well-heeled citizens."

CHAPTER FIFTY-EIGHT

$\mathcal{A}$ soft, foggy morning greeted Roz when she hopped to the window. The garden was peaceful, but branches snapped off during the earlier storm littered the grass. The view, the air brought bittersweet feelings welling up.

There was a smoothness to the air here, maybe honed by so many centuries of human habitation and history and she'd miss this comfort. But she was anxious to get back to her own fog, a tougher setting with a sense of adventure. She let her mind spin in idle, wondering how she could combine the best of both worlds.

"Saying good-bye?" At Hal's voice Roz whipped around, grabbing the edge of the desk for balance.

"Yes, I guess so." She cleared her throat, wanting to dislodge the frog that had suddenly crept in. She certainly wasn't going to cry, not now, not after all she'd been through.

"I am going to miss you. I wish we'd met under different circumstances." He walked to her and wrapped his arms around her waist, pulling her to him for a brief second then releasing her.

Roz nodded her agreement. "If I were freer, didn't have ties and people I cared about I could have figured out ways to build a life here. There's much to recommend it." She turned to sit in the desk chair. "I hope we can stay in touch and remain friends, though. You took such good care and showed me so much of your home, I'll never forget it."

"Have you had coffee or breakfast yet? I can ask Brenda to bring something over."

"That would be wonderful it it's not too much trouble." Roz thought that there wasn't much that would be too much trouble if Hal was involved but kept those thoughts to herself.

"Done, then," Hal said and sent a quick text. "What else do you need to do before your flight. It's day after tomorrow from Heathrow, right?"

She glanced at him then realized she'd made the final arrangements while he was off looking for the remaining gang members. "Yes. I've called for a car service in the morning. My flight's at 1 p.m. and I'm scheduled to get in late evening in Portland, changing planes in New York. Liam will be meeting me."

"There's no need for a car, I'll drive you to the airport."

"That will take up your whole day, I can't ask you to do that."

"It's not an imposition, you'll be helping me out."

Roz stared at him. Was he going to spring something on her?

He watched her expression and grinned. "Nothing to onerous. If you're up to it, I'd like you to come down to the station tomorrow. Meet some of the other members of the team, give us a statement, both about your kidnapping and your finding Ilic's body. That will tie up our open cases."

"Of course, it's the least I can do." Roz smiled ruefully. "Since Winston was killed I've spent a great deal of time in police stations."

A tap at the bedroom door and Brenda stuck her head in. "I've put a pot of fresh coffee and plate of scones in the kitchen," she said. "I'll bring soup and a sandwich for lunch. Will both of you be here?"

"No, I'm at the station all day," Hal said, "but I'm planning to come back for dinner, if it's something I like."

Brenda gaped at him, then, "Oh you! I'm making prawns scampi so you better like it." She smiled, tossed her head and left.

Roz watched the interaction with a secret smile. She wasn't wrong about Brenda's interest and judging from Hal's teasing, he reciprocated.

The shipping company had earlier picked up the crates of glass, tools and completed sample window and she wouldn't see them again for a month or so, until she flew to Wisconsin for the formal review and signing of the commission. She was satisfied but not complacent about this project and once the contract was signed, she had close to a year's worth of work in front of her.

With things tying up, she decided to treat herself to a lie-down, not realizing how tired she still was. She jumped a little when Brenda knocked and announced dinner. "And wonder of wonders," Brenda said, "himself is on his way home to eat with you."

"You're not eating with us?"

"No, have to get back and feed the mob at the pub, but I'll come over later and get the dishes. May stay for a nightcap," and she was out the door.

Roz grabbed her crutches and was in the kitchen when Hal came in.

"Ahhh, I smell Brenda's been here already. She always says 'it's just pub food' but she's a great cook and has a reputation all along this stretch of coast. I hope she doesn't get so well-known that one of those chi-chi restaurants that cater to the tourist crowd grabs her."

After they ate, Hal filled her in on what to expect the next day.

"We have three officers from the **Sûreté**, a representative from the Foreign Office, two EU reps and one guy from Interpol. They'll want you to tell them your story so they all have the same information when they interrogate the last two we picked up. The EU people will also be working with the Bulgarian and Romanian national police to try and shut down those scammers and kidnappers who prey on poor families."

******

The next day went as Hal had lined out. Roz recounted her entire story, from finding Ilic's body to Hal asking her to work with them on the stained glass theft, to the escalation when the bosses discovered she was working with the police.

They asked her several times about her "accident" on the French coast, the attacker who'd come in to her hospital room, the attack and thwarted kidnapping by the "beekeeper" who turned out to be Josef, and the attack on the night of the storm. And the Interpol officer asked her about Liam and Sam's poking around in the dark web, which caused one of the Foreign Service guys to blanch with horror at the thought that Her Majesty's Government could have been hacked.

When she got a chance, she asked about the two young Romanian women. One of the EU representatives, a middle-aged woman with an Eastern European accent, said they were still in the hospital but recovering. Their family had been notified and their mother was on her way to England.

"This is always a problem with poorer nations," she said. "It's such a lure to think they could go to a rich neighbor country, make some money and send it home. Many of them are so naive they can't tell the scammers from the legitimate offers."

Roz left, sobered with the understanding that terror lurked in inconspicuous places.

******

Tapestry of Tears

On the drive to Heathrow, Roz and Hal chatted about the wrap-up. In the silences, she wondered how her life may have changed if she'd chosen to stay in England. Hal would certainly be in the picture, but what else might it hold? Idle time spent on the "what ifs" that could never be answered.

As though he read her mind, Hal said, "Oh, about those two teachers, Jocelyn and Phoebe? We had them checked out thoroughly and their story was true. As games mistresses, they were stuck in a rut, other faculty thinking they were glorified jocks. They wanted to prove they had brains and were capable of scholarship so saw a well-researched and written book on the Battle of Hastings and the Tapestry as a ticket to advancement."

Roz felt a sizzle of relief wash over her. The women's offer of a place to stay and recuperate was so kind that she didn't like thinking of them with ulterior motives.

At the airport, Hal insisted on getting her a wheelchair and attendant and she was silently grateful. She hated to make a fuss, but he was right, this was the best way. Changing planes in New York, the airline made sure there was a wheelchair attendant to transfer her to the next flight and as the plane filled up, she was startled at the voices around her, more nasal and louder than she'd been hearing in the last months in England.

They chased the setting sun west and landed in Portland before midnight, with Roz on the edge of exhaustion.

Once again in a wheelchair, Roz spotted Liam pacing around the baggage carousel from her flight and her heart squeezed with happiness as he raced over, lifted her from the chair and hugged her so hard she thought her ribs would crack.

"You have no idea how glad I am to see you," he said, his grin so wide his eyes wrinkled. "I was worried I'd get a phone call that either you weren't coming home, or you'd been hurt again or worse."

She laughed with pleasure. It was so comforting to be home and with him again. "What now?"

"We're going to my place here in Portland for two days. I found an appointment with an orthopedics guy here for tomorrow to have him look at your ankle and foot and let us know what to expect to get you back whole and moving again."

Roz had a small qualm about Liam taking over parts of her life but admitted to herself that she enjoyed someone taking on her responsibilities during this time. She'd gone to England to stretch her creativity and build her self-sufficiency and now found that there was solace in letting go of some things.

As Liam wheeled her luggage cart and the attendant wheeled her chair she asked, "Where's Tut? You did bring him, didn't you?"

Before Liam could get the pickup door fully opened, a lean, 80-pound body came boiling out of the car, dancing in circles and trying to get into Roz' lap, wheelchair armrests and all.

"Oh Tut, oh Tut my boy, I've missed you so much!" Roz crooned into the greyhound's ear as he licked, licked and licked, giving her big doggie kisses.

"Well," Liam said, "let's go home."

CHAPTER FIFTY-NINE

Two weeks before Christmas, Roz and Liam flew to Wisconsin.

She was out of both a boot and cast and walking well, although she had occasional twinges of feeling—not as bad as actual pain. She'd joked with Liam about being one of those older people whose injuries presaged a storm or change in the weather.

Getting back into her routine gave her days a comforting schedule. She was catching up on the mail orders for kits and ordered more supplies. She unpacked and rearranged tools, glass, cames and cartoons, preparing to work on the Tapestry commission. And if she didn't get it? Well, she had other ideas for commissions, perhaps even for the small church in Lympne to replace the ones that were clear glass.

St. Gertrude's University, just outside Appleton, was a small private school heavily into the liberal arts with a student population from around the world. It shared some facilities with the city so when they embarked on a project to construct their own museum, they designed it to be an attraction for the larger area.

Roz had little concern that she wouldn't be awarded the commission, she'd had assurances from Dean Longe that it was a done deal. The Dean invited her for a pre-holiday event, featuring the sample window she'd made in England as well as an exhibit of sketches and cartoons.

She knew the Dean planned her to be the center of a fund-raising cocktail party announcing the commission—

and incidentally bringing in more donations. Mildly uncomfortable, she was expected to give a short presentation on why she'd chosen the Tapestry and how she'd done the research and design.

"Public speaking isn't my best foot forward," she said as she and Liam were escorted to two visitor's rooms in a dorm.

"Maybe not, but I know if you launch into stories about stained glass, you can go on for hours." He smiled and held the door to one of the rooms open. They were slowly getting reacquainted, deepening their interest in each other, but Roz was not yet comfortable enough to commit to sleeping together. Maybe, probably, one day, not today.

The party was in the President's House, a massive Victorian surrounded by gardens on the edge of the campus.

"Very English," Roz commented as they entered the foyer.

Dean Longe and the president greeted them with handshakes and hugs and brought them into a large, open area filled with people, sound, Christmas decorations and easels dotted around holding elevations and renderings of the proposed gallery as well as a sampling of her own sketches. Her sample window was propped on a table against one wall, back-lit with lights to make the colors throb.

She sucked in a breath, said, "They've done a great exhibition and I'm stunned how good it looks!"

"Why?" Liam's eyes squinched together in surprise. "You made it, you've seen it."

"But it's been a few weeks and I forgot how well I like it."

The Dean came over and took Roz' arm. "There's someone I'd like you to meet," she said, and Roz assumed it was a large donor to the project.

Instead, as she crossed the room, she saw Hal, chatting with the president, looking proud, a bit smug and at ease in the mix of town and gown.

"Inspector," she said as she leaned in to kiss him. "What a surprise! I'm so please to see you, I had no idea you were coming to the States."

"It's a fairly quick trip," Hal said, his soft British accent a rich remembrance of their time together. "It was primarily to give you this." He pointed to a small box wrapped in Christmas paper on a table. "Is Liam here? I'd like to meet the man who…," he caught himself and finished with "tried to help us out."

"Yes." Roz waved at Liam, who made his way across the room.

"Liam Karshner, I'd like you to meet Detective Inspector Hal Fitzroy. Hal, this is Liam." The two men eyes each other for a brief second then Liam reached out and took Hal's arm.

"I'm so happy to meet you," he said. "And to thank you for taking such great care of Roz. She can be a prickly patient, I know, but she's safe at home now. And I'm glad that the bizarre case wrapped up so well."

"As are we." Hal clasped Liam's shoulder and the two shared a fleeting hug. "And I've brought a little present for Roz as a thank you from the Crown for her help in uncovering a theft of English heritage."

He handed her the box, Roz carefully unwrapped it and found a wooden box with a hinged lid.

She opened the box and on a piece of white velvet, twenty pieces of the Westminster glass lay snuggled, red, blue, green, gleaming like gems.

"Oh Hal! These are priceless! Thank you." Color washed across Roz' face at the richness of the present.

"Without you, we may never have been able to present this to anyone," Hal said. "It's the least we could to."

Roz couldn't speak, she was too busy mentally fitting the pieces together into a window.

The Village

Books don't get written in a vacuum; just like a child, it takes a village to see a book through from idea to an object that takes flight.

Tapestry of Tears had a village including critique partners Linda Townsdin, Tarra Thomas, June Gillam, Cherie O'Boyle, Catherine McGreevy, Danna Wilberg, Karen Trinkaus, Kim Wiley and Pam VanAllen.

Add to them the best beta readers around; Judy Wyland, Martha Kelly, Elaine Faber, Darcy Olander and Emorey Macadangdang-Drier.

The cover is the work of Karen Phillips, who started out as an artist and ended up as a friend and resource, and formatting is by Rob Preece, who always catches a pesky typo or so that gets through.

Thank you to all!

Thank you for reading *Tapestry of Tears*. If you enjoyed it, please consider leaving a review on Amazon or Goodreads. Authors depend on reviews to help in becoming known.

Coming up

For 2021, two new books are in the pipeline: the third book in the Stained Glass Murders, *Resurrecting the Roses* and the eleventh in The Kandesky Vampire Chronicles, *SNAP: Pandemic Games*.

Please get in touch at mjdrier@gmail.com, or www.micheledrier.me or on Amazon,
https://www.amazon.com/Michele-Drier/e/B005D2YC8G?ref_=dbs_p_ebk_r00_abau_000000 or Goodreads, https://www.goodreads.com/search?q=michele%20drier

My facebook fan page is
https://www.facebook.com/AuthorMicheleDrier and I'm also on Twitter, Linked and Instagram.

Keep reading for an excerpt from *Resurrection of the Roses*

CHAPTER ONE

"I don't know why I come." Roz slammed through the door and tossed a pile of papers on the desk in the living room. She and Liam arrived at the apartment on the Ile de St. Louis two days ago and today she attended her first conference seminar.

"Probably because th

ey paid you?" Liam looked up from his laptop and grinned at her. "You know it's an ego stroke, being asked to give a paper and be on panels."

Roz blew out a breath. "I know, it's a big boost and an honor. But after a day of saying hello, standing around drinking coffee, wandering through the place looking for room numbers, being stopped by students asking questions," she shook her head. "I get exhausted. My feet hurt. It saps energy that I don't have to spend working alone."

Tut, her greyhound, looked up, his tail thumping on the floor. "My boy." Roz reached down and ruffled his ear. "I'm glad we brought you, but you may get bored here in Paris. It'll be better when we get out into the county."

As an internationally renowned stained glass artist, Roz Duke was invited a couple of times a year to address conferences on medieval life, medieval stained glass, future designs in glass. She didn't usually accept, preferring to stay at her seaside home in Oregon and work, quietly and alone, on her creations and commissions.

When this invitation to address a conference on replicating medieval stained glass in Paris came, it was too big a draw. There might be forces at work, an undercurrent of malevolence, in the world of stained glass that worried her.

After Notre-Dame burnt, and then the cathedral of Saint Peter and Paul in Nantes, and those two fires only a couple of years after a hoard of medieval stained glass from Westminster Abby was stolen, Roz felt her superstitions tingle. She didn't believe in conspiracy theories, but there seemed to be more coincidences popping up than fit random events.

She'd give her keynote talk, "New Life for Old Glass", tomorrow, outlining how British craftspeople were repurposing some of the stained glass hoard found at Westminster. What she would leave out was that more than 15,000 pieces of the glass had been stolen, held for ransom and recovered.

She was ready for tomorrow, but tonight was Paris.

"What are you working on? Are you at a point where you can stop?" She sat on the edge of a chair, slid her shoes off and rubbed her aching feet.

"Just some notes on what I want to cover when we begin the rest of the trip."

When the invitation to give the keynote at the conference arrived at her home in Hamilton, Oregon, Roz' first inclination was to turn it down. She hadn't finished the commission for the university gallery in Wisconsin, a piece she'd researched and design last fall during an extended stay in England.

She'd left the invitation on the kitchen counter, intending to write a polite "Thanks, but no thanks" to the organizers when Liam spotted it.

"What's this?" He'd come over to her house, to take Tut out for a run on the beach, a habit they'd established when Roz was in England. And now Tut was in heaven, usually two runs a day, one with Roz and one with Liam.

Roz looked up from the sink where she was washing lettuce for a lunchtime salad. "I'm going to say no. Last fall in England was enough travel."

"That was almost eight months ago, and besides this is another country." Liam reached down to stroke Tut. "Is this a pretty influential bunch, the conference organizers?"

"Yes, they have a hand in most of the large-scale public commissions." Roz paused. Should she go? What would it benefit? Her reputation was secure, and she got more inquiries about commissions than she accepted, but there was constant pressure to maintain her presence. A major commission could bring public acclaim as well as up to $1 million in fees for up to a year's work.

"Maybe I'd go with you." Liam tapped the invitation. "I've only been to France once. Maybe we could make a longer trip out of it, do some traveling around the countryside, Burgundy, the Loire Valley. I could get a couple of travel pieces out of it."

Roz stared at him. Travel? She and Winston, her late husband, used to spend two or more months every summer in Europe. As an art historian at UCLA, Winston visited museums, galleries, cathedrals, gathering information and slides for his classes. Roz spent her time in cathedrals and churches, soaking up the stained glass windows and finding glass workshops she could visit. Would traveling with Liam drown her in bittersweet memories?

"I suppose we could." She was hesitant, not wanting to immediately take on something so intimate. She and Lima were probably working toward some kind of relationship beyond friends, but they still weren't lovers. Logistically, how would this work? And who would watch Tut? While she was in England, Liam, took on the task of surrogate dog owner to heart and he and Tut had become second-best friends.

Made in the USA
Columbia, SC
18 February 2022